THE SHADOW
OF
SILVER TIP

Also published in Large Print
from G.K. Hall by Max Brand ™:

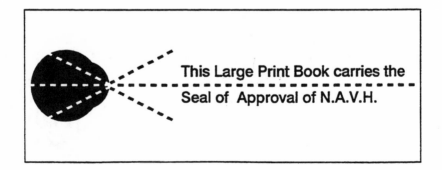

THE SHADOW OF SILVER TIP

Max Brand ™

G.K. Hall & Co.
Thorndike, Maine

Published in 1995 by arrangement with
Golden West Literary Agency.

Acknowledgment is made to Condé Nast Publications, Inc.,
successors-in-interest to Street & Smith.

The name Max Brand ™ is a registered trademark with the
U.S. Patent and Trademark Office and cannot be used for any
purpose without express written permission.

G.K. Hall Large Print Western Collection.

The text of this Large Print edition is unabridged.
Other aspects of the book may vary from the original edition.

Set in 16 pt. News Plantin by Rick Gundberg.

Printed in the United States on permanent paper.

Library of Congress Cataloging in Publication Data

Brand, Max, 1892–1944.
　　The shadow of Silver Tip / Max Brand.
　　　　p.　　cm.
　　ISBN 0-7838-1470-4 (lg. print : hc)
　　1. Large type books.　I. Title.
　[PS3511.A87S38　1995]
　813'.52—dc20
　　　　　　　　　　　　　　　　　　　　　　　　　　95-31607

THE SHADOW
OF
SILVER TIP

Chapter One

The Shadow Reappears

Unquestionably the town of Silver Tip lay in a region somewhat beyond the law; for the law, after all, likes smooth going. It does not care to sail across the sea to pursue its proper errands, and neither does it wish to bark its shins climbing over bramble and stone in the mountains. And Silver Tip lay in the most chopped and broken region one could imagine. A town was there because, in the first place, a perverse evidence had chosen to streak the rocks in the mountains near by with gold. The mines quickly played out, and afterward Silver Tip continued to exist for no particular reason, like a thousand other towns west of the Rockies. But Silver Tip was even more without excuse for life than most other villages in the sweep of the mountain desert.

The vicious said that Silver Tip only continued to drag out its life because there were pooled in it various elements highly prejudicial to the well-being of the law-abiding citizens of the country. They declared that rustlers, crooked gamblers — meaning, thereby, all gamblers — out-worn road agents, desperate train robbers, yeggs, and sneak thieves — all congregated at Silver Tip to find safety in their numbers.

And at least it was well proven that, once a criminal reached the environs of Silver Tip, it was a well-nigh impossible task to locate him. He faded among the sun-blistered houses and was lost to view.

Men of Silver Tip countered all these bitter accusations by pointing out that there was never the slightest sign of trouble in the streets of the town itself. How, they asked with a great deal of point, could the sweepings of the range be gathered in one place without explosions occurring every day? And such explosions never were witnessed in Silver Tip. There was no doubt about that. Men did not fight in Silver Tip. They might bluster and brawl, but knife or Colt were never drawn. The death list was free from gunpowder and cold steel in the number of causes assigned. And the great reason could be found in the form of Sheriff Algernon Thomas.

The great man sat on a chair on the neat little veranda of his own house and looked up the street with his gray eyes, somewhat sad and misted from staring for many an hour into the horizon haze. He was neither large nor young. He was not even in that hardy middle age. In fact, "Algie," the terrible Algie, was a little withered man full 65 years old, with bony shoulders bowed forward over a sickly chest, and with pipe-stem arms at the end of which were age-calloused hands perpetually shaking in a slight ague, so it seemed.

His face was the mildest face that ever delighted inquisitive children. They went to him instinctively with their questions, and the great Algie would answer them at endless length. Yet Algie Thomas was the power which kept Silver Tip quiet, and men said that strange, strange things indeed could be done by those same tremulous old hands when the need came. Indeed, such a need did arise every two or three years, and the sheriff exhibited a sign of his prowess. His fights were all short — disgustingly short from the viewpoint of a historian.

He asked no questions. He went by the shortest line to find the man he wanted, and when he reached the objective he was instantly on the firing line. Words were rarely exchanged.

In front of the veranda stood a sun-faded buckskin horse, ugly, but as durable as leather. Its head hung low in utter dejection — or relaxation — and only occasionally it shifted from foot to foot and squeezed the liquid-thin dust into spurts of vapor. Perhaps those meager dust clouds set up by the moving horse provided the air with its never-dying scent of acrid alkali, that stung the nostrils of the unaccustomed and dried the throat to a famine-strong sense of thirst.

So intensely hot was it that heat waves rose even in the scant distance across the street — heat waves that made the roof-ridges of the opposite houses run in foolishly uncertain waves. So consumingly dry was the air that the perspiration which started under the heavy leather band of the sombrero was dried to salt before it trickled to the chin.

Algie's guest stirred a little from time to time, even getting up and walking back and forth the length of the porch. Then he would come back and resume his chair beside the imperturbable sheriff. Algie did not so much as stir to roll a cigarette. He sat like a carved creature — except for that eternal tremor of his hands.

It was the quiver of those fingers that so worked on the nerves of the visiting officer of the law that the latter had to rise now and then and make a trip up and down the veranda to pacify himself. Otherwise, he felt that before long he, too, would begin to shake a little from head to foot.

"Now I'll tell you what really brought me down here," he said after resuming his seat at the end of one of these trips on the porch. "I have news about The Shadow!"

As he deliver the words he leaned briskly forward with his hands clapped on his knees, very much as a man looking to see the effect of a shot on a target; but Algie did not stir. He only moved his misty gray eyes toward Federal Marshal Jeff Hall and nodded.

"Is that boy at it again?" he asked mildly.

The marshal settled back in his chair with a sigh. It was like the escape of air from a punctured balloon. He seemed to grow smaller in size.

"You beat me, Algie," he said at length. "I sure thought that that news would wake you up and start you talking!"

10

"I'm tolerable wide awake," said the gentle old sheriff. "But how come you to be sure that it's The Shadow himself?"

"By the hoss," said Marshal Jeff Hall. "It's the same dappled chestnut, finished off with dark points."

His own horse, at that moment, danced into view, sidestepping at the hitching rack where he was tethered. It was a slim-legged bay with the head of an Arab and the Arab's human-bright eyes.

"Steady, Mary," said the marshal soothingly. "I know, Algie, because I give him a run with Mary, and The Shadow walked right away from me on his red chestnut. I seen the hoss tolerable clear. Yep, it's him."

The sheriff clucked to himself in quiet surprise.

"Him all healed already? Why, the boys said he left a trail of murder a mile wide. I thought it'd sure be a long time before he was around again."

"Healed already?" exclaimed the marshal. "Why, man alive, it's full two years now!"

"Two years?" said the sheriff. "You don't tell me! Why, it don't seem no more'n last week, hardly. Two years!"

He seemed so taken with surprise at this matter of the intervening time that all thought of The Shadow himself had passed from his mind, and Jeff Hall, with a frown, leaned a little forward and stared sternly into the face of the old man. Ever and anon persons were in the habit of staring

11

at Algie Thomas in this manner, as though to see if the imbecility of age had not at length gained a grip upon him.

Such news as the marshal gave should have made the sheriff pass his hand toward his gun and jump from his chair. There was only one Shadow, and that was synonymous, well nigh, with the devil. From holdup work to safe-blowing, there was nothing that The Shadow could not take in hand and manage with the skill of a consummate craftsman. There were peculiarities about him which accounted for the fact that the law could never come to grips with him.

For one thing, there were no "handles" by which he might be seized. He had no pals. He never worked in concert with others. His trail was always a single trail. Also, no one had seen him unmasked, and for that reason the only way to identify him was through the vastly conflicting descriptions with which the country was flooded. Some called him slender, others called him broad; some said that he was gigantic in height — but all that was accurately known was that he rode a black-dappled chestnut.

A little over two years before, it became known that pretty little Sylvia Rann, far back in the mountains, was receiving a mysterious visitor. He was seen to arrive by moonlight on a black-dappled chestnut, and Sylvia's guardian, with whom she lived, waited to hear no more. He gathered for the purpose no less than three youths of the neighborhood, who had been ardent suitors of

Sylvia for years. He told them what he had seen, and, as a result, young Jess Sherman, Harry Lang, and "Chuck" Parker lay in wait for five nights until, on the fifth, the strange rider came once more, masked, riding the black-dappled chestnut, and met Sylvia in the clearing among the trees. They saw her run to his arms, but before she reached them three rifles spoke, and The Shadow sank to the ground.

At that, being young, the hunters left cover and rushed to get at him, but the moment they were under way he fired from the ground, dropped Jess Sherman with a bullet through the leg, Chuck Parker with another through the shoulder, and felled Harry Lang with the weight of sheer terror. In another moment, delaying only to hurl a curse and a denunciation at the girl he thought had betrayed him, The Shadow dragged himself from the ground into the saddle and was gone.

Afterward they trailed him by a terrible series of crimes, but the trail did not bring them to the outlaw.

A month later a letter was received by Lang, Parker, and Sherman, threatening each that The Shadow would some day return and take full vengeance on them for their cowardice in veiling themselves behind a girl. In the meantime, Sylvia Rann had been plied with questions to learn from her any possible details concerning the personal appearance of the terrible man. But she had refused to reveal a single point of his description, and her lips had been securely locked on that subject ever since the disappearance of The Shadow.

Two years had slipped by, and The Shadow was rapidly becoming rather a figure of legend than of fact, when Marshal Jeff Hall dropped in on the redoubtable sheriff of Silver Tip and made his startling announcement. No wonder, then, that he was chagrined when Algie Thomas accepted the news in such a matter-of-fact manner.

Chapter Two

A Stranger in Town

"Green old age," was the marshal's explanation of Algie's indifference. "The great man ain't what he used to be once."

He added aloud, with a touch of vindictiveness: "But I guess it don't mean much to you. All you want to do is to keep this little town quiet. What happens in the hills around it, don't matter much to you."

For a moment the age-misted eyes of the sheriff dwelt tenderly on the blue-brown summit of Mount Samson; then he glanced at his companion.

"I guess that's my job," he said. "I'm an old man. Before they elected me in this county, I up and told 'em plain that I wouldn't do nothing but stay here in town. Deputies would have to take care of everything else. They seemed to want me just the same."

Marshal Jeff Hall flushed. He was remembering some dozen men before the sheriff who had attempted this same task of controlling Silver Tip. All of them had come to a sudden and untimely end.

To change the subject, he looked eagerly up the street and down — down until he saw two horsemen jog their horses along opposite trails and meet in the center of the street. There, obviously greatly surprised at encountering each other, they drew rein with such a jerk that the cow ponies were flung back upon their haunches. Jeff Hall no longer needed to hunt for a new topic for conversation. He found two new ones sitting their horses in full view.

"By the Eternal!" he cried. "If there ain't old 'Timber' Johnson and Alec McGregor!"

"Where?" asked the mild sheriff.

"There! There! Sittin' on their hosses right in the middle of *your* street, Algie!"

He placed a little more emphasis on the personal pronoun than was strictly necessary. To his surprise, and somewhat to his anger, the sheriff did not directly answer. His mind was still working on the subject preceding the last one.

"Suppose we was to see a fire bust out on the top of Mount Samson," said the sheriff. "That'd be a sort of a thrill for the folks in these parts, Jeff, eh?"

He referred to the vow which The Shadow had made that when he came back he would announce his coming by building a fire on the top of Mount Samson, that everyone in the mountains would be forewarned that he was among them, and that the three specified objects of his wrath might be prepared to fight for their lives.

"Fire on Mount Samson!" exclaimed the marshal. "Fire in perdition, Algie! I say that there go Timber Johnson and Alec McGregor!"

"Timber and Alec?" said the sheriff turning his head and clucking in a deprecatory manner he had. "Why, Jeff, you plumb surprise me! Them are two boys that've been living over to the hotel for a couple of weeks, and nobody ain't heard a bad word out of either of 'em!"

"You ain't?" groaned the marshal, realizing that he had no direct evidence against either of the two notorious ruffians. "Well, the rest of the mountains has heard plenty, and a pile more'n plenty, about them two, partner! Alec and Timber, as sure as I'm a foot high! Lord, how I'd like to nab 'em!"

"Go just as far as you like," said the sheriff pleasantly, and he took off his hat and smoothed his silken white hair with his trembling hand. "Go as far as you like — with me or without me, Jeff!"

But Jeff had settled back in his chair with a groan.

"There ain't any use," he said. "I've seen 20 hard eggs in your town today, sheriff. I've seen yeggs and guns of all the kinds a gent could shake a stick at. All I need is a little evidence. I could stock a penitentiary with a tidy lot of cutthroats right out of your own little town, sheriff. Is that another — coming in broke, and expecting to fit up here and get ready for the road again?"

Jeff pointed to the figure of a third man, who appeared down the road beyond Timber Johnson and Alec McGregor. This was a young fellow who swung down from the hillside, leaping from rock to rock during the last part of his descent with the nimbleness of a goat, and landing in the deep dust of the road. He now faced toward the town and came with the peculiar half-swinging, half-gliding stride which announces an expert and trained pedestrian. Not one cow-puncher in a thousand, or in ten thousand, perhaps, could step out in like manner.

He walked unencumbered by a pack of any kind, though there was that about him which, even in the distance, clearly proclaimed one who had come from afar. The very look of the dust upon his clothes told of distant places, and the acceleration of his gait as he came up the single street of the town was the increased pace of one happy in a goal achieved. There was meaning, therefore, in the question of the marshal: "Is that another?"

The sheriff regarded the pedestrian with his usual glance of mild indifference.

"I never seen him before."

"Not that you remember, eh?" said Jeff Hall suspiciously.

"I always remember right," answered the sheriff. "I never in my life seen a face once that I wouldn't remember the next time I laid eyes on it. By Jiminy, that's a nervous-looking lad! I'd of hated to hunt trouble with a gent like that, even when I was as young and as spry as him!"

It was an astonishing confession for such an able old warrior as the sheriff. It made the marshal glance askance at him, and look again, with real interest, at the youth about whom he had made his spiteful chance observation. The latter was still too far away to be examined narrowly, at least by his eyes. It was astonishing indeed if the sheriff could see anything of importance while the youth was so far away.

"Yes, sir," went on Algie Thomas. "Young and spry and quick as a cat. That's the sort of gent that ought never to use weapons. They got too much advantage over ordinary gents with just their bare hands!"

"Are you guessing?" asked the marshal.

"Tut, tut," clucked Algie. "I don't never guess, Jeff. Guessing don't help nobody much. Does it? I'm talking straight facts — without chasers!"

"H'm," muttered the marshal. "And you don't figure to get much interested in The Shadow, then? I'm sure surprised, Algie. I thought for once you'd prick up your ears."

Algie merely shook his head. "I might get interested if The Shadow crossed my trail, but he ain't never done that, so I'll let him alone if he lets me alone. He's bad medicine, Jeff. That's why I don't bother him none."

Of course this was understatement, for every one in the mountains knew well enough that Algie Thomas feared nothing that breathed. An exclamation from the marshal now gave a new twist to the conversation.

"Trouble down there, Algie! Better step sharp!"

"Trouble?" echoed the sheriff. "Well, well! What do you know about that!"

19

The trembling old hand moved back, dropped onto the finger-worn bone handle of his revolver, and froze to the solid steadiness of a rock. The marshal observed and wondered, and in the depth of his calloused heart he prayed that the incident might give him an opportunity to see the famous gun fighter in action.

Far down the street three men were in commotion.

It had begun simply enough. The man on foot, reaching the two horsemen, had stepped aside to avoid them, whereat the bay pony of Alec McGregor reached out with slashing heels which ripped through the air an inch or so from the head of the stranger. Whereupon Alec and Timber Johnson rolled back their bearded heads and laughed uproariously at the sight of the man on foot leaping out of the way.

Apparently the latter was perfectly willing to accept the affair as a jest at first, whether because the ominous appearance of Timber and his companion over-awed him as well they might — or because of inherent good humor. He put back his head and laughed at the dangerous escape as heartily as either of the mounted men. But it was a different matter when Alec backed the savage bay toward him and the quick-footed beast let fly again.

It was at this point that the marshal called the attention of the sheriff — just in time, in fact, to note the singular agility with which the tall youth side-stepped the drive of the hoofs and shook his fist in the face of the horseman. It was not a familiar gesture in a country of guns. One's heart might be shot out while one's fist was poised in midthreat.

This was the juncture when the sheriff let his hand dart back and rest on the butt of his revolver. Would he, if need should arise, attempt a pot shot at even that great distance, the marshal wondered.

There was no need. At least, events among the three happened with such dizzy speed that there was no chance for any human being to interfere with such promptness and precision that a calamity could be averted. Alec McGregor answered the threat of the shaken fist by slashing the stranger straight across the face with his heavy quirt. The counter to that blow came with the remarkable speed which the sheriff had foreseen in the youth.

The latter left the ground like a catamount and landed on Alec before the man could raise his whip a second time or change his mind and slip out his revolver. An instant later both men were off the horse, out of the saddle, and rolling over and over right under the heels of the horse of Timber Johnson. The latter deftly pulled his animal out of the way, and, as he did so, one man arose and the other lay flat, crushed, shapeless, in insensibility, into which he had been so quickly wrenched and pounded. The man who lay still was Alec McGregor, and the man who arose was the cat-footed youth.

His rising, however, did not put an end to his activities. Like a tiger who has made a killing, he turned from one victim to another. As he rose he whirled a little and made for Timber Johnson.

That gentleman was no easy prey. He had the shapeless bulk, the apparently unwieldy and really deft power, of a grizzly. He met the sudden spring with a downbeat of the loaded handle of his quirt, a blow that skidded from the head of the youngster as though from a rock. Then, in turn they were locked together, swayed to and fro, and fell to the earth.

Marshal Hall was shouting with excitement. So were half a dozen or more others who streamed out from the veranda of the hotel farther down the street.

"He's picked a handful of work," observed the old sheriff, who had not budged. "Timber'll squash him in them big bear arms! No, by cracky!"

That exclamation signalized the point at which the youth extricated himself from the gripping arms of Timber and they both got to their feet. They came together again, the youth dancing and erect, Timber with a downheaded rush — which was met by a tearing, lifting blow that straightened him as though he had butted a rock wall. While he hung half dazed, unbalanced, another blow of the same kind, short, fast as a wink of light, and with the same tearing upthrust, caught Timber full on the point of the jaw.

He lurched forward on his face and lay inert, while the dust cloud raised by the battle lifted lazily, slowly, and melted into the white-hot air.

Chapter Three

Man to Man

Justice in Silver Tip was personified as may have been suggested before, by the renowned sheriff himself, and the methods of that dignitary were, to say the least, antique.

Two minutes after the conclusion of the conflict, a score of men, in answer to the terse bidding of the sheriff — who had not budged from his chair on the veranda from first to last — rushed down the street, scooped up Timber and Alec and the conqueror as well, and bore them all before Algie Thomas, where he sat in state.

It was the habit of the sheriff to conduct what might be termed extra-legal investigations before he acted in official capacity. The sheriff was very grave, so grave that the onlookers fell back in a solid semicircle and, in their turn, frowned at the three culprits who were left thus exposed to the terrible, dim eye of Algie Thomas, who saw all things and knew the soul of a man at a glance. One could never tell how the old fellow would act. The marshal looked on in keenest interest. He would have sold half the coming years of his life for a tithe of such power over the rough men of the mountains as this withered relic of a sheriff possessed.

Timber Johnson and Alec, equally huge, whether in height or in girth, had very much the air of men struck recently by lightning, and were still inclined to stare blankly up, wondering how such a calamity could have descended upon them out of a clear blue sky. As for the youth, he was neither proudly buoyant because of his victory nor savage because he had been interrupted in the course of conquest. In fact, he was oblivious of the entire group and busily dusted himself and produced a newly washed handkerchief to rub the fresh crimson off his knuckles. The gashed faces of Timber and Alec showed from what sources that had come!

The sheriff maintained a silence which grew and grew in solemnity until all were breathless. It was the first time in months that there had been a brawl of such dimensions in Silver Tip. Would he put the youth in jail for a year, or would he merely fine him heavily and send him on his way with a warning? He was capable of anything. Now he began to speak.

"Alec," he said, "what you got to say for yourself?"

"The skunk hit me from behind," said Alec, intelligence rapidly returning to his ordinarily ferocious eyes. "He hit me before —"

"You lie," said the sheriff, as mild as ever. "How did it start?"

"You seen for yourself," said Alec, grown sullen. "I can't help if a hoss has a pair of bad heels."

"I ain't asking you how the fight begun," said Algie Thomas. "I'm asking you how you happened to get licked — by a kid like him!"

He pointed. Plainly, as he indicated, there was a great difference between them.

"He used to trick —" began Alec.

"Do you want to fight him over again — man to man?"

Alec whirled as though to rush into battle immediately, but the open, steady blue eyes of the youth stopped him with an uncanny power.

"I'll pull guns with any gent in Silver Tip," he said. "I ain't no prize fighter."

The old sheriff clucked softly and wagged his head.

"And what about you, Timber?" he asked.

Timber was of different metal. "Lemme at him again," he said. "I ain't through with him — not if he lives to be a hundred, I ain't nowheres near through with him. Fists, knives, guns — I don't care how he wants to start!"

"Well, kid," said the sheriff to the youth, "what d'you say?"

"Me?" said the latter, looking up from the scrubbing, of his knuckles. "Why, any way you say goes for me!"

The sheriff pondered; but when he spoke, it was not to give signal for battle.

"He'd kill you in ten minutes, Timber," he said. "You take my advice and keep offen him — you and Alec, both of you. I seen you hit him with the butt of your quirt. I bet they's a knob on his head like an egg; and they's the mark of Alec's quirt on his face, too. Now, you —" he jerked his head suddenly at the youth "— what you got to say for bringing fights and brawls into a peaceful town like Silver Tip?"

The boy looked steadily into his eye. "You saw it from first to last," he said. "What do you think about it?"

The direct query seemed to bring the sheriff up short; but when he spoke, it was not to the youth.

"Alec and Timber," he said, "I been watching you a long time, and what I seen ain't pleased me none. I've knowed some folks that was fond of riding by night. Well, I figure it might be healthy for both of you if you was over the hills by morning. Understand?"

"Look here," began Timber, "I can stand for a lot, especially from you, sheriff; but I want to say —"

"Don't say nothing, Timber," said the old man wearily. "I know about the gray hoss you used to ride, and what become of it, Timber. You and Alec shut up and get out."

Whatever the innuendo of the gray horse might have been, it carried enough significance with it to shut the mouth of Timber as though with a lock. With Alec McGregor behind him, he turned, burst through the inclosing semicircle, and disappeared a moment later into the hotel. It left only the youth as the center of interest, but the sheriff quickly removed the audience to other scenes.

"Shoo!" he said as though scattering chickens. "I got some business with this gent. The rest of you — g'wan!"

They melted away, but from the veranda of the hotel they watched. Even the marshal did not feel that he was invited to linger. He retreated down the veranda and sat on the edge of it, patting the nose of bay Mary. But from the corner of his eye he watched a scene which he could not overhear.

As for the sheriff, he stared fixedly at the youth. He exhibited a change and variety of interest as great as though he were turning the pages of a book; yet the face which he looked into was by no means extraordinary. It was merely the clear-eyed, bold, healthy face of a young man, strong featured rather than handsome. The stern gaze of the sheriff at length brought a flush into the face of the boy, so deep a flush that the mark of Alec McGregor's quirt stood out in dim gray relief against it. At this the sheriff leaned back in his chair once more.

What he said was: "Son, how old are you?"

There was such a wealth of kindliness in his voice that the features of the other relaxed, and by their relaxation they showed the degree of strain under which he had been laboring previously.

"Twenty-three," he said.

"Twenty-three? Well, well!" The sheriff laughed softly as though the answer afforded him cause for pleasant mirth. "And what might your name be?"

"Thomas Converse," said the other.

"Tom Converse? There's a right good name, now! Step up here and set down and rest your feet, lad. How far you been coming?"

The youth started to answer, changed his mind, and looked sharply at the sheriff.

"I've come quite a ways," he said, and leaned back in his chair with a sigh of pleasure as the top rung of the back fitted into the muscles behind his heavy shoulders. He seemed to be relaxing in sections; only his eyes remained bright.

The sheriff smiled, both at the reticence and the weariness. Suddenly he thrust out his trembling hand.

"Lemme see your Colt, son."

Tom Converse started. "I don't pack a gat," he began.

"Tut, tut," clucked the sheriff with a suggestion of a frown. "One like you don't need a gun, but you'd rather appear among folks undressed than without your gun. Lemme have a look at it!"

There was something so crisply businesslike in this address that Tom Converse, after a moment of hesitation, reached behind him and brought forth a revolver which, up to this time, had been out of sight. He slipped it over his flat palm to the sheriff, all the time probing the old face with his keen young eyes. Where the revolver had been concealed was a mystery, for the gesture of the youth had been as swift as light, though perfectly smooth and casual. The sheriff now chuckled in delight.

"You've practiced up a pile, I see," he remarked.

"Practiced what?"

"That draw. Oh, I know it don't come by nature. A gent has to work on it to get it down that fine. Why, son, most of 'em with a gun hanging in a holster at their side can't get their guns out much quicker than that."

A glint of satisfaction came into the eye of Tom Converse. "They ain't half as fast, most of 'em," he declared.

"Then why do you practice so much?" snapped the sheriff. "Are you aiming to pick a fight with a gent and kill him?"

The youth flushed and blinked. Apparently the matter had never been put to him before in this manner.

"I've never shot a man," he said. "I hope I never have to."

The sheriff was still half stern, half sad.

"I'd ought to take this gun away from you," he said. "But, if I did, you'd go and get yourself another."

He restored the weapon reluctantly.

"Tom," he said, resting his hand on the shoulder of the youth, "will you let me talk like an old, old man — not like a sheriff?"

"I'll sure listen to you," said Tom Converse as he made the big gun disappear with uncanny adroitness. "You can't talk too much for me!"

"Thanks!" and the sheriff smiled. "What I want to say is: You'd be better off without that gun altogether. But, if you ever pull it out, for Heaven's sake don't shoot to kill!"

He spoke with profound solemnity.

"I know you," he went on, "pretty nigh as well as though I'd raised you, because — well, because I've been pretty much like you myself when I was a kid. I know that you've come out of a good home. I know that you've worked on your dad's ranch handling the cows and riding herd ever since you was knee-high to a grasshopper, and I know that pretty soon you got terrible tired of the ranch and wanted to see things — wanted to see girls that you hadn't danced with a hundred times before at the schoolhouse dance, and wanted to see gents that you hadn't growed up with, so's you knew just which ones you could lick and which ones could lick you — or maybe none of them could lick you?"

The youth flushed. "I guess you're laughin' at me," he said gently. "But I guess, too, you're wise enough to go right on laughing. So go ahead, because I don't mind it from you."

"You've come out hunting for excitement," went on the sheriff as kindly as ever. "But excitement most generally, sooner or later, means trouble. Now, Tom Converse, mark what I say!" His voice changed, rose, and rang. "If they's a gent killed in a gun fight around these parts before long, I ain't going to ask no names — I'm going to send for you!"

Tom Converse blinked.

"And d'you know who I am?" continued the terrible old man.

"I don't."

"I'm Algernon Thomas. Maybe you've heard tell of me."

He had; the little gasp of wonder attested it. But suddenly he reached out and laughed as he wrung the hand of the sheriff.

"You're a white man to waste so much time on me, Sheriff Thomas. But I'm sure proud to have talked to you."

"You run along," said the sheriff joylessly. "Lord, I wish I had the authority to send you back home!"

Tom Converse turned his back with another nod and laugh and strode across the street, while the sheriff still gloomy, watched him going.

"Jeff!" he called. "Jeff Hall!"

The marshal came at a run.

"Well?" he said. "Who is he?"

"Look him over. You've seen him coming. Now look at his back, Jeff."

"Well?"

"I'll tell you why, son. You may need to be able to recognize Tom Converse before very long. If ever I seen a gent all labeled and staked out for raising tarnation, there he goes."

He turned with a sigh and walked into his house; the screen door banged heavily behind him.

Chapter Four

Absurd Betting

As for Tom Converse, if he were aware of the interested eyes which bore upon him from behind, he was still more concerned with the hostile battery which played upon him from in front. On the veranda of the hotel across the way and a little down the street were lined the major portion, so it seemed, of the men of Silver Tip. Hardy men, he thought — hardier men than he had yet encountered in any group in his travels, and they glowered upon him in sullen silence as though every one of them yearned to be at his throat.

How could he know that there was hardly one of them who was not a malefactor fleeing from justice, or one who had fled not long before? Hardly one but had served his term; hardly one but had watched the terrible old sheriff dealing kindly with the youth, and hated the sheriff for his forbearance and the youth because of his favor.

What if Tom Converse were a spy sent among them by the wily sheriff? In their innermost hearts they knew well that Algie Thomas did not have to stoop to such methods as this, but they hated Tom Converse, nevertheless — on general prin-

ciples. He could sense the antipathy without being able to arrive at an explanation for it.

As he went up the steps, they glared at him like dogs at a stranger. Had it not been for the injunction of the sheriff which still weighed a little upon his mind, he would have picked a quarrel with one of them at once — the biggest one, of course — and had the matter out with him just to clear the air and get at the root of things.

That injunction made him merely pause and say to the first man he picked out — a slender, sallow-faced man with rather sad eyes, "What town is this, partner?"

The sallow-faced man did not join in the general scoffing outburst of laughter at this query. He looked the youth over slowly from head to foot. He and the sheriff had been the only men in Silver Tip who remained in their chairs after that brief fight began.

"This town is Silver Tip, son," he said at length, and then licked his cigarette, lighted it, and drew the first breath of smoke deep into his lungs, all the while without removing his dull eyes from the face of Tom Converse.

"Thanks," said Tom, and, after hesitating a moment and running an uneasy eye up and down the line of scowlingly hostile faces, he went on into the hotel to secure a room for the night.

"And to think," said one worthy as Tom disappeared, "that we got to sit here like so many chunks of mud and watch a kid like that walk

heavy and talk big! I say it makes me crawl inside — makes me plumb sick!"

"It ain't the kid," remarked a companion. "It's old wisehead across the street — old sure-shot — old Algie Thomas that keeps a couple of dozen of us from eating that kid!"

He of the sallow face now closed his tired eyes and blew toward the ceiling a stream of smoke, so much of which had been inhaled by the long sojourn in the lungs that now only a thin blue mist went up.

"As long as I ain't got the job," he said, "I'm just as well pleased."

"How come?" someone asked. For there was that about the sallow-faced man which commanded respect. "You figure him to be pretty hard — even with guns?"

"I dunno," said the other. "I don't waste much time thinking about things!"

So saying, he rose, stretched himself, and went toward the door, hobbling with a heavy limp in the left leg. In fact, he gave the impression of a sadly worn man the moment those wise dull eyes were turned away. He disappeared through the door.

"Who is he?" asked half a dozen voices in chorus.

No one knew.

"But he's a wise one and a hard one," ventured a lounger. "I seen him rolling dice with 'Bud' Masters this morning. Bud can't make the dice talk, but you all know that he can darned near do it. Well, this gent kids Bud along for a while and drops a couple of hundred to him. Then he turns around and trims Bud worse'n I ever seen. Bouncing every shot, too. Darn 'f I could see how he done it, but he seemed to be calling every wallop. Got back his two hundred, and then sunk into Bud for five hundred more before you could turn around hardly. Cool, too. Took it as though it was hardly worth while wasting his time to pick up a measly five hundred like that. Bud is still mad enough to bite the sight offen his gun."

Talk strayed to other matters as talk will in that universal Western symposium of the hotel veranda. It was far later in the afternoon when someone who had gone inside came out again and winked to the others about him.

They went down to the farther end of the veranda and peered through the door into one end of the barroom. There sat he of the sallow face and Tom Converse on opposite sides of a little card table. In front of the sallow man was a liberal stack of money. In front of Tom Converse was a watch.

Presently the watch disappeared and joined the stack of money.

The onlookers turned away, laughing silently for fear lest noisy mirth interrupt the trimming of the obstreperous youth.

"Raw?" said one. "I never seen nothing rawer'n that. He palmed a chunk of cards thick enough to choke a mule with 'em, and then he turned around and started feeding the dead stuff to the kid. It sure tickled me. But the kid must be blind."

"Blind nothin'," said another. "You'd be blind, too, if you was opposite that little worker. He's smooth, son, take it from me. Only he ain't working no harder than he has to work. That's all."

In the meantime, in the barroom, that consummate workman with cards, whose craftsmanship had called forth such enthusiastic praise from the vagabonds and "stickup artists" on the veranda, was now proceeding to weigh the watch in his hand after the manner of one who wished to make the former owner consider fully the extent of his loss.

"Maybe you got a knife?" he said.

Tom Converse disconsolately shook his head. It meant a great deal to him, the loss of that small capital which the crooked gambler had just won. To be sure, there was not so very much of it, but there was enough to have secured him freedom of foot for a few weeks, or even months, if it were carefully handled. But now it was gone, and he must descend again into the mild torment of daily labor. Not that Tom Converse was peculiarly lazy, but he had worked too long on his father's ranch not to acquire a detestation for labor as hearty as it was permanent.

"I haven't a knife," he said, "except this one."

He showed a worthless old tool with the blade all worn away from much sharpening.

"That's as good as a dollar," said the gambler.

"Why, it's not worth fifty cents," protested Converse.

Such foolish honesty made the sallow-faced man stare more fixedly than ever at Tom, and his lip curled slightly as he answered: "I feel like rattling the cards a little. Come on, kid. Call the knife a dollar."

Accordingly, it was called a dollar — and as such it was immediately lost.

"Never seen such a run as I'm having," commented the gambler blandly. "Anything else, son?"

"Nothing else I want to lose."

"What? Going to quit now? That's plumb foolish. I've been in a winning streak. All you need is to hit the same kind of a streak, and you'll get back everything and a pile more — whole pile more, so far as you know."

"Sorry," said Tom. "I can't play again."

"What about your gun?"

"Gun?"

"I saw you show it to the sheriff. He sure seemed to be interested in the make of it."

Tom flushed a little. "That gun," he said coldly, "ain't going to be staked." He even shivered slightly at the mere prospect.

"But why not?"

"I'll tell you," answered Tom. "It's because I got a gun that The Shadow used to use!"

At this the lame gambler started fully as violently as Tom could have anticipated.

"The Shadow? How come? I thought you were

never up in these parts before?"

"That's right. I don't know The Shadow. Never laid eyes on him. But an uncle of mine did, and got his gun. You maybe heard of the stage holdup in the Black Mountains in the road near Garrisonville?"

"Don't think I have," said the other thoughtfully. "What happened?"

"The Shadow stuck up the stage. He cleaned the party of their loot, and he was about to swing onto his hoss when my uncle made a play for him. The Shadow brings out two guns and lets fly. He dropped my uncle, but my uncle had a lucky shot and knocked one of the guns out of the hand of The Shadow. When he come home and got cured of his wound in the leg, he give me the gun. Why, I pretty near learned to shoot with it!"

He spoke with a semireligious passion, as a violinist of his favorite instrument. The other nodded. Then he shrugged back his shoulders.

"Let's play for anything, then," he said. "I want to use up this lucky streak. You see?"

"Name a stake that I've got," said Tom cheerfully, "and I'll sure go the limit with it."

"Twenty dollars," said the gambler, and looked around for a wager with wandering eyes that at length passed through the window and dwelt on the mountains, "against a ride to them mountains. That's a good fifteen miles, I take it, and it's worth twenty."

"Sure. Sounds like a fool bet, but I'd take it,

if I had a hoss," and Tom smiled.

"Ride a hoss of mine if you want," said the other carelessly.

Tom rehearsed the bet, shaking his head. "You'll bet me twenty dollars against a ride to the mountain — on your hoss?" He laughed at the absurdity of it.

"I'll bet anything with anybody," snapped the other, irritated. "Take it or not?"

"Sure," said Tom. "If you got the time of a hoss to waste, I guess I can waste the time to ride it!"

Of course there was something behind the absurd proposition. But, as he leaned back in his chair and studied the thin face of his companion, he could not imagine in what the catch lay. Why should this man have inveigled him into a card game to win his money and then put up to him as foolish a bet as this? What was behind it?

"How'll you know that I've ridden all the way?"

"When you get there — say to the top of Mount Samson — you can light a fire big enough to be seen down here."

That was the goal, then — to induce him to ride to the top of the mountain and light a fire? But what harm could that do him? He studied a moment.

"Deal," said Tom. "I take the bet!"

Chapter Five

Perfection in Horseflesh

Never had Tom followed a hand of stud poker with an interest so intense, and the hand was exciting enough for the prize. The lame man was dealing in the most masterly fashion, literally "reading the mind of the pack," and pulling his cards from the very center in order to fill his own hand and deal with corresponding strength to Tom Converse.

The cards flicked out in swift succession under the fingertips of that master. To Tom he slipped an ace as the buried card, and then three jacks in a row, followed by another ace. Never had so pat a full house been presented. On top of the gambler's "show" stood only three wretched little treys, but the turn-up changed matters sadly, and the treys grew to a tremendous four-of-a-kind.

Stunned with surprise, Tom Converse watched that card turned. He had had twenty dollars and a change of luck inside his very grip, so it seemed; but now the prize eluded him, and he found himself condemned to ride on a strange mission to a mountaintop and there ignite a fire large enough to be seen from the village.

While he was playing for the hand and the prize, it had not seemed so strange. Anything goes about a gambling table. He knew men who had gambled for their shoes or for the houses over their heads, so the stake for which they had just played seemed more or less a matter of course — until it was won and lost. Then it seemed strange indeed.

Looking across the table, he seemed to see glints of a yellow light playing across the black eyes of the lame man, and a hint of excited color coming into his cheek. Under the glance of Tom, the color faded, and the eyes became as dull as ever; but in that instant Tom had guessed at many things — and among the rest he knew that he had been tricked. Yet there was no way in which he could back out. He had been raised and trained by a stern schoolmaster — his father — who taught him that the most pressing of all debts are gambling debts, and, firm in that belief, Tom determined to put through his half of the bargain.

It raised his gall to know that the other had so wound him about his fingers.

"Friend," he said, and his square chin jutted out a little as he spoke, "I guess I've been the fool; but, after I've come back from this ride, I'll have a little talk with you — about cards!"

It seemed to Tom that in the very face of this threat the other smiled; but here again the expression was a mere flitting shadow of which he could not be sure. Moreover, the next moment the lame man was as courteous as ever.

"Talk to you as long as you want, partner," he said, "and about anything you want. Now let's eat. You'll sure need food before you start out on that ride. Riding raises a powerful appetite from my way of thinking."

It was growing late in the afternoon. In another hour it would be dusk, and though Tom felt a sudden and singular aversion to remaining longer in the company of this stranger, he could not deny that riding 20 miles uphill and down at night on an empty stomach was no pleasant prospect. He conquered his scruples, therefore, and they presently were out of the hotel and down the street in the eating room kept by a Chinaman who had won fame in the kitchen of an adjoining ranch, and who now, in his old age, was capitalizing on his reputation. They ate a leisurely meal here.

The gambler, in fact, seemed bent on urging on Tom Converse every dish of which he could think to flank and fortify the central masterpiece — the steak. Not only did he do this, but he supplied, in addition, a steady stream of conversation. He talked well, Tom thought; so very well that before long Tom had half forgotten the strange circumstances under which they were eating together.

Afterward, through the gathering dusk, they strolled down the main street, cut across between two of the houses, and, after continuing for the space of a mile, in a dead silence, they were brought up a steep grade and dipped down into a shallow gulch on the far side.

Here, as the complete blackness of the gully swallowed them, the lame man, who had kept up with surprising patience and agility during the walk, now whistled a note both piercing and small, and very like the note of some strange warbler.

He paused, whistled again, and was presently answered by the whinny of a horse — a guarded sound, Tom could not help feeling.

If there had been mystery about the lame man before, it was instantly increased a thousandfold. Instinctively Tom reached for his revolver. The first touch of its warmed steel reassured him, but nevertheless he was tinglingly on his guard. Where there were horses, there might be men. But who and what power could have conveyed a horse up a slope which men could barely climb; or, still more impossible, who could have lowered a horse down the dizzy descent from the edge of the cliff above? Certainly no beast could have managed the climb up or down unassisted. At least, so Tom Converse would have vowed.

His guide now turned up the gorge.

"I'm going to show you your hoss," he said, "the hoss for you to ride tonight."

"You keep a queer stable," answered Tom, and then, remembering that there was no reason on earth for this fellow to harbor enmity to him, and surely no way in which he could profit by a mischance that might come to Tom, he swallowed the burst of other questions which rose in his throat.

His companion now produced an electric torch from his pocket, and, having gone for some distance in the direction from which the neigh had come, he flashed the light on, let it glow for a bright instant on a white rock at their feet, then raised it and made it instantly play on the horse.

In the clear circle of light Tom Converse looked upon a picture of equine perfection. Lover of horse-flesh all his life, he had made it his diversion to train them, and his pleasure had been to handle them, once trained. But never in his experience with the half-breed stock on his father's ranch had he encountered such a specimen as this.

All his previous life with horses he had been gradually building up, feature by feature a picture of what an ideal horse should be: A horse large enough for a lengthy stride, but not too bulky for mountain work — say fifteen three or even sixteen hands at the very upper limit — and so powerfully and compactly made that it could endure the crushing impost of such weight as clothed the big frame of Tom Converse; large where the front cinch runs; deeply sloping of shoulder; having tapering legs of mighty bone and perfectly placed muscle; also a long neck, strong but not so heavy as to make the forehand overweighted and clumsy — such was the picture that had grown in the mind of Tom Converse; but, above all, his thoughts had dwelt on the head, that center of interest.

Now he found that the circle of the pocket lantern embraced all that he had dreamed. Point by point, the horse for which he had yearned, was before him! The very color was perfect — a dappled chestnut.

So long did he continue his silence that the lame man, who himself had looked on the horse with a flaming eye and then half faced his companion, now cried: "Well, partner, what you think? Think that hoss can make the trip with you and bring you back?"

"Lemme have the light," gasped Tom faintly. "Give me the light."

He tore it from the hand of the other and approached the stallion, speaking husky, broken words of pleasure and endearment such as the wildest horse recognizes, and the dappled chestnut stood like a rock while Tom went toward him.

"Easy!" exclaimed the lame man. "I know that hoss, son, and he'll tear you to bits if you fool around with him. He ain't no lady's pet."

"Shut up!" answered Tom tersely. "He'll stand for me. I know him; and he knows me. I've met him in my dreams. Steady, boy. Steady, old-timer!"

And, while the lame gambler cursed under his breath in astonishment, Tom Converse came beside the stallion, patted his head, and then went over him inch by inch, the wonderfully rich color of the red chestnut, dappled with black, shining like polished wood as the light came close to it. At length Torn stepped back and he shook his head.

"I can't find it," he said.

"Can't find what?"

"The flaw in him. But maybe it'll show up when he starts working."

"Not if you do a hundred miles with him at a stretch," answered the gambler. He added with a touch of feeling that surprised Tom: "You seem to know hosses uncommon well for a kid!"

"H'm," said Tom. "What sort of price would you put on that hoss, partner?"

The other paused, then began to laugh; and never in his life had Tom heard a sound more dryly mirthless than this laughter.

"He couldn't be bought," said the gambler. "I — I'd rather give him away than sell him!"

There was something about this speech — a suggestion of grief and rage combined — that made the heart of Tom Converse leap in sympathy and awe. He said no more, but picked up the fine saddle — far lighter than the average range saddle, and apparently made to order by a master workman — and threw it on the back of the horse. In a moment more he was on the chestnut.

"I'd only like to ask," said Tom, "how this horse was brought here."

"Look up," answered the gambler.

Tom raised his head. The sheer cliff beetled above him, an ominous wall in the blackness.

"I rode him down that," said the gambler simply.

Suddenly Tom knew, beyond question, that it was true. This pair together had accomplished the impossible, and something about that answer made him realize, also, that the ride he was about to undertake was a grave thing. The lame man would not lightly intrust his horse to a stranger. Behind the veil was a mystery well worth penetrating.

"I thought you were going to show me some trick way of riding out of this cañon," said Tom. "But I suppose I'm to ride him right on down the slope — over that slippery rock?"

"Give him his head. Let him get it as low as he wants, and don't bother him none with spurs or reins. He'll take you down. You won't need a whip on him. Speak to him, and he'll do what you say."

"What's his name?"

"First name that comes handy to you."

"Well," said Tom after a short pause, "I'll make a fire big enough for you to see. So long!"

He was about to ride on into the dark when the gambler hobbled suddenly in front of him and caught the head of the chestnut in his arms; and it seemed to Tom that a groan came from the lips of the man. Then he stepped back and snapped out the electric light. Walled in by the darkness, Tom sent the horse on, but he wondered grimly to himself what purpose that bonfire on the head of Mount Samson would serve.

One thing at least was certain: It was no mere jest. He wished that he could discard some of his pride and turn back and fire a volley of questions at the lame man; but pride restrained him. No matter how foolish he had been to take the bet, it had been made, and now he must stick to it. No doubt the gambler had counted on that very pride in approaching him, but — he summed up his argument with a curse and gave his mind to the immediate work before him.

Chapter Six

Fire on Mount Samson

That work was no slight thing. The wall of the cañon on the lower side was simply a small precipice, yet the chestnut traversed it with the agility of a mountain sheep. Tom felt under him a quivering strength such as he had hardly dreamed of before.

They tipped over the ridge and were confronted at once by an even more difficult task. The side of the hill dipped away in the sheer slope up which he and the gambler had labored with such trouble a few minutes before. The only thing to do was to trust the stallion with his head and hope that he could see better than his rider. This, accordingly, he did, and the wise horse dropped his nose far down as though he would smell out the best course.

The place immediately in front of him was not to his liking, and therefore he edged off to the right a matter of a dozen yards before he began to descend, throwing his forefoot so as to bring the cushion of the frog to bear on the slippery rock. At the same time he gathered his quarters beneath him and flattened down toward the slope with the deftness of a cat.

But even this dexterity in mountain work could not bring them safely and smoothly down the entire course of the slope. Presently Tom felt the stallion slipping, swaying — and suddenly the wise fellow rose from his crouched position and bounded into thin air. For a moment Tom's heart was in his teeth, but then the stallion landed catlike, bounded to a new foothold, and a moment later was trotting smoothly on the level ground beneath.

Far away and above them a voice was shouting a cheery greeting, and, as Tom's pulse began to settle, he shook his head and then chuckled. It was going to be strange work, to be sure; but it was also going to be the finest ride he had ever had in his life.

There would be traveling that would take the best out of the chestnut before they came back. Far above them rose the ragged head of Mount Samson, outdistancing its nearest peaks. In the darkness it seemed sheer cliff. But he had noted by daylight that there was a steep trail winding toward its top.

In two hours he should be able to make it. In fact, it was two hours and a half before they gained the top, and yet the time seemed far shorter to Tom. All the way he was marveling at the patient address with which the stallion went about his work, so that he quite forgot all the strange and threatening cirtumstances under which he himself had undertaken this night excursion. It was only when he came to the crest of the rise,

51

where the night winds played freely about him, that he remembered that there might be danger connected with the trip.

He paused for a long moment on the peak and looked and listened; but there was nothing to be seen save the noble forms of the mountains rolling away like black, frozen waves on every side, and the pale, small lights of Silver Tip glimmering in the deep hollow out of which he had climbed.

Where was the lame man at this moment? Did he sit at some window of the hotel, with his elbows resting on the sill, and with his intense, stern eyes directed in expectancy toward the top of Mount Samson? Or was he among a crowd in the barroom telling the rest how he had made a fool of the youngster?

Something told Tom Converse that the former was far more probable than the latter. Then, turning to the work at hand, he swung from the saddle, taking with him the small hatchet which the gambler had pointed out to him before he started. With it he cut a quantity of young pitch-pine saplings and built them up layer by layer into a tall pyramid. In the center of the pile, and around the edges, he placed some dry shrubs, then continued to pitch saplings toward the top until the mass was towering 20 feet aloft.

It had reached that height before he lighted the pile of leaves which sent a small yellow tongue of flame up, and this in turn caught in a mass of dry pine needles and cast a sprinkling of fire through the heap. That sprinkling turned, in a few moments, to a rush of fire that vaulted presently a dozen yards above the top of the pile, snapping off great masses of flame into the black night.

Tom Converse drew back, pleased as a child over the heat and the brilliance of the flame. Then he craned his neck to peer down at the village, as though he could see the results of that signal light on the inhabitants of the little town where now the lights had gone out in various windows as the occupants went to bed.

Presently, to his astonishment, he did see results and very definite results. There was at first a sprinkling of not more than half a dozen lights in windows. But now, within ten seconds after the time when the fire on Mount Samson soared to its full pitch, window after window added a yellow ray to the illumination of the village.

Before long it seemed that every house in the town had awakened, so that, if he could have heard at such a distance, he might have distinguished the excited voices of men and women, muffled within doors as they dressed, and then bursting loudly into the street to compare notes with neighbors and point to the fire on the height.

Since he could not hear, his imagination served him well enough — and how truly it was serving him he could not guess! He drew back from the heat of the fire, however, and tried the whistle which he had heard the lame gambler use as a signal for the chestnut.

53

When Tom Converse had duplicated the whistle quite exactly, he was rewarded with a low neigh of response, and the beautiful horse came glimmering into the firelight and paused beside him. He patted the neck of the animal, enjoying the silken smoothness of the hair, and all the time thoughtfully watching the spread of lights in the village.

Was this a signal to confederates of the lame man far away? But if so, why did the fire on the mountain so alarm an entire sleeping community?

Let that be as it might, though they sent to inquire as to the source of the fire, they could not reach him in much under an hour and a half, even if they rushed their horses as he had refrained from doing with the chestnut. So he waited there complacently, with the fragrance and the warmth of the yellow fire blowing about him in waves from time to time as the wind veered; and it seemed that the stars had never been closer overhead than they were this night, and never had the purity of the mountain air meant so much to him, or the quiet stolen so deeply into his heart. As he stood there he determined solemnly that this was indeed his country, and that he could never leave it.

How long he remained there, he could never have told, for he had fallen into one of those waking dreams which are, perhaps, the pleasantest parts of our lives. But from those dreams he had now a rude awakening.

There was a grating sound down the mountainside, not in the direction of Silver Tip, but from the opposite side; and next he distinctly made out the grunt of a man as his foot slipped on a stone.

Tom Converse crossed to the far side.

"Who's there?" he called out.

Then he saw for himself. There was not a single climber. Up this steep slope — far too steep for a horse — came a group of a dozen men. In answer to his hail they halted suddenly, and he could make out — as the outer rim of light from the bonfire reached down to the climbers — that they raised rifles as he spoke. At the same time, before they could respond with guns or words, there was a yell from the Silver Tip side of the mountain, and two rifles roared behind him.

The gun of Tom Converse was in his hand as he whirled, and yet he did not fire. The men who had stolen up slumped forward to the ground, their guns at their shoulders; but they were so utterly exhausted by the climb, and so shaken by their panting, that their shots were far wild.

Tom himself rushed for the chestnut, his revolver poised, and behind him the guns of the first group he had seen spoke in a volley. But already the edge of the hill was a screen behind him, and their bullets shrilled up harmlessly toward the stars.

He reached the stallion in a lunge. The way to Silver Tip was closed. So was the opposite side; and the third slope was a sheer cliff. There was nothing for it, then, but to escape through the fourth side of the mountain unless this, too, were blocked.

No time to ask questions of these madmen. One bullet clipped past his cheek. There was a tug at his shoulder as another slug tore through his coat at the armpit.

Then he was in the saddle, with the chestnut instantly in full stride. So quickly was he under way that Tom Converse, expert horseman though he was, was flung far back in the saddle. And in this manner, thrown so far off balance that he could not use his gun, he crashed into a third line of silent climbers, hurrying at the sound of the volleys already fired at the top of Mount Samson!

They had only time to yell once and pitch their guns to their shoulders before the stallion — the steep slope giving him almost veritable wings — was through them, and away!

Vainly they let drive in pursuit. A knoll was already between them and their target, and Tom Converse, wondering if that fire, like black magic, had raised a thousand devils out of the very ground, leaned far forward in the saddle and rode on like mad, calling to the stallion to give of his uttermost.

Chapter Seven

Fear

Well did the chestnut answer the plea of his new rider. Otherwise, Tom Converse would never have escaped from the top of Mount Samson with his life, for it actually seemed that the mountain was alive with men.

The explanation came to him as he hurried his willing horse along. Of course these were not men from the village of Silver Tip. But there might well be half a dozen villages nearer than Silver Tip itself, or solitary dwellings of trappers who might have gathered at the signal of fire on the mountain.

No matter from where they came, they were as savage as wolves behind him. They were shooting steadily, and shooting to kill — perhaps a score of men in all. Only the wildest combinations of good luck had preserved him thus far, he was aware; and good luck still favored him.

The suddenness of his descent carried him down from the rugged crest of the mountain and onto the broad, smooth shoulder to the north, communicating with more easily negotiable hills in that direction. Behind him the shouts and the noise of shooting died out, and he brought the stallion back to a more reasonable pace. Even that controlled gallop was bearing him through the night faster than any other animal he had ever bestrode.

Now he could think, and he had such food for thought that his mind whirled. What had they yelled?

"It's him! Drop him, for Heaven's sake! Kill the devil now that we have him! Now's our one chance, boys!"

They had screamed their words half in frenzy, it had seemed to Tom Converse. They hunted him, not like a dangerous man, but like some poisonous beast, too vicious to be given a sporting chance for life.

It seemed to him that he must have dreamed his way through that day. What had he done to awaken such frantic wrath against him? What had he done in the village of Silver Tip? He had met and fought two huge bullies, each of them armed, each of them a larger man than he. Surely he had fought them fairly and squarely. Had one of the men died as an after-effect of the beating, and had this posse ridden out to find him?

No, such presumptions were absurd. They had come because of the fire, and the fire was a trap which the cunning of the lame gambler had prepared for him and driven him into. That was the reason the sallow-faced man had flung his arms around the beautiful head of the chestnut and given it a farewell as affectionate as another man would give to his closest relative. He, Tom

Converse, had been chosen as a sacrifice by the wily rascal, and for some mysterious reason the scoundrel had sent the horse he loved to share the fate of Tom. But why?

It was a mystery past solution. What he must do first of all was to get out of the vicinity of these raging madmen who shot at sight and shot to kill; and, having got his bearings in a new place, he would then set about seeking explanations. Above all, he would hunt out the sallow-faced man. That face haunted him; the thin cheeks; the lean, handsome features; those dull black eyes with the glints of yellow light that played across them from time to time.

Full of these reflections, he paid little attention to the direction in which he rode, and let the chestnut fall back to walk and trot through the difficult going. He was only aware that they were keeping steadily to the north and west, drifting in and out among the ragged-sided mountains.

So, in the early dawn, he looked off of a chilly summit, and his eye plunged down to a new mountain town. It was a welcome sight to him. He rode straight for it, but the clear mountain air had deceived his eye, and it was twice the distance he had calculated. The sun was up, and the people of the village with it, before he dropped down into the street of the town.

That was all the better, for he would have a chance to ask a few questions before he found a bed and tumbled into it. He waved to a wide-shouldered fellow of about his own age who lounged out of the door of one of the houses and stooped to gather an armful of firewood from the pile.

"Hello!" called Tom Converse. "Which way is the hotel?"

"Hotel?" repeated the other.

Then, as he turned his head, his originally bright, intelligent face changed and became pale, expressionless as the face of a half-wit. The pieces of firewood tumbled out of his hands, and he straightened suddenly with a strong twitch of his arms as though — absurd to state! — he were about to fling his arms above his head. Yet he was hardly able to stammer: "Hotel — right down the steet — right down the street!"

With that he leaned suddenly over the woodpile again and began scooping up pieces of stovewood with hands so clumsy that the pieces fell out of his fingers as fast, well nigh, as he picked them up.

"Plain idiot," said Tom Converse, his anger melting at once into pity. "Funny I didn't make out the silly look right off. He seemed nacheral enough when I first seen him."

He went on toward the hotel, found it around the next turn of the winding street, and led his horse to the stable behind the building. There was no one near at that early hour, so he pitched a portion of hay into the manger for the chestnut and scooped a generous feed of barley out of the feed box. The stallion had come the last part of the journey so slowly that he was cool enough to eat grain at once.

These duties performed, and the chestnut duly unsaddled, Tom entered the hotel and advanced at once to the breakfast room. It occurred to him as he was sitting down that he had no money to pay for the meal, but that was a small burden. He would pay his bill when he left the hotel, and in the meantime he would find some way of raising a few dollars.

There were others trooping into the dining room by this time, big, hardy men of the mountains who all sang out a cheery good morning when they saw the newcomer. Tom, whose anger over his last night's adventure increased as the day wore on, refrained from telling his story to the first men who appeared. It would not do, he knew, to tell so wild a tale to the first men who came under his eye.

The credence of a man's best friend, as a matter of fact, would be sorely tried by such a narrative. A fire on a mountain — a sudden appearance of men with guns — men who shot to kill without first asking for any explanation — surely such a tale was woven of flimsy fabric. It gave him a shivering feeling of unreality even after all those hours of riding. As for the opening chapters of his adventure — gambling with the sallow-faced man whose very name he did not know — that also was a story too odd to be repeated except to a most trusting comrade.

He proceeded to attack a huge breakfast of hot cakes, bacon and eggs, and endless cups of coffee.

In the midst of his repast a stammering boy burst into the room from the outside.

"D-d-dad!" he cried, rushing for that portly, white-whiskered individual in a corner of the dining room. "They's a hoss in the sta-stable that l-l-l—"

"Whistle, son," said his father, making a great wedge out of a stack of hot cakes disappear. "Whistle and then try it again."

"A d-d-dappled chestnut hoss with black p-p-points and j-just l-like —"

"Eh?" gasped his father.

Every man in the room suddenly stopped eating.

"That's my hoss," said Tom Converse. "Anything gone wrong with him?"

All heads jerked around at him. It seemed to Tom that all eyes widened as they looked.

"Your h-h-hoss?" stammered the boy, and over his face, as he looked at Tom, passed the same white, idiotic look which he had noted in the face of the other youth down the street a few moments earlier. "They ain't n-n-nothing wr-wr-wrong w-with it. It — it's a fine h-h-hoss, that's all!"

Tom nodded and turned back to his food, bewildered. Was this a town of idiots?

Suddenly he saw that the big brown hands of the man directly across the table from him were shaking so violently that the coffee slopped heavily from side to side in the cup he raised to his lips. Tom looked up. The same white, stupid look was making the eyes of his opposite table companion wide. No, it was not stupidity.

It was rank, staring fear!

Chapter Eight

The Scented Note

In a blur of conflicting emotions Tom finished his breakfast. Why was it that they dreaded him the instant they laid eyes on him. No, it had something to do with the horse.

The matter had better be slept upon. He rose as he finished, and stalked across the strangely silent room, where men glanced up at him with furtive eyes as though afraid that, if they looked steadily, he might turn and blast them with a frown. Beside the proprietor Tom paused.

"I want to get a room," he said. "Got one for me?"

The fat man gaped, and there was a gasp behind Tom throughout the room.

"Ain't that plain?" demanded Tom angrily. "I want a room. I want a place where I can turn in. I've been riding pretty near all night. Can you put me up?"

The fat host moistened his colorless lips.

"Sure," he said. "I'll put you up, if you say so." He pushed back his chair slowly.

"Never mind," said Tom. "No hurry. Finish your breakfast. I can wait that long, no matter how sleepy I am!"

The fat man looked up at him in astonishment and, it seemed to Tom, redoubled fear. Then he bounced to his feet.

"I'll have you fixed up as well as I can," he said; "and I'll have you fixed up in a jiffy."

"I haven't much cash on me," Tom told him honestly. "I may have to look around for a little to pay you."

"Cash?" said the other, and summoned a sickly smile. "You don't have to have no cash here."

"Why not?" asked Tom, sharp with suspicion, bewildered by the manner of the other.

"Why, I take gents by the looks of 'em. You see?"

He led the way out of the room up the stairs. Halfway up the flight, Tom paused. In the dining room there had broken out a clamor of deep voices as many men spoke toegther, each one letting out his voice more and more. He could not hear what they said, but it stood to reason that they were talking about him.

He was led forward in the upper hall and shown into a large, neat room.

"I don't need to hold down two beds," said Tom. "I can get along with a smaller place than this."

"Smaller? Oh, no," said the host. "I guess you're used to having lots of room — lots more room than I can give you. I'm just doing my best to make you comfortable." And he broke into laughter which squeaked up into a high key, and threatened presently to become hysterical.

Tom advanced and raised a threatening forefinger. At the gesture the laughter was cut short, while the fat lips froze white and stiff around the next guffaw.

"Look here," said Tom, "who do you think I am anyway?"

The protestations of the host were frantic. "Who are you? I dunno. How could I guess who you are? I don't ask too many questions. I ain't one of them fools that has to ask a bunch of questions of everybody that comes along. You're just a — a miner out prospecting."

"A miner without a kit?" Tom sneered.

"Well, a cow-puncher out to see part of the country."

"That's exactly what I am — a cow-puncher out to see part of the country."

Again the hysterical laughter threatened to attack the fat man, but he choked it back with writhing features.

"Sure," he said. "Anybody could see at a glance that that's what you are!"

"Then get out of the room and go down and tell those gaping idiots downstairs what I've told you. You hear?"

There was a nod, and then the proprietor backed to the door, partly leaped and partly fell into the hall, and was gone with scurrying footfalls.

"You'd think I was the devil, and that he'd just got away from me." Tom Converse grinned; and then, overcome with bewilderment and irritation, he slammed his hat on the bed. "They're crazy — all plumb crazy!" he said as he closed the door.

For a moment he was on the verge of striding downstairs, seizing the first man he met, and demanding an explanation of the mystery; but weariness began to exert a mighty influence over him.

He sat down to draw off his boots, but waves of sleep swept over his brain. Presently he leaned to one side, dropped his head on the pillow, and was instantly sound asleep.

Downstairs, men moved back and forth in an increasing commotion, but Tom Converse heard not a sound or a shadow of a sound, so profoundly was he plunged in sleep.

When he wakened, in the center of the floor a pool of golden light from the western sun was sloping farther and farther toward the wall, and Tom came to with a start, his head spinning from the uncomfortable position in which he had slept, and because he had been asleep through the heat of the day.

He rose and staggered to the washstand, where a hastily-performed toilet cleared his mind enough to let a few of the experiences of the past night return to him. He turned away, shaking his head to clear his mind still further, and, as he turned, he kicked a small rock halfway across the room — a small rock with a piece of paper attached.

This he picked up. The paper was a pinkish gray, and it had a faint scent, the last breath of a perfume which had been ghostly thin even from the beginning. He unrolled the paper from the stone and found within a portion of swift, delicately clear writing.

There was no signature, there was no address; only:

I suppose you no longer care about yourself or for me. Otherwise, you wouldn't have done this wild thing. Perhaps you take this as a joke, but it isn't a joke. You think that you can walk right through the men of Wentworth as you have walked through other towns. But you can't. They have sent away. An hour ago Algie Thomas came from Silver Tip. They have surrounded the hotel. Heaven alone knows how I shall get this message to you, unless I can manage to throw it through the window, and Heaven alone knows why I am sending it.

If this is the end, it's only right, however, that you should know something that you have caused. I suppose your shoulders are broad enough to carry this burden. You will only laugh at it, perhaps. But I want you to know that Ben, who you know has always worshiped me, decided that you could not be altogether bad, simply because you cared for me, and that your ways must be justifiable. No, he began to hero-worship you like a silly child and he's hardly more than a silly child, you know. He decided that he was going to make himself a man — such a man that you would notice him and perhaps make him your partner. He used to talk to me about it, but I always thought it was only a make-believe dream.

Then one morning we woke up to learn that a safe — an old safe in a grocery store — had been blown in the next county, and that Ben was suspected of having done the work. By noon came the report that he was captured in a fight in which he wounded two of the posse that took him.

Perhaps you know all this, and you don't care. But I tell you that, if Ben is sent out of Carlton Jail and put into the penitentiary, the guilt will belong partly to you.

Oh, if you could do something to help him! His father looks at me every day and says nothing, but I know he thinks it is my fault because I cared for you, and because you had done such things —

But why should I talk of it any longer! You are smiling already.

If I could only learn, once for all, that you have really a heart, or that there are only cold veins in your body —

Good-by, and Heaven help you and me and Ben. I think we must all go down together.

Tom Converse sank upon the edge of the bed and ground his knuckles into his forehead.

"Ben is in jail because he blew a safe," he

groaned, "and he blew the safe because I set him a bad example. And I'm in this cursed hotel with all the men in town waiting for me to come out and get my head blowed off — and Algie Thomas, that old eagle, waiting for me along with the rest of 'em —"

He broke off and straightened to his feet.

"I'm crazy. I'm plumb crazy. I'll wake up pretty soon and find out that I've dreamed it. Who am I? Who's Ben? And who wrote this letter?"

He was about to crush it to nothing, but his fingers, as though with volition of their own, refused to smash it, and, instead, folded it neatly. He raised it again. The fragrance was something to be guessed at rather than known. But out of it stole the subtle thought of a woman, and spread pleasantly around him.

"I'll get out of here," said Tom abruptly, "and go down and have an explanation with old Algie, because he'll put me right."

He strode to the door, turned the key, and pressed on the knob, but the door didn't budge. It was heavily braced from without.

At the same time a voice said — the voice of old Algie: "That you, Tom?"

"Sheriff Thomas!" cried Tom Converse. "Thank Heaven that there's one sane and sensible man within a thousand miles of me! Sheriff, lemme come out and have a talk with you!"

The answer was, first of all, a soft, low laugh; then: "You start your talking on the other side

of that door, son. I'm sure against taking un-
necessary chances."

"Sheriff," cried Tom, "you don't think I'm —"

"I don't think nothing — I don't think nothing," broke in the sheriff. "I just know that you've
reached the end of your trail, son."

"Good Lord!" cried Tom. "Are you going
to act as though I've done something terrible
and —"

"Tush — tush!" said the sheriff. "I'd ought
to of known it the minute you showed me that
gun. But I wasn't watchful. I sure wasn't watchful.
I didn't dream that even you would play a game
as bold as that, Tommy!"

Tom Converse stepped back, and, so doing,
he placed himself in line with the window. Instantly there was a ringing report, and a bullet
hummed past his head and crashed against the
wall.

It was true, then, that they had him perfectly
surrounded.

Chapter Nine

Weakness and Rage

Tom side-stepped into shelter, while a dull shout of excitement rode outside of the building and faded away again.

"You got to watch out and step lively, son," said the quiet voice of the old sheriff beyond the door. "But maybe it'd be better for you to have it done with right now than to have to wait until you get starved weak and desperate."

"What do you advise me to do?" asked Tom.

"Come out and surrender to me, and take my word to keep you from the crowd. They're a hard gang, and they mean bad by you, Tommy. But, hard as they are, I'm a mite harder, and they won't lay a hand on you if I say so. You just come out and surrender to me, Tommy," he coaxed, "and I'll see to it that you get your trial and have your picture took by all the reporters and get hung nice and quiet and proper. Why, Tommy, papers all over the world will want to come and send reporters to hear what you got to say. And maybe you'll have time before you swing, to tell the story of your life and all your killings to one of them smart writer gents that can fix up your yarn in fine words, fine as gilt. Might make you so much money that out of that book you could have a hospital built, or something like that, eh, Tommy?"

The union of seriousness and mockery in this speech convinced Tom Converse that it was useless to argue, but he tried one other step before he gave up.

"Sheriff," he said, "you call me Tom?"

"Yes."

"You admit that my name is Tom Converse?"

"I admit that it's anything you say it is."

"Will you get in touch with my folks at the address I give you, and prove my identity?"

"Come, come," said the sheriff with a touch of irritation, "ain't we carried the fooling far enough? They's only one hard thing about your case, Tom, and that's to get you safe to a jail. You can have time to prove you got ten names, once you're there; but, every minute you hold out, that crowd out yonder is getting bigger and worse tempered. They want your body now. But they'll be plumb crazy for it if you don't give up right quick."

"Will you answer one question?"

"I'm a patient man," said the sheriff. "Talk away!"

"Who do you think I am?"

The sheriff laughed. "What man d'you think would take me out of Silver Tip, that I ain't left inside these ten years? On account of what man would I ride all the way across these consarned mountains? They's only one man in the

73

world that's worth it — and that's The Shadow!"

The color rushed out of Tom's face. Then he steadied himself. His voice, as he pleaded, became shrill.

"Ain't you going to use no common sense, sheriff? Ain't The Shadow a middle-aged man, anyways? And ain't I barely twenty-three?"

"Lord! Lord!" The sheriff sighed. "D'you expect me to be took in as plumb easy as all that? Why, The Shadow started working about five years ago. Well, that ain't too far back for you. Look at Bill, the Kid. He was thirteen when he started to get famous. He was a man's-sized man, when it come to reputation, by the time he was sixteen. No, you've had plenty of margin to work in. Now I ask you for the last time, Shadow, are you going to act like a gent with sense and give up to me, or are you going to hold out like a fool and get yourself all shot to pieces?"

Tom Converse, though his brain was reeling, understood why that plaintive note of pleading was in the voice of the sheriff. Great as was the name of Algernon Thomas, slayer of criminals and gun fighter extraordinary, the taking of The Shadow alive would at a stroke eclipse all of his other deeds, and the old man was naturally anxious to finish his life in this last and greatest blaze of glory. It was worth waiting half a generation in order to come to this great moment.

While Tom turned away in silence, the sheriff called to him again and again, until convinced that there was nothing more to be gained by talk.

74

Tom, in turn, had been convinced of the same thing. Words could not avail him in his struggle now. Then a flash of inspiration came to him. He whirled again toward the door.

"Mind what I tell you," he shouted. "You laugh at me now, but, when you've murdered me, you and the rest of your gang of dirty cutthroats, you'll find out that The Shadow is still alive. And you'll find that The Shadow is the yaller-faced, half-sick-looking gent that won my watch from me in Silver Tip — him that walks with a limp. You hear —"

But the laughter of the sheriff silenced him, and this time other, heavier voices joined in the laughter.

"He's losing his nerve, now that we got him cooped," said one. "Hark to him beg — the dog!"

The sheriff answered the last insinuation. "We ain't plumb fools, Shadow," he said. "The gent you say is The Shadow, is down in the stable right now, making friends with your hoss, 'Captain.' "

"Is that the name of the chestnut?"

Another laugh.

Tom Converse bowed his head and gritted his teeth, for it was almost more than his nerves could hear. No words more. They had doomed him to die, and, if he could not die like The Shadow, he would at least die like Tom Converse, who had never been known to show fear of the inevitable.

Yet it was terribly hard! The faint scent of

perfume rose from the paper in the breast pocket of his shirt, and that fragrance seemed to be the incarnation of all that was beautiful and worthy to be enjoyed in life. The fading light of the sun — now a patch high on the wall, turning to dim, reddish gold — was symbolic of the night which was about to end his days forever.

Far and near, now, he could hear voices of men. Once, he thought, he could make out a woman laughing in the distance. How horrible that any living creature could laugh at a time when another had been doomed to die!

All at once he found that it was necessary to sit down. The wind was rising as the sun declined, and the sharpening wail of the wind's voice sent a thrill of hollow weakness through him. His knees buckled; it became very, very difficult to stand and endure the weight of his own body. Sitting in the chair with his head bowed in his hands and the knuckles ground into his eyes, he felt, rather than saw, that it was becoming dark while he weighed the chances.

Should he take the old sheriff at his word? No, the rising voice of that wind, now already increased to the force of a storm, warned him that the anger of the men who waited outside was up to the boiling point.

And was it any wonder? Suppose that he himself had received word that The Shadow, the devilish, murdering Shadow himself, had been caught in a room. Would he not have rushed to the attack, and would he not have taken the first opportunity to drive home his bullet into the body of the outlaw? Yes, and there were a hundred — perhaps five hundred — men in the little town who would take advantage of a similar opening at his expense. He could not trust even the formidable sheriff to protect him. He could trust only his own skill in keeping himself out of the hands of the enemy.

Something brushed against the window.

He looked up to find that the room was immersed in darkness. The sunshine on the wall — how kindly it had been! — was gone. Never again would he see the blessed sun rise or set, or kindly human faces about him. All of that was at an end. There remained only a brief span of darkness and hate — then the cold and the dark forever.

The muscles of his throat constricted. It was increasingly difficult for him to swallow, and he had a great impulse to go to the door, beg them to open it, and, when they opened, fall on his knees, throw his arms above his head, and beg them not to shoot until he explained — that he was an honest man, of an honest family, and that his father could be found at —

No, no. They would laugh. They would answer each word with a dozen bullets. A feeling that he was about to rush at the door, beat at it with his hands, and shriek like a hysterical woman, brought Tom Converse to his senses with cold sweat on his brow.

"Am I a coward?" he asked himself. "Isn't this

cowardice to sit here trembling, afraid of the dark like a baby?"

Dread that he might shame himself was instantly greater than his dread of death. He forced himself to rise from the chair and walk a pace here and there. With the motion the terrible coldness of fear diminished. His heart no longer beat and choked him in his throat. His eyes cleared. The weakness and tremor left his hands. Instinctively he reached for his revolver and was comforted by the touch of it.

There, if need were, lay six lives. He could only pray that he should not be forced to spend them for his own liberty. At the thought of how he had been cornered, he called up the picture of the sallow-faced man who had driven him against the wall. How cunning he had been! How devilishly crafty! Yes, it was The Shadow. He had never heard The Shadow's horse described before, but then, he lived far from the range where the outlaw had performed the majority of his feats, and The Shadow cunningly had found out his ignorance. That was why he had played on him.

In the person of Tom Converse, he was allowing an innocent man to be slaughtered for his crimes so that he himself might have a free hand. The very life of the horse which he had risked with Tom, was now restored to him! In rage, warmth spread through Tom Converse, and, throwing back his head as renewed life breathed in through his nostrils, he shook his fist in the darkness at the thought of The Shadow.

Chapter Ten

The Shadow Outdone

Anger had nerved many a man before him. Now it raised the ordinarily brave spirit of Tom Converse to its usual pitch, and even above. He stepped to the window and peered cautiously into the night as though they might see even through the darkness and make him a target.

There was no sign of life, however, beyond the house, saving the increasing activity of the wind, which now carried along gusts of rain from time to time, and rattled it heavily against the side of the old hotel. The force of the rain and wind again and again brushed the very tip of a bough across the window. It was this which had caused the brushing noise that attracted the attention of Tom a little earlier.

The storm, it seemed to his rising spirit, would serve as a mask through which he might well be able to break through the lines of the watchers. But that hope had hardly been roused in him, than it was extinguished again by the appearance of a glow from above. Whether well lanterns or electric lights had been suspended from the roof above him, he could not tell; but certain it was that the light broke in a cold and uncertain stream, which plainly showed the great, swinging bough, wet, and agleam with rain drops. It rushed past the window with a swish, and then returned and danced high above his head — a tantalizing ghost of a bridge by which he might cross to safety!

There was an open door in the loft of the barn. He crossed to the far side of his window and was able at once to look down through the barn door and into the lighted area within, for a dozen lanterns must have been there, to judge by the brilliancy of the light which showed him, for the first time, a considerable group of his besiegers. In the space of one minute he saw 20 men!

But what fascinated him most of all was the center of interest around which these men moved — for that center of interest was no other than the black-dappled chestnut, the magnificent Captain, as Algie Thomas had termed the horse. High-headed, patient under the scrutiny of the many, he turned his head not a fraction of an inch from the man who stood at his head. That man was the sallow-faced, dull-eyed one who had brought all the danger to Tom Converse. That man was, Tom felt certain, the terrible Shadow himself! He whipped out his gun.

Something which Sheriff Thomas had said, restrained him. No, it was not right to shoot at even a complete villain like The Shadow unless the fellow were first warned that he was in danger. Even a snake played fairer than that. It rattled before it struck.

How perfectly The Shadow had planned, and

what victory had come to him as a result! In spite of himself, Tom could not help but admire, and though he cursed the outlaw, he found himself nodding in wonder and admiration. There he stood, surrounded by 20 men, each of whom would have risked his heart's pulsation to kill The Shadow, and he calmly patted the head of his own horse!

"I'll get one thing out of this if I come out with my life," vowed Tom Converse, his heart swelling as his eye drank in again the perfect lines of the chestnut, "and that one thing is you, Captain!"

Now the sallow-faced man stepped aside, appeared again carrying a saddle, and swung it onto the back of the stallion. Tom Converse could hardly keep himself from cupping his hands at his lips and shouting as through a trumpet: "You fools! Are you giving his own horse back to The Shadow?"

He restrained himself, still grinding his teeth with rage. Then, as he leaned a little farther out of the window two rifles exploded from the opposite side of the barn, and two bullets hummed wickedly close to his head.

With an oath he started back. Could they have seen him by the feeble and ghostly light which streamed from above? It did not seem possible.

He began pacing up and down the room. If they were watching that window as closely as all this, he would have a difficult time indeed in getting away.

The two rifles exploded again, and two more bullets hummed through the square of the window and crashed against the opposite wall.

Suddenly he understood. Unable to watch that window closely, owing to the torrents of rain which were now falling, and to the brushing of the bough back and forth, the guards had taken to firing random braces of bullets through the dark square of the window in the hope of driving the occupant back from any attempt at escape in this direction.

He stepped boldly back to the window. The horse was saddled, and The Shadow, if this were indeed he, stood beside Captain, with one hand resting on the neck of the magnificent animal. The heart of Tom Converse swelled. He was seeing the horse of his dreams for the last time.

How The Shadow had regained possession of the animal, was not hard to guess; he had simply outbid the others. But once he was past that farther door of the barn and away into the night, no man would again see the chestnut so close, for The Shadow would be back at his old trails to mischief. Thirty seconds more, and horse and man would be gone. Were they all mad to let them depart in this manner?

The great bough swung across the window, obscuring his view, and suddenly Tom Converse acted — blindly and without forethought.

He sprang onto the window sill and cast himself far among the small branches of the bough — a leap such as he had never made before! There was no chance that he might make it unnoticed. Instantly a score of voices shouted beneath him, and a roar of guns sent bullets whistling through the leaves, but they had no target save the whole branch.

They had seen him leap, but they could not locate him in the bough; and the branch, now on its backward swing toward the barn as the wind let up in its terrific pressure, was given redoubled impetus by the leap of Tom and his weight. That weight depressed the whole bough several feet, and swung Tom squarely at the dimly lighted square of the door which opened to the loft of the barn.

As he shot through the air on the swinging bough, he saw every man in the barn turn, at the sound of shouts and guns without, and make for the barn door. Even The Shadow came with the rest, and left Captain standing.

The bough hurtled to within four feet of the door. Indeed, its outer branches scratched the side of the barn, and, before the impetus of its swing was lost, Tom Converse leaped. Fair and true his feet struck the ledge beneath the loft door, and the force of his drive threatened to topple him headlong into the well-nigh empty space within, a fall that could not have failed to break his neck, for it was a great, 120-ton mow. As it was, he reached out with his left arm barely in time to catch the board in that direction, so that he was whirled suddenly into safety along the narrow ledge.

He clung there, hardly able to breathe with excitement. Had they seen him jump?

No; guns were roaring, voices were shouting outside, but never a shot whirred near him. They were shooting at the tossing bulk of the great branch, which dodged and whirled in the storm as though purposefully attempting to make them miss their targets.

He looked down. There stood The Shadow at the door of the barn, with his arms folded, and a sinister smile barely perceptible on his lips as he watched — waiting every moment to see the body of his dupe come crashing out of the tree and fall to the ground.

So enraged was Tom Converse by what he saw that he barely withstood the temptation to whip out his gun and fire down at that calm figure. But how sweet — how ineffably sweet it must have been to the outlaw to see the power of the law working its hardest to execute his own will!

These observations Tom made in the space of a single breath. Then he stole down the ledge and began to work his way across the braces which, in a small forest of rising upright beams and crisscross timbers, supported the far-flung sides of the barn. A hundred men were shooting at his shadow outside, and it gave him an eerie feeling to be safe inside this shelter.

Swiftly, but not too swiftly, lest that quiet figure at the door be attracted even though his back were turned, Tom tiptoed across the beams until he was directly above — not more than five feet, at that — the back of the stallion. There he lay flat along the timber, but, as he did so, Captain tossed up his head, and one of the long line of horses, in stalls down the barn, neighed loudly.

The Shadow whirled at the door.

All the breath was squeezed out of the lungs of Tom by terror. Would the shadowy light save him — that and his obscure position, lying flat along the beam? Perhaps this was what did it, for the eye of The Shadow no doubt plunged among the dim spaces of the barn searching for an upright figure in the act of flight, not a stationary one lying flat and plainly in line with his eye.

He did not see Tom Converse, for the gun which he flicked out of a holster was not leveled or discharged. He did not see Tom, but he seemed suddenly to have guessed where the fugitive might be.

"Halloo!" he shrilled. "Come in here, half a dozen of you. Maybe he got off that branch and into the barn through the open door."

They came in a rush — a dozen wild-eyed men, swarming through the open doorway. How much more formidable was the solitary form of The Shadow standing before them! The great outlaw turned toward the others. The moment his back was turned, Tom slipped down, hung an instant, and dropped snugly into the saddle on the stallion.

His fall was seen, but before a yell could apprise The Shadow of what was going on behind him,

Tom Converse had twitched the head of Captain around and had struck his heels into the flanks of the horse.

The Shadow whirled — but it was only to see Captain flash through the opposite door of the barn with the form of the fugitive bent low over his neck!

Chapter Eleven

Work of Revenge

When the rest of them, groaning and yelling their rage, flung themselves on horseback and plunged into the wild night, The Shadow did not stir. There was agony inside him to think that Captain was gone from him again, just as his heart had been growing big with the thought of repossessing the peerless horse. But he knew the folly of pursuing a man who bestrode the dappled chestnut. Too often he himself, on that safe back, had laughed at pursuers mounted on the fastest horses in the mountains.

In three minutes there were few sound men remaining in the village, and then The Shadow turned disconsolately from the barn and walked into the deserted hostelry. It would be interesting to see the room where the youngster had slept that day. He climbed the stairs, his mind full of Tom Converse.

In all his life, so far as he knew, he had never done a thing so utterly calculated and treacherous as the trap into which he had plunged Tom Converse. But since three men lay in wait and shot him from ambush while he came to the girl he loved — since that time all human kindness had vanished from his mind. All men were enemies, all in one degree; yet there was something about this youth that made The Shadow shake his head, partly in pity and partly in concern.

He himself had reached the advanced age of 24 — he was exactly a year older than Tom Converse. But in experience there was a difference of centuries between them. Every man who has killed is a generation older than his law-abiding companions, and The Shadow had killed many and many a time, carelessly, risking his own life as freely as ever he took the lives of others. He had always consoled himself with the thought that he had not once slain through taking a cruel advantage.

But could he keep that consolation any longer? He had trapped Tom Converse as a man would trap a stupid beast, and at first he had said to himself that it made no difference. Tom was simply a heavy-handed clod; his life and his death meant nothing to the world. But it was turning out that Tom was something more. This episode of the escape from the hotel was as cool-nerved an exploit as he, The Shadow, had ever performed.

A grisly, chill feeling that, in some manner, his fate was wrapped up in the destiny of Tom Converse, came to the outlaw. He climbed the stairs, turned down the hall, and stepped into the room recently occupied by Tom. To his surprise there was a lighted lamp in it, and suddenly he was confronted by Sheriff Algie Thomas.

The old man was nodding and smiling.

"Look at that!" he said. "He didn't try no fool stunts. He didn't try to cut a hole through the ceiling or tear up some of the boards of the floor. No, siree! He just waited until he got his chance and came right where we expected him to come!"

He shook his aged head in wonder, and The Shadow fixed upon him black eyes from which the dullness was quite gone; glints of yellow lights were showing in their depths. How strange it was that he, The Shadow, should be standing here quietly, at liberty, and talking in peace with the most formidable upholder of the law in the mountains! Where was the strength in the withered body of this old man? Where was the strength that had made him dreaded for so long, and kept him dreaded even now when he was on the verge of his dotage?

"Tell you what, sheriff," he said maliciously. "I'm sure sorry that he's slipped through your hands. This is the first time you've ever met up with The Shadow, and I sure hate to have it said that he beat you. First time anybody has ever got the best of you, ain't it?"

The old sheriff caught up the lamp and raised it high above his head. He stared fixedly at the outlaw.

"You're a wise boy," he said slowly, regarding The Shadow closely. "You ain't been off gallivantin' around and tryin' to catch The Shadow on a night like this, have you?"

"No," said The Shadow. "I seen it wasn't any

use. I seen his hoss."

The sheriff nodded. "So did I," he said. Suddenly he reverted to the first remark of The Shadow.

"I've been beat before, son. Don't ever go around saying that this is the first time that I been beat. Why, I was raised on beatings. I learned how to shoot a gun by being shot down by other folks. If I have nine lives, I've sure lost eight of 'em by means of powder and lead!" And he laughed with the most perfect good nature.

The Shadow watched him as one would watch a curious relic saved from the grave. Somewhere in those withered muscles was a force to be dreaded. Where was it? He began to guess that there was only a mind in little Algie Thomas, and that that mind forced a feeble and unwilling body to do great things. Dazzling and swift as had been the actions of Tom Converse that night, it seemed to The Shadow that he was now facing a greater power. But in the meantime he must be about his work. Before long Converse would be back among his own people with his identity established. Jess Sherman, Harry Lang, and Chuck Parker must die before that time came.

"Well," he said to Algie, "so long. I'll be on my way."

"Wait a minute," said the sheriff. "Seems to me you and me might exchange a few words. I misrecall seeing you around many times, son."

An imp of the perverse rose in The Shadow. There was no reason in the world why he should antagonize the old hunting hound of the law who had run down so many a difficult trail. There were a thousand reasons against it. Yet The Shadow snarled with a sudden hatred in his voice: "I don't aim to hang around crossroad saloons talking about myself. Maybe that's why you ain't seen me before!"

So saying, he turned on his heel and stalked out of the room. The sheriff followed softly to the door, and, raising the lamp high, he stood there peering after the departing form and clucking softly to himself. He made a half pitiful and half ridiculous figure, standing there in the doorway. However, had The Shadow known what was going on inside that old mind, he would probably have turned short on his way down the stairs and finished the debate right there with a slug from his active Colt.

He did not turn. He continued down the stairs, and, going into the barn, he took his horse.

It was a long-legged, clean-cut gelding with plenty of speed, and, though the bay lacked as much endurance as the outlaw would have liked to find in him, yet it was an honest horse, and could turn a dizzy five or six miles of sprinting that would shake off a host of mountain ponies. Once with a comfortable lead behind him, The Shadow knew the country so well that he could be tolerably sure of ducking to one side and escaping the most vigilant posse.

He saddled the bay slowly, for he was by no means eager to save time. When the saddling was ended, he went to the door and watched the storm until the drum of rain abated. Then, with the wind dying and the noise quieting, he swung into the saddle and slipped out of the town at the very time that the first of the disappointed pursuers of Tom Converse began to stream back toward the village.

It was a gravel trail that The Shadow took, and, riding at a slow, comfortable jog along it, with the slicker rustling and gleaming under the lightening rainfall, he topped the first range of hills and dropped into a gully beyond. Here, under an oak whose foliage was especially dense, he paused; fumbling in his saddlebag, he brought out some paper and a pencil. He also brought out a fragment of paper covered with the same delicate script which Tom Converse had seen on the note that was thrown into his bedroom at the hotel.

He studied the latter carefully by the light of his pocket electric torch, and at length began to scrawl on the blank paper before him. It was some time before his hand was running smoothly enough to please him. Then he took a fresh sheet and dashed off a more than creditable copy of the handwriting which Tom Converse had seen. The note read:

JESS: Something terrible has happened. Come to me at once. And hurry, hurry, hurry! I'm waiting for you in the old hollow.

He paused here, and regarded his work with considerable complacence.

"That's exactly the way she chatters — curse her!" he muttered. "Only I hope that she ain't fallen out with Jess before now!"

So saying, he sent his horse on into a long, striding gallop, and at this gait he dipped down the valley until, through the night before him, rose the outlines of a ranch house. Here he reduced the pace of his gelding, and after a time swung out of the saddle, hurried on foot to the house, and stole noiselessly along the veranda. At one of the windows he paused, crouched, and became cautious as a great cat. Then, gently, very gently, he pried it open and raised the sash, leaned far in, and tossed the note onto the chest of the figure which slept in the near-by bed.

There was an instant commotion.

He heard the man sit up, heard the exclamation in the voice of Jess Sherman, and heard the crunch of paper under excited fingers.

The Shadow wanted no more, but, slinking away to the side, he rounded the corner of the house, remounted the waiting bay, and galloped off again into the night.

He headed straight for that fateful hollow where, two years before, he had ridden to see the lady of his heart, and had been greeted by bullets instead of her voice. As he waited there in the shelter of the trees about the hollow, his anger increased steadily. What a consummate, treacherous witch the girl was! Oh, to be able to draw down on her head as much misery as she had drawn upon his!

The train of thoughts broke off short. In the distance he heard the quickening beat of the gallop of an approaching horse.

Chapter Twelve

One of the Three

The storm-wind had rushed out of the northwest; the storm had diminished as the wind swung toward the full west, and, now that it was fanning pleasantly out of the south, the heavy rain clouds were tossed apart and driven in great herds into the northern sky. All the southern sky was now pale with moonshine, and toward the north the light broke through the gaps and shone fitfully, picking out a hilltop here and a hollow there.

By this light the bandit saw the horseman racing in answer to the treacherous message which he had sent. Jess Sherman was riding to meet his end, and riding joyously, no doubt.

Yes, here he reined his steaming horse in the center of the hollow. His slicker was blown back from his shoulders by the wind of his gallop, like the cloak of a cavalier, and the wide brim of his sombrero was curled back into rakish lines. He made a splendid figure — a big-shouldered, handsome man of something past thirty. Now he turned his head here and there, calling eagerly: "Sylvia — Sylvia — dear Sylvia! I'm here, honey! Are you waiting?"

The gorge of the outlaw rose. How utterly he

hated the big man! Besides, he knew the inside history behind that handsome mask of a face. He knew how the fortune of the prosperous rancher had been started in cattle rustling. He knew how the mining ventures of Jess Sherman had been made successful by his grasping tactics. But now that he was established, how easy it was for him to play the part of the generous gentleman!

"Bah!" sneered The Shadow aloud, then spurred his bay savagely so that the tortured brute gathered its weight and burst into the hollow with a single bound.

As Jess Sherman turned in the saddle, The Shadow raised his sombrero and pushed it far back so that the moonlight would shine clearly on his face.

There was a startled exclamation from the other. "You — why, I was thinking that — Who the devil are you, friend?"

"I'm not the friend you're looking for," said The Shadow with much composure. "But I'm a gent you'll be a pile interested to hear from. I met you once before down here in the same place."

"What the devil you're talking about," said Sherman, "I can't make out. Who are you?"

"A man you tried to murder down here! You hound, I'm the man you sent for by the name of my girl — just as I've sent for you tonight by the same name! I'm The Shadow!"

Disbelief, anger, and then swift fear flashed

across the face of the wretched Sherman. His big right hand made one furtive move toward the butt of his revolver, and then, seeing that The Shadow did not stir a hand in answer to the move, the calm of the outlaw seemed to have an effect more terrible than the presented muzzles of a dozen guns. The surety of the sallow-faced man tied the hands of Jess.

"I dragged myself off yonder," went on The Shadow. "I lay down like a dog and got ready to die, but I didn't die. Some unknown destiny wouldn't let me. It was saving me until I finished you up. Sherman — you and the two other skunks that lay yonder with you and plugged me after you'd made the girl —"

Jess Sherman found his tongue. "We didn't make her," he said. "I swear to Heaven we didn't, and she hadn't any idea that we were laying there waiting for you to come. That's the straight of it."

The outlaw smiled. He had thought that he would have to do with a brave man at least, but cowardice was thickening the tongue of Jess Sherman. With disgust The Shadow shivered. Then he sneered: "You'd swear to a lie like that?"

"Lie?" echoed Jess Sherman. "It ain't a lie! It's gospel truth, I tell you!" Hope was putting a ring in his voice.

"She didn't know you were there," said The Shadow slowly. "She sent for me, and then you simply up and blew blazes out of me without her knowing what was to come?"

"That's it; and the reason I was with 'em —"

"Don't talk no more," said The Shadow suddenly. "I'm thinking."

He actually dropped his head, and again the hand of Jess Sherman went furtively toward his gun — only to be withdrawn. It could not be that the terrible Shadow was actually off his guard. No, it was only a trick to entrap him into trying to draw his gun, so that the outlaw could have the pleasure of killing his man in a fight. He brought his hand well forward again and waited — waited, with his wretched, guilty heart thundering high in his throat.

"Well," said The Shadow at length, raising his head, "I'll tell you what I been thinking. I been thinking that the gent that told me that Sylvia didn't really double cross me, had ought to get off light, and I tell you straight, Sherman. I know you're a skunk; but I'd let you go clean if it wasn't for one thing. You've seen my face."

Jess Sherman stirred his lips twice before he could speak, so hard had the cold of fear frozen his mouth.

"I don't know nothing, partner," he pleaded. "I've seen your face, but I ain't ever going to talk about it and —"

"Shut up," said The Shadow. "I begin to feel sort of like a skunk just because you're a man — the same as me! Don't talk that way. You know and I know that as soon as I'd gone out of sight you'd be riding for Sheriff Algie Thomas —"

"My sacred word —"

"You ain't got any sacred word. Didn't you give your sacred word to your old partner — the fat gent, Chalmers?"

"Partner? He was no partner of mine."

"You lie!"

"He tried to double cross me," whined the big man.

"That's another lie, and a bad one. He didn't try to double cross you. He done the work and located the stuff, and then you up and beat him out of his share. Why, if the inside story of that deal was to be known throughout the range, folks would just as soon have a mangy dog around as have you in their houses, Sherman. But we've done a plenty of talking — and too much. Pull your gun, you rat, and die like some kind of a man."

"Heaven help me!" groaned Sherman. "You know I ain't got a chance agin' you!"

The teeth of the outlaw showed.

"I'll give you a chance, then," he snarled. He thought a moment; then: "I'll even turn my back on you, Sherman!"

A flash of incredulous joy convulsed the face of the big man for a moment. He stared at the outlaw with loose-mouthed joy, like a man dying of thirst in the desert who sees blue, cool water in the near distance and tries in vain to shut the mirage of hope out of his mind.

"Turn your back?" he echoed.

"I said it, and I mean it. Sherman, I'm going to make my hoss rear and turn around. While he's rearing and swinging clear around, I'm going to try to kill you, and you can try your best to kill me. Why I'm giving a rat like you such a chance to murder me is more'n I know. But I can't, somehow, kill a gent in cold blood. Sherman, will you fight that way?"

The coward nodded convulsively and then cried: "I'll fight you that way. Are you ready?"

"I'm ready, but you ain't," said The Shadow calmly, almost gently. "You're still shaking all over from being scared. And you one of the bullies of the town! Sherman, suppose somebody should ever find out about you, and what you are! Wouldn't even the dogs slink away from you?"

Sherman blanched and blinked under the insults, but his jaw gradually thrust out. Anger was warming him, and hope of killing the outlaw in this strange duel was also lifting his spirit.

The Shadow, who knew what to expect, waited until the gleam of Sherman's eye satisfied him. Then he raised his left hand.

"Get ready, Sherman. Get ready, shoot fast, and shoot straight — or Heaven help you, because, when I come around out of this turn, I'll go for you!"

Instantly, with a wrench of his body, a twist of his legs, and a violent tug on the reins, he drew the bay gelding back so that its quarters were well gathered under him, and then whirled the tall animal around.

Mid-turn, the gun of the big man leaped from its holster, and, as the back of the outlaw was squarely turned for the split part of a second, he fired. But The Shadow had no intention of sitting bolt erect in the saddle during this maneuver, like a drum major before the band. Instead, he ducked far over, just as his turn presented the broadest rear target to the enemy. The bullet of Sherman whistled above his head, and, before the unhappy man could fire again, The Shadow, shooting under his own left arm before the bay was completely turned around, sent a forty-five-caliber slug through the forehead of Jess Sherman.

He turned again as the body hurtled out of the saddle and struck the ground with a loose, jouncing thud, like the fall of a skin of water. Jess Sherman lay flat on his back with his arms thrown out crosswise, and in the center of his forehead there was a red blur. So the first of the three had fallen, and a two-year-old vow had been one third fulfilled.

The Shadow looked down on the fallen man without regret and without remorse, but very critically he noted that the shot had struck the center of the target with perfect precision. With a compass and ruler one could not have found the exact center of the forehead of Jess Sherman with greater accuracy.

He now turned the bay in an opposite direction, and sent him off at the long, rolling gallop which was the best feature of the animal's ability to go. It swept The Shadow over a mile and a half of hill and dale, and brought him at length in sight of a modest ranch house with only a meager maze of surrounding fence, that sure token of prosperity.

He paused on the top of the hill for a long moment, letting the familiar scene roll pleasantly back upon his eye. How well he knew it, and how well he loved it, for somewhere in that low, squat, black-walled house was Sylvia Rann!

Chapter Thirteen

Sylvia's Test

What wakened Sylvia was a disturbing dream rather than any sound made in her room. But waken she did, of a sudden, as clear minded as though she had never slept at all since that eventful night began. Indeed, it was hardly more than an hour since the incredible news of the escape of The Shadow from the hotel had enabled her to close her eyes in peace.

Now she sat up in bed, and instantly she heard a light hushing sound from the center of the room. She looked in that direction and saw at once the shadowy form of a man. In that light, or absence of light, he looked taller than humanly possible, but she knew before he raised a hand, before she heard his voice, that it was The Shadow and she cried "You? Jim, it is you?"

It was characteristic of him that he did not rush to her with an enthusiastic outburst of joy. Instead, she saw him drawing off his hat, a shadow in the shades; that was a rare and important tribute of respect, coming from him.

"I knew you wouldn't get hysterical. I knew you wouldn't start throwing no fits when you seen me," he said. "You sure pack a level head

103

around with you, Sylvia."

"Not so loud!"

"They can't hear me. Better to talk out loud, pretty near, than to whisper. Whispering would wake up a thousand men on the other side of a stone wall. Leastwise, it would wake me up on the other side of a stone wall!"

He did not move toward her as she caught up a bathrobe and swept it around her, and stuffed her feet into slippers.

"I sure got to apologize for coming here into your bedroom like this, Sylvia. But you ain't taking it wrong, I guess?"

"I know you couldn't come in any other way, very well. But oh, Jim — Jim — Jim, tell me everything!"

She ran to him, and he felt her small hands fumble for his and then hold them strongly. A fragrance such as lingered so faintly about her writing paper, blew toward him and set his heart beating wildly. He stepped in, leaned to kiss her — and then found that she had evaded him with the suddenness and the perfect evasiveness of a thin mist. There she stood, all at once, far off among the shadows, and when he attempted to come near again she warned him away.

"You mustn't do that," she commanded. "You know you mustn't act that way, or I'll have to send you off! And now, Jim — my poor dear! — tell me how everything happened — how you were healed, and how —"

He waited a moment until his mind could clear

of the sudden rosy cloud of happiness in which it was whirling.

"I thought you'd helped 'em trap me, honey," he said at length. "I thought it for pretty nigh two years. But when I come back and got close to the house, all at once I just simply knew that you couldn't do a thing as yaller as that! You might leave me and give me the go-by if I was up and around, but you wouldn't have gents go and lie in wait for me like that!"

He thought of the dead man, from whose lips he had learned that truth, and he was thankful for the darkness which covered his smile.

"I knew you'd give up that wild idea you first had," said the girl. "But before you go on, tell me how you got out of the hotel first, Jim. Was it my note that made you determined to fight for your life? Was it that?"

So she had sent a note, and thrown it into the room of Tom Converse. All at once he locked his jaws. It would certainly not do for her ever to meet that reckless young fire-eater. She loved daring with all her heart. What she chiefly worshiped in the world was courage. Because of courage she had smiled on even the terrible Shadow, and had refused to believe the tales which were circulated about him.

But what would she feel and do when she met Tom Converse, with no shadow upon his past save what the outlaw himself had artificially placed there? In the meantime, what was he to say about the escape from the hotel? Dared he tell her now of the trick which he had played?

No, he knew that, if she learned how Tom Converse had been beguiled, she would despise the outlaw for it.

"Of course it was your note, Sylvia," he answered. "Sure it was that. I was tired of living, pretty near, until I got that note, and then I made up my mind to do my best — and so here I am! And — and I want to see you, Sylvia. Can we manage that? Will you risk that for me?"

"If you want to — of course."

He scratched a match furtively, then stepped close, and, cupping his hands dexterously, he threw a broad flush of light across her face, pale with excitement, eyes wide in preparation for the dazzling light. Feature by feature he drank in her beauty. Even her fear was dear to him.

The match burned his fingertips and made a red streak to the floor. He did not say a word for a moment; then: "It's worth waiting two years for, Sylvia — just for one look like this one! But I want you to tell me one thing right now: Is there any more hope for me now than there was in the past?"

"Have you changed your mind, Jim?"

"I've changed it. I used to think that I couldn't live a regular life the way other gents live, but I've changed from all that. I see how plumb foolish that would be; you see, Sylvia? Besides, I know that I can get back into the world as a law-abiding gent, because nobody has ever seen my face, honey!"

"Not even today? Why, didn't you come to the hotel yesterday morning like a madman with no —"

He had forgotten. He had forgotten the rôle of that cursed Tom Converse, which he was supposed to play as well as his own.

"They got just a glimpse of me," he said; "and they were all so excited that they didn't know what they were seeing."

"Yes, yes," and the girl nodded. "They were so afraid that they described you as being two inches taller than you are, and a great deal heavier and younger looking, Jim."

"That's it. My idea is that if you sneak away and go East, honey, we can be married and settle down, and nobody'll ever ask us no questions. Would you do that, Sylvia?"

"Don't ask me now," she urged. "I just want to be happy in having you back with me."

"But you got to tell me something, Sylvia. You got to hold out some kind of hope to me. Do you remember that you promised once if —"

"I know," she broke in. "But something holds me back, Jim. I suppose it's the horrible stories that they tell about you; and of course they've hunted me out during the last two years to tell me such stories."

"The hounds!"

"I've tried to shut my ears to them, but in spite of myself the stories would sink in. I couldn't help hearing them. Oh, I know that you wouldn't take advantage — you wouldn't kill coldly and calculatingly, as they've tried to accuse you of doing. I know that they've saddled a lot of things on you that you never did —"

"They've laid murders to me, honey, that they say were done when I was with you."

"I know that. Haven't I laid that comfort to my heart a thousand times in the last two years? And every minute of that time — twenty-four long months, Jim, without a word from you, but knowing that you were hating and suspecting me — twenty-four months, Jim, I've kept true to you. Not that I ever told you I loved you, and I don't — the way you want me to. But I've never spent any other time with other men. I've kept waiting for you to come back, and when you came back I told myself that I would try to get one great proof from you. You understand, Jim?"

"Understand? Name a proof, Sylvia. Name any proof you can think of, and I'll do it — I'll do it happily."

"I couldn't think of one for a long time. When just lately one came to me — the one I mentioned in my note that I threw into your room today."

"Confound that note!" thought The Shadow. He said aloud: "Say it over again now."

"You haven't forgotten, surely!"

"A note is one thing, and what you say aloud is a whole lot different; you admit that! Besides, things were happening so fast to me just then that all I could think of when I read that note was what a terrible pile I love you, honey!"

108

She laughed softly. "I'll tell you again. It's Ben."

"H'm!"

"You never liked him. I think you've always felt that I was too fond of poor Ben. But let me tell you, Jim, that, when he found out about you and me, he made up his mind that you must be all right. He refused to believe anything against you — any more than I would believe!"

"The deuce!"

"Yes. He said if I cared for you, you were good enough to suit him. So he began to pick up stories about you, and he carefully shook out everything that was bad in each story and left only what was good, so that he collected a tremendous lot of stories about your courage, and all that. Finally he made up his mind that there was only one thing in the world worth doing — and that was to be a robber!"

The teeth of The Shadow clicked. No matter how true the name might be, it cut him as with a lash to hear it from her lips.

"He started to learn things, Jim. He studied patiently. He practiced with revolvers and rifles for hours every day. He watched good riders and imitated their ways of riding. He learned all about safes, and how to make 'soup,' as he called it, out of dynamite, and how to make molds to run the nitroglycerin out of soft yellow laundry soap —"

"That little shrimp of a sawed-off kid — he learned all that?"

"He's not so small. He was seventeen when

you last saw him or heard of him. He's nineteen now, and he's grown a great deal in the last two years. He — he's big enough and old enough to be sent to the penitentiary!"

"Eh? I didn't foller you there, Sylvia!"

"In a single word, he's blown a safe, and he's in the jail at Carlton! Oh, Jim, what can be done?"

In the silence he could feel her strong hope turning to lead.

Then he cried softly: "Is this the test you were going to put up to me? Is this jail-breaking test the one you want — to make sure that I'll be able to go straight?"

"Not to go straight. I want you to make one effort for the sake of that boy. Somehow, if you do that, I'll know that you can be trusted with all I have — with the rest of my life, Jim."

"Gimme a chance to think," muttered the bandit, striding swiftly and silently to and fro in the room. "Gimme a chance to think!"

He stopped and caught her hands with both of his, and she felt the lean, agile fingers cut into her flesh.

"If I got him out, you'd marry me, Sylvia? You'd run off with me and marry me, honey?"

Her voice shook. "Yes," she said. "I'd do anything. I tell you, Ben's father looks at me every day with a curse in his eye. He knows that through me Ben went wrong — began to worship you. And you know what they have done for me here — what a home they've given me?"

The outlaw nodded. "Sure. I guess I know.

Only, honey, Carlton Jail is the strongest jail inside of five hundred miles. It's worse'n that!"

"How can it be?" exclaimed the girl. "Haven't I heard of a dozen jail-breaks in the last five or six years?"

"Sure you did, and more than that, maybe. That's why it's strong now. They learned that it wasn't so easy to keep folks inside walls as it was to put 'em there. So they just laid out a pile of money and built a jail that couldn't be blasted open, let alone dug out of! Honey, give me some other job — anything else you can think of. I'm willing to do anything —"

"Anything but this," she said. "And you won't even try this? You won't even try? Oh, Jim, I know of some of the terrible and wonderful things you've done. Think of how you broke out of the hotel today, even when that Sheriff Thomas was there —"

"They've got a man pretty near as bad as Thomas in Carlton. They've got Joe Shriner over there. He's a devil; he never sleeps!"

"You won't try?"

A wave of hot irritation swept through his mind. How willfully blind she was to the facts of the matter! How like a woman!

"I'll try," he said.

"With all your heart and all your might?"

"If it makes you any happier to have me say it — yes!"

"Jim!"

"Well?"

"If you do that — if you save that boy from being sent to the penitentiary, where his mind will be stamped with crime —"

"Well?"

"Then — then I could love you with all my soul!"

Chapter Fourteen

Bill M'ginn's Guest

Out of town Tom Converse darted rapidly, swaying a little from side to side as the deft-footed
stallion picked his way among the fences behind
the hotel stable. What a horse, what a horse Captain was! He had the eyes of a cat to see in the
dark. He had the brain of a man to think and
choose his way. He ducked about like a sprinting
back in a broken football field. Then he rose
and soared as on wings over a tall fence, the
sudden rise nearly shaking Tom out of the saddle.

Plunging into a tangle of trees, the wise animal
cut down his pace to just that gait which he could
maintain while still keeping his impetus under
control, so to speak, and managing to dodge about
among the trunks even on a footing of wet, slippery pine needles. The fragrance of the pines
soaked into his lungs as he worked down through
the forest.

In another ten minutes, with the roar of the
pursuit beginning to break up or roll off on either
side, as men fired blindly at every chance target
that came into their way in the darkness, Captain
swerved out into the open again. Through the
tumbled masses of clouds in the southern sky a

shaft of moonlight fell squarely upon the head and shoulders of Tom.

In moments of great peril, and peril avoided, men grow simple of mind, and to Tom Converse it seemed as though this sudden burst of radiance from the moon was a promise from Heaven that he would succeed in getting back unharmed to his father's ranch and into the land where he was known.

In the meantime, there was no particular hurry, surely. There are few games so delightful to the heart of a child as the game of tag, and Tom Converse in many a way was simply a child grown large. This game he was now playing was a game of tag, also, save that one would be slapped with a forty-five-caliber slug instead of a hand.

There is no fascination in the world so great as the fascination of the near presence of death. In the days of dueling, the first encounter was sufficient to give many men a taste for the terrible sport and send them out sooner or later to hunt for trouble again. Many and many a worthy man — in other respects — had been turned into a confirmed duelist by being forced, for the sake of honor, into two or three encounters.

If Tom Converse could have gone through the icy joy of the moments which followed his escape from the window to his burst through the door on the back of the dappled chestnut, he would almost have been tempted to place himself back in the room of the hotel — that room which for a time had seemed to him well-nigh synonymous with a coffin.

That thought was far behind him now. Why should it not be? Charles XII., when he first heard bullets on his landing in Denmark, chose that eerie music for his own; and Tom Converse, now that bullets for the first time had hummed past his ears, felt that he would have paid in gold for a repetition of the experience.

How strangely his attitude toward the entire world had changed during the past few hours! He had walked into the town of Silver Tip with not a care in the world save a desire to see more of this little round planet and the men who reside on it. Now behold him some 24 or 30 hours later, dreaded and hated by thousands of sturdy mountaineers! But what had their dread and hate accomplished, aided and abetted by the machinations of the most daring and skillful of criminals? They had all availed only to place him in a specially constructed saddle built as though to order for him, and they had put the saddle on the horse of his dreams.

Suddenly it came to him that, if he gave up the identity of The Shadow, he must give up Captain at the same moment and turn the wonderful stallion into the hands of the officers of the State, to be used by them as they saw fit, or sold at auction.

It was a very strange position, and, as has been said, it was not at all unpleasant. He balanced it here in solitude, delighted with himself and his adventure, and he had a strange feeling that the world owed him something. Having attacked him for no good reason, they should now pay him back in some manner or other.

In the meantime, he would not be in any vast hurry to get out of that country and go back to the hills where he was known as Tom Converse. They were hundreds of miles away, for that matter. If he bolted toward home he might be headed off by telegraph even if he could not be run down by horses. He had had enough experience already, under the name of The Shadow, to be perfectly well aware that in a pinch men would not waste time over the niceties of the law. They would simply shoot him on sight and ask their random questions later!

He came, in the midst of these thoughts, to a clearing, with a shanty in the center of it. The shack was black with quiet and sleep through one half of its ragged roof line, and white with moonlight and peace in the other half.

The pseudo-Shadow paused and seriously considered. If he rode on until the morning before he stopped somewhere to get food, that stopping place would give everyone the direction of his flight. If he stopped here, he would be inside the circle of their first search, for surely no one would stop to hunt for the marauder at this short distance from the scene of his latest escape from death.

No sooner than that daring thought entered the brain of Tom Converse, he decided to act upon it. He went to the corral. In it he found two horses which, by the moonlight, he could tell to be ancient nags. Promptly he put up Captain in a shed near by, hunted about until he had found feed for the stallion, and then, carrying his saddle and pack, he turned and made for the house.

The opening of the door released a long shaft of whiteness into the midst of the shack, that fell on the form of an old graybeard in the act of sitting up on his pallet. Tom strode through the door.

"Old-timer," he said, "most of the gents in the next village have been shooting at me lately, because they figure that I'm The Shadow."

There was a convulsive movement of the old man in the bunk.

Tom continued: "Anyway, I've ridden as far as I feel like riding away from them tonight, so I'm going to stay right here until the morning. I got my blankets. You lie down and go to sleep. I'll lie here and go to sleep, too. But, mind you, I'm a terrible light sleeper. Why, a cat is a pig when it comes to sleeping sound — compared with me. Now don't you forget that. And if I was to wake up in the middle of the night and find that you'd started for the door to go out and spread an alarm — or if I found that you were snooping over there toward the wall to get one of them big rifles of yours that are hanging there — why, old-timer, I'd have to plant you with a dose of lead and my regrets!"

While a groan of terror came from the old fellow, Tom calmly made up his bunk near the door, lay down in it, and almost instantly was sound asleep.

Not that he needed real rest after his sleep which had lasted during most of the day, but he was determined to travel by daylight; and now he was sleeping in order to have a surplus of energy. It delighted him past mention to find that sleep swept over him at his will. Every part of his body and brain was beginning to function perfectly.

He wakened in the morning with the faint scent in his nostrils from the writing paper in his breast pocket, and when he rose accordingly and stretched his big arms and faced the hollow-eyed ancient on the far side of the room, there was only one great determination in the mind of Tom Converse. That was to ride to Carlton, as the mysterious woman had indirectly begged in her note, and there liberate Ben, whoever he might be, from the jail.

But where was Carlton?

"Cheer up, father," he said to the old man. "I've never hurt old fellows like you, no matter what they may say about me. Cheer up, and show me what sort of breakfast you can fix for me!"

He left the cabin, saddled Captain, and brought him back to the shack. When he went inside, he found the finest breakfast that trembling hands and limited resources of larder could furnish, and he delivered such an oration in praise of the flap-jacks and the crisped bacon that the

118

old man began to brighten.

"I'm coming back," said Tom genially, "and I'm going to pay you for this a dozen times over. You understand? Going to pay you big for it. Roll a smoke and tell me about yourself."

He threw the makings to the veteran, and, while the latter smoked, Tom poured at him a series of questions about the country. It was difficult to do, because the questions had to be so veiled that they would not be questions; they were rather comments which drew out further remarks from the old man. By this means he learned that Carlton lay beyond the western range and down in a snug valley beyond — a matter of 40 miles.

It was 40 miles into an agricultural valley, where a heavier loam soil and more frequent rains had brought the plow and the fruits and prosperity of the plow. Had the news of the escape from the hotel penetrated as far as that town?

"I s'pose you've had dealings with Joe Shriner down in Carlton," said the old man, "the new assistant sheriff they got, who runs the jail? I suppose you and Joe'll meet up one of these days."

"Maybe," said Tom Converse. "We might meet up."

"Then before you start shooting, just give him best regards from old Bill McGinn, will you?" The ancient was beginning to lose his terror of the outlaw. "I've knowed Joe ever since he lived next door to me in Crayville. I remember when he busted his arm from falling out of the cherry tree. Always getting hurt or hurting other boys;

119

and as far as I can make out he ain't changed much from that day to this. I lost sight of him pretty pronto. Him and his folks moved out of Crayville and come up to Carlton. I guess Joe was no more'n ten when I last seen him, but he'll recollect how I picked him up and brung him into my house and made him comfortable till the doctor come."

He was still chattering about the old days and the broken arm of Joe Shriner when Tom swung into the saddle.

The old man then came out and dropped his hand on Tom's knee. "You don't look up to half the things that I've heard about you," he said, "and I don't noways believe you are. I've always found out that a man is as good as the best you can think of him. I've always found that, because no matter what he might do here and there — well, we've all got the leaning toward bad things in the bottom of our hearts. Maybe I'd be a gun fighter if I was a little mite faster on the draw. Well, what I want to say is: I sure hope that you'll drop out of the habits you're following now, son, and start in trying to live up to your looks, because, if ever they was a clean-eyed boy, I count you as him. Now you're laughing at an old fool like me trying to give you advice?"

But Tom leaned and clapped him on the shoulder.

"I've written every word you've said inside of my head, and I'm going to think about it often. You be sure of that!"

He turned Captain's head and started off at a swinging gallop toward the west and those blue-brown hills which screened the rich little valley where Carlton lay.

Chapter Fifteen

Tom Comes to Carlton

The valley was not more than ten miles long and five wide, and from the top of the range of hills Tom could see every tree in the entire range of the valley when he came in view of it that afternoon. He had put 35 miles behind him to get there, but Captain was as strong on the bit as when the ride began. Never was there such a horse! His ordinary lope, with which he ate up the distance hour by hour, was faster than the sharp canter of an average cow pony, it seemed to Tom. More than once he got off the stallion and looked him over in astonishment, to make sure that he was really not more spent than he seemed.

Gradually he began to understand that this was simply a different type of horse. Not only did Captain maintain an incredible pace, but he kept up the most perfect good humor. He continually canted his head a trifle to one side, and cocked back the ear on the side which was turned in, so that he gave the appearance of looking back at his rider and preparing an ear for him. There was a friendly way he had of tossing his bit and of pushing out a little on the reins from time to time — not as though trying the grip of his rider, but in the effort to show that he was in touch with the will of the master.

The heart of Tom Converse went out to the beautiful animal more and more as the day progressed. So, fresh as a lark, Captain stood on the crest of the hill and whinnied softly with pleasure at the sight of the green little valley below him. Carlton itself was a substantial-looking village with important roofs here and there — a schoolhouse, a bank, perhaps, and another, which might be that famous Carlton jail.

Tom Converse drew a great breath. Surely never a mortal rode toward a crime with so joyous a heart as he rode, for it seemed to Tom that it was not a crime. It was only another move in that deadly game of tag which he was playing with civilized society. They had routed him with volleys of lead from his own peaceful course of living. Now he would slip around and slap them on the other cheek, so to speak. So delighted did he grow at the prospect that he actually burst out laughing as Captain swung down the trail, and he laughed so hard that the horse tossed up his fine head and snorted a query.

Laughter is the one human expression that dumb beasts dread, because they cannot understand it.

There was only one question of importance: How was he to get Ben out of jail? One glance, from the distance, at the barred windows and the stone walls of the jail told him that this would not be any case of a hammer and a jackknife. There was only one way in which a single man could extricate another from the cells of that prison, and the key he must use would be impertinent courage and ready wit.

As for the wit, Tom had not the slightest idea what he would do, even should he succeed so far as to get past the first door of the jail — even though that door did not then fold back and hold him a prisoner forever! But he rode on. Impudence must be his aid. Had he known Hermes, he would surely have sent up a prayer to that saucy deity; but that section of Tom's education had been exhausted, and he contented himself with patting the shining neck of the dapple chestnut and asking those sharp, pricking ears to understand and help him.

One thing was certain: If anyone from the last town had come to Carlton this day, he was no better than lost. However, 40 miles was 40 miles, and there was only one Captain!

Straight down the main street of Carlton rode the adventurer, just as he had ridden down the main street of another village the morning before, but he had been in ignorance of his danger then. Now he was fully awake and aware of the imminence of death about him.

Yet, just as he had expected, they could not believe their eyes! Not even The Shadow would venture to ride down their street in the open day! He had come in a circuit around the town just before entering, also, and that slight difference of direction — small thing though it was — might prejudice men in his favor. They would be thinking of The Shadow, if at all, as having taken the opposite direction.

It was a child of nine playing with a dog in the white dust of the street who saw him first, gaped, screamed, and then — just in the act of fleeing — stopped short and turned around to gape again with a pale face. Tom Converse stopped the horse.

"What's the matter, son?" he sang out.

"Nothing. I — I just was thinking you might be somebody that you ain't."

"You keep your thinks quiet, then," reproved Tom. "You pretty nigh scared my hoss into jumping out of his skin. Come here and pat his nose. I sure don't like to have him get scared of folks."

Slowly the boy approached, fascinated. Almost simultaneously there was a shout from the distance, echoed on either side of the street. Plainly the crisis was about to descend on him.

The crisis developed into the slow approach of a sweaty blacksmith and his helper out of the nearest shop — a patriarchal gentleman upon the right, with a beard which divided at the end into two prongs like the divided root of a carrot. Half a dozen young idlers came thronging behind. Every one of the outfit was armed. The broad-faced blacksmith was spokesman.

"Howdy, stranger," he said. "Where might you be from?"

"Down by Crayville."

"Crayville?"

"Yep. I was drifting along toward Waterbury and —"

"Why, Waterbury ain't in line with Carlton. You're plumb out of your way."

The others were packing in, yet each man left himself plenty of room for his gun hand, and every pair of eyes was bright and stern. They distinctly meant business, if once they should find a weakness in what he said.

"Sure I'm out of my way," said Tom Converse instantly, though secretly cursing the inaccurate information which he had drawn from the old man that morning. "I turned out of my way on purpose. I wanted to see a gent in town here, that used to live down to Crayville."

"Who's that?"

"Joe Shriner."

"What!"

He had scored a great stroke. They gasped, then laughed. Certainly their eyes and their suspicions must have played them false. A man who wanted to see the formidable deputy, Joe Shriner, could not be The Shadow. Yet they kept up a lessening siege of questions.

"What's the name of your hoss?"

"Dandy. That's what we call him."

"He looks like a dandy, right enough. How old is he?"

"Six even."

"Pretty well set up, ain't he?"

"I'll tell a man he's well set up! He wasn't took off of pasture till last spring!"

"You don't say! Well, well! Son, d'you know why we all come flocking down here to talk to you?"

"I dunno. I thought maybe it was a habit here in Carlton."

There was a sympathetic guffaw at this feeble jest. They had been thinking of bullets and death ten seconds before. Now that they began to feel that they were wrong, they wanted to laugh for relief.

"I'll tell you who," shrilly shouted the boy, who was still monopolizing the nose of Captain. "We thought you was The Shadow!"

Tom Converse was prepared for that exclamation, and he had been mustering his energies ever since the boy began to speak. The result was a veritable facial explosion, so far as silent expression went. He performed so admirable an imitation of fear and astonishment that the little group was entirely satisfied and burst into a roar of laughter.

"That's all right to laugh about," said Tom, apparently beginning to breathe again with ease — and indeed a great sense of ease was spreading over him; "but it ain't any light thing to be took for The Shadow. It might of got me shot — that's what it might of done. How do I look like The Shadow?"

"Ask Mr. Williams. He was stuck up by The Shadow."

The white-bearded man stroked and combed his whiskers, much pleased at becoming the center of attention.

"I was just waiting till you youngsters got through being foolish," he said, "before I spoke up. This ain't much like The Shadow. The Shadow is a couple of inches taller and about fifteen pounds heavier, and Captain — why, Captain is seventeen hands if he's an inch. I seen him clear and full —"

"I thought it was after sunset?" asked a voice.

"The sun was barely down. They was plenty of light. I thought I'd let you kids go on and have a thrill for a minute or two."

"Well," said Tom Converse, "I'd like to see the sheriff and get fixed up — with a piece of paper saying in big letters that I ain't The Shadow."

"It's all because of that hoss," said the old man. "Captain is the name of The Shadow's hoss, and it's a dappled chestnut just like yours. You see, that color's rare. You go look up Joe Shriner. He's the deputy sheriff. He runs the jail."

Two of the youths, and the little boy who had first discovered him, led Tom Converse down the street toward the jail and only left him when he had come in front of that structure.

It was a formidable building. Some bits of architecture have expression as clearly defined as that of an animal, and the squat, heavy front of Carlton Jail, with the broad, protruding steps, looked remarkably like the face of a fighting bull-

128

dog. It looked as though a prisoner, once swallowed by those doors, could never issue forth again.

Meanwhile, a tall man stepped from the shadow of the doors above with a grunt, and the grunt stopped the companions of Tom Converse as they were on their way back down the street. Tom himself looked up sharply, and he knew at once that this was the man whom old Bill McGinn had called Sheriff Joe Shriner — the man who loved battle for its own sake. He knew also that he would have to be sharp indeed if he wished to circumvent the man who stood above him. But he had come to deliver the unknown Ben from Shriner's stronghold, and deliver Ben he must.

Chapter Sixteen

Passable Deceit

At 25 Joe Shriner had commenced to turn gray. At 26 he looked ten years older, and no sooner did he commence to look old than he began to act old. Some men have that way. They are what they seem to be. Cut the long hair of a musician, and he might be forced to become a tired business man.

At least, it was true of Joe Shriner that he could not resist the influence of his face. He had a big jaw, square at the end, and jutting out. In his youth, when people had laid eyes on his face, they had exclaimed: "There's a young Trojan for you! There's a fighter, I'll wager."

To save his face, Joe Shriner had to live up to his reputation. He was champion among the hardy fighters of his period in the little town of Crayville. He became champion in a more extended and exclusive sense when he reached the years of manhood and, with those years, the deadly weapons of matured men. He took to revolver play as easily as he had taken to fisticuffs. He was still looked up to as the leader in combats, and force of public opinion made him become what it wanted him to be — the foremost warrior in the adopted town of Carlton.

Here he had achieved name and fame, and, when gray hair came to him at the age of 26, Joe Shriner became instantly as hard and middle-aged as his looks. He was now 35, and for fully nine years he had demanded — and received even without demand — the respect due to white hairs and physical prowess, combined.

That combination would have made a stronger-minded man than Joe Shriner vain, and Joe was very vain indeed. He believed that he should be enumerated among the great heroes of the early frontier — men who had dared death by thirst, death by cruel Indian warfare, death by a thousand privations and accidents. Because books were not written about him, Joe Shriner carried in his heart a great empty place that required filling with daily adulation, a great sorrow which was too deep for expression. How can a man tell the world that he is far, far greater than the world sees him?

Joe Shriner received praise with a shrug of the shoulders; so he gained a measure of content. The shrug was because the praise he received was far below the praise he merited in his own estimation; but those shrugs were accepted by Carlton as proof positive that their celebrated deputy sheriff was a man above being moved by flattery.

At least, so aloof and so formidable did he seem to Tom Converse, as that cool-headed young rascal stood at the bottom of the steps and looked up at the combined seer, man-killer and egoist, that Tom's nerve trembled and nearly failed him for a moment. Then he seized opportunity by the forelock.

He rushed up the stone stairs of the jail and caught the limp hands of the deputy sheriff in both of his.

"By the Lord, Joe Shriner," he said, "you ain't changed so much as they said — not half so much!"

"Ain't I?" said the deputy sheriff, by no means overpleased. "And who might you be, friend?"

"I'm the son of Tom Campbell up Crayville way. I was heading for Waterbury, and dad told me sure not to miss looking you up! Dad was one of them that always said you was going to do big things when your time come!"

"Huh!" grunted the imperturbable deputy as this libation of praise splashed and sank noiselessly in the great hot desert of his vanity. "You come up here out of your way, did you?"

"I did."

"That's quite a hoss you got," said Joe Shriner.

"We thought he was The Shadow, first time we seen him — on account of that hoss," cried the boy, whom Tom had met coming into town.

The deputy started. "The Shadow — in Carlton?" he said.

Tom Converse saw that the idea had not entered the brain of the great man before. In spite of the respect which he felt for the formidable deputy sheriff, according to the account which he had received from old Billy McGinn, it occurred to him that in this one particular Joe Shriner had been just a trifle obtuse, just a shade slow in putting two and two together for the purpose of making four. But he forced himself to say heartily, as he saw the deputy sheriff start and look sharply first at Tom and then at Tom's horse: "It's sure a crazy idea to think that even The Shadow would have nerve enough to come into the same town as Joe Shriner!"

The deputy blinked, but he managed to swallow the compliment without choking. He even turned and bent upon Tom Converse a look in which there would have been open approval, if he had not been forced to make at least a summary examination before he dismissed all suspicion and, through his indorsement, opened all the doors in Carlton to the stranger.

Down the steps he strode and proceeded, without a word, to go over the shining chestnut. A growing concern took possession of Tom Converse. He had felt, a moment before, that his compliment had not been altogether wasted; but now the sharp-eyed deputy was prying into the secrets which might be marked on the hide and hoofs of the outlaw's horse. What marks were there on Captain?

Ah, there was only one that he could recall, and even now the deputy had arrived at it. As his hand swept over the croup of the horse, there was a slight change in his expression. His eyes darted a glance toward Tom and then became a blank. He had felt a certain scar, now overgrown with hair.

"They was a load of piping standing in the corral about three years ago," said Tom, "and Dandy was in the corral with it. He got to r'aring around, and pretty soon one of the older hosses took a swipe at him. Dandy tried to back out of the way, and he backed right into the sharp end of one of them pipes. He got cut there. I guess maybe you can find the place, but if you're looking him over for blemishes, you won't find none, sir, none but that — if you can rightly call a cut like that a blemish."

Here the formidable Joe Shriner grunted again. He dismissed the bystanders with a single wave which served to announce to them that their suspicions were ridiculous, and that he himself would take care of any shadow of suspicion which might rest upon this stranger. Then Joe came slowly up the steps again.

"Old men and boys," he said, "are a pile like women. They're just plain foolish!"

Tom was a trifle astonished by a declaration which so casually established the folly of three classes of mankind — old men, boys, and women — but he managed to sustain a smile.

"They're always looking to find things," said Joe Shriner, "where there ain't nothing to be found. Take a man's wife. If you ask her where your hat is, first thing she does is to start hunting in the same places that you've just told her you've been over. That's the reason that they all flocked around and thought that you might be The Shadow." His facial contortion was more a sneer than a smile. "As if even The Shadow would ride right into a town in plain daylight!"

"He did that yesterday, I guess," said Tom, "so I suppose they thought he'd turn right around and do it again today. But the town he rode into yesterday didn't have no Joe Shriner in it."

The deputy dismissed the compliment gently with a deprecatory wave of the hand.

"Come in," he said. "I got a new box of Havanas that ain't to be sneezed at. Come in and try one and tell me about things at home. I always look back on Crayville as being home for me, somehow, though I guess they've plumb forgot me down there long ago!"

Tom accepted invitation of the door which was left so wide ajar.

"Forgot you? They still talk about you as the most promising kid that ever give the other boys in Crayville black eyes."

"They do?" said the deputy, brightening in spite of himself. "Well, well! I was a quarrelsome kid in them days, I guess!"

They passed through the heavy doors. Down a narrow hall they advanced. Presently, this opened, in turn, into the gloomiest office that Tom had ever seen. It was literally a cell. Great bars of tool-proof steel ran up on all sides and made a network across the ceiling above. Tom paused, shuddered, then stepped through the door and heard it close behind him with a clang of metal.

He caught the uneasy, shifty eye of the deputy upon him and he explained as casually as possible: "Looks so much like a cell that I was sort of afraid to step inside it!" And he laughed foolishly.

The deputy nodded in his usual superior manner. "Mostly all folks feels the same way," he said. "It sure amuses me to see 'em come into my office. But what I say is: None of my prisoners are going to find the way out of this prison through my office!"

As he spoke, he struck his fist with grave dignity upon his desk.

"Why," murmured Tom, "I guess there ain't no crook so plumb foolish that he'd try to force his way through the office of Joe Shriner!"

A shadow of a smile of gratification crossed the lips of the deputy.

"Leastwise," he said, "there ain't been a man got out of this here prison since I took hold of it! No, sir, not one! And they used to be busting out every three or four months. You see, Carlton lies about halfway between the W. & W. and the C. & S. lines. The crooks drop off the freights along about here — if they want to mix up their trails plenty — and they cut across country to hook on at the next line. And so they been picked up pretty regular in Carlton. We don't have no ordinary bunch of cattle-rustling, small-time crooks. We got the real gents, son! I could show you —"

"I wish you would!" exclaimed Tom with heartfelt eagerness. Then he paused. Had he been too eager? The snake-bright eyes of Joe Shriner were fixed steadily upon him.

Chapter Seventeen

Carlton Jail

That suspicion held Tom for a long moment before it relaxed.

"Well," said the deputy, "maybe that might be done. We got a fine gang of 'em in here now, I'll tell a man! We got 'em from Chi and New York and New Orleans. We got 'em from El Paso and Frisco. All the long roads cross at Carlton sooner or later for a gent that's in the crook world! We'll have a look."

He pressed a button. There was the faint murmur of a bell in the distance, and presently two men, carrying huge sawed-off shotguns under their arms, made their appearance. They looked like business — they were business, and no mistake. It did not need a word to tell Tom Converse that these were guards, and that they would shoot sooner than talk. They turned their brute faces upon him with a curious and disgusting hunger, as though they expected that here might be another bit of grist for their mill. But the deputy at once enlightened them.

"I'm going to show an old townsman of mine through the place."

So saying, he unlocked a cabinet, took out a

bundle of massive keys, and passed through the tall, steel office door leading to the interior of the prison.

"These two men keep watch," said the deputy, "and we have one more on guard who never comes away except for a special signal."

Tom, in the meantime, was waved forward by the guards, and he stepped through the door. It was closed behind him with a loud clangor, and he found that the two guards had taken up their position, one on either side and slightly to the rear, with the hideous muzzles of their shotguns presented even with his back, ready, beyond doubt, to blow him to smithereens at the first suspicious move on his part. So the inspection began.

The jail was of singular construction. The cells were so arranged that no two of them looked in upon each other. They lay in a queer hodgepodge, twisting this way and that on the capacious floor of the prison. Light and air were admitted through two skylights high in the roof above, so that these orifices might not be used for purposes of escape. All around the room — for the body of the jail was a single apartment subdivided into the individual cells — ran a promenade about two feet in width and perhaps ten feet above the floor.

On this promenade now walked another man with one of the sawed-off shotguns. He was slightly bent over, because the beams of the ceiling came close to his head. Moreover, the width of the promenade was so slight that he had to go with a sort of sidling motion.

He was pointed out at once by the deputy, and with a great deal of pride.

"Every thirty seconds," said the deputy, "the guard looks into every one of the cells from his runway, and the runway is purposely made so narrow that he has to keep wakeful and alert to save himself from making a misstep that would throw him down into one of the cells. If he landed in one of the cells, the relations of our guards and our prisoners are so far from amiable that the question of who survived would probably be the question of who got the first advantage in the matter of a strangle hold. Anyway, that would just about sum it up!"

He chuckled, then laughed, and the two brute voices behind Tom Converse obediently echoed that brute laughter of their master. They made Tom think of two brainless dogs held on a leash.

The farther he went in the jail, the more his heart failed him. He was planning to do his best to break the law, but this was the danger he ran — the danger of being cast into a living death such as this! Surely he was seeing the teeth of the law.

With only half his mind he listened to the remarks of Joe Shriner as they passed cell after cell.

"That's 'Blinky' Davis. He done for two in Chi. We're cooling him off here for a while and getting him ready to be shipped. He was sort of wild when we got hold of him, but we're whipping him into shape."

Here the deputy chuckled, and the two brute voices in the rear echoed the sound once more.

"There's 'Denver' Rathbone. He killed his first wife and murdered his father-in-law — so they say. And what they say is most generally right when they talk about a gent that has the looks of Denver. Look at his eyes!"

They were the eyes of a hungry pig — greedy, wickedly cunning, inhuman.

And so the story went on in its brief chapters. At length came the remark:

"Here's the prize of the lot. Here's our beauty!"

He stepped forward and struck his bunch of keys against the bars. There was a snarl of rage from within, and Tom Converse saw a man inside raise his head and look out from between his hands.

What he saw in that face made Converse step back. It was not settled viciousness that he found. It was insensate rage and the desire to kill.

"That's Ben Plummer, old man Plummer's boy. Come out of a good home, then stepped over here and blew a safe, got cornered, and here you are — all ready to raise Cain the rest of his days! Ain't you, Ben?"

But Ben Plummer, after that first snarl and that first glare, dropped his head back in his hands and would not stir, would not speak.

So this was the man he had come to rescue!

"Mostly the worst crooks come from outside parts," said the deputy, "but this here nacheral and native-born flower is sure in a class by himself. He eats murder; he lives, sleeps, and dreams murder, just like a mountain lion, only he's got more sand than one of the big cats!"

They passed on, but Tom Converse saw little of what followed. His brain was whirling, and when they returned to the deputy's office, he sat down weakly. Was it the innate viciousness that made the boy what he was, or had he been tormented and given that third degree in the jail until he was reduced to this state?

Tom raised his hand; the paper in his breast pocket crinkled slightly and brought back to him with a rush that first emotion of hope and the desire to fight for life which the note had given him. When would he be able to see the writer of that letter, and what would the emotions of that writer be when she saw Ben Plummer at liberty if he, Tom Converse, could surmount the apparently invincible obstacles which began to loom in his path in the person of the deputy, to say nothing of the strength of the jail and the danger of the three big guards?

But try he must. He made up his mind to that! In the meantime, he must do his best to secure a few more minutes with the deputy while he made his plans. Now that he was inside those heavy outer doors of the jail, he had better take his try at once rather than delay to scheme.

The deputy himself afforded the opening.

"What part of Crayville did you and your folks live in?"

"Down at the end of town," said Tom noncommittally.

The two guards were retreating through the door to the interior.

"End of town?" The great Joe Shriner frowned. "I dunno how there can be an end of a town that's built as round as a ball as far as I can remember it. You mean on the other side of the Creek, maybe?"

"Yes, right near the bridge."

The deputy gaped again.

"Bridge?" he said. "What bridge? There ain't no bridge over that old dry slough!"

Desperately Tom fought to recover the lost ground.

"It ain't much of a bridge, not much more'n a culvert; but they put it up last year because folks was always cussing that dip in the road just as they come into town."

"H'm," said Joe Shriner, and he fixed on Tom one of those ferret glances which probed deep into his very soul.

His glance wandered away, then suddenly it became fixed.

"Who done the building of it?"

"I — I dunno," said Tom Converse wretchedly.

He saw the deputy sit suddenly erect in his chair, staring at him from beneath black brows. The climax had come, and his deceit was about to be revealed.

Chapter Eighteen

Ben is Pleased

That miserable moment was one of the longest that ever passed in the life of Tom Converse.

"D'you know what I'm thinking?" said the sheriff at length, his pugnacious lower jaw thrusting out farther than ever.

"Can't guess."

"I'm thinking that you ain't no more lived in Crayville than you've lived in heaven."

The least flicker of an eyelash would bring about gun play. The hand of the deputy was already back, the fingertips touching the butt of his weapon, and Tom's own hands were folded in his lap. He could not possibly get out his gun as fast as Joe Shriner from such a start. Moreover, he did not want to make it gun play, for gun play meant death for one of them, and, much as he despised and hated the guardian of the jail, he did not wish to be the one who ended the life of the fellow.

Only one shift came into his mind. That was to put back his head and laugh; and hysteria, or the near approach of hysteria, enabled him to laugh with something like reality. Yet, from the corner of his eye, he noted the right hand of the deputy slowly come away from the butt of his gun.

Joe Shriner was by no means entirely blinded by this ruse, but he was willing to delay for a moment of talk and hear what the stranger could say.

"I'll tell you," began Tom, leaning forward in his chair and thrusting his hands still farther out, away from any weapon.

In spite of himself the deputy made an answering move of his body, leaning forward with a frown to listen to the joke, or the attempted joke, of Tom. As he leaned, the big brown right fist of Tom Converse dipped up and across, and his shoulder dropped behind the punch. It was a very short blow, but it landed opportunely an inch to one side of the very point of Joe Shriner's jaw.

The latter sagged back in his chair, but, though his body was unnerved by the shock, he still made a desperate effort to fight back. His eye still lived and struggled, and his right hand made a clumsy effort to get at his gun. A tap across the wrist ended that effort. His right hand hung limp. An instant later Tom was master of the deputy's gun.

Afer that, he worked with frantic speed, for who could tell when the guards would return, or when someone would come up from the street? The arms of the deputy he twisted behind his back, and clamped onto them the pair of handcuffs which lay prominently on Shriner's desk. A bit of cord fastened his feet, and then a wadded bandanna was made to serve as a gag.

With an easy effort Tom lifted the bulk from the chair and deposited it to one side, behind the desk, so that only a person standing in the center of the room could see the form. Then he leaned over the body. The eyes of Shriner were wide open, awake. He had recovered from the effects of the blow, and now he was patiently waiting, biding his time.

"Hark to me sing, partner," said Tom through his teeth. "I've heard you talk. You sound like bad medicine to me, and if I hear you open your mouth to yap again, I'll shove this gat down your throat and feed you some lead. Understand? I mean a pile of business!"

He turned again to the desk, having seen that the warning was heard, and he pressed the signal which would call in the two guards.

"Shriner," he said, while he waited for them, "I'm getting two guards. If you make a move when they come in, they'll get me, maybe — or else I'll have to kill both of 'em. But if I do, I'll shoot first at you — you hear?"

He had hardly ended when steps approached and the guards came in.

It was amusing to see the expression of smug obedience fade from their faces when they saw that the master was not there.

"Joe stepped out for a minute," said Tom. "He asked me to call you in while he was —"

"He stepped around the corner and asked you to call us in?" echoed the larger of the two in amazement, as though such a thing had never been heard of before.

"Exactly right," said Tom. "Sit down a minute. He left me a message for you."

They nodded, and, as they sat down, naturally enough they put aside the shotguns. When they looked up, it was to stare into the muzzles of Tom's own gun and the revolver he had taken from Shriner.

"Hands up, boys," he said. "I mean you no harm, but if you give me trouble, I'll finish you. I don't want a killing on this trail if I can keep myself clean of it, but, if it comes to a pinch — I'm The Shadow!"

The effect of the name was magical. Their hands were already above their heads, and the work of shackling their arms behind their backs and then coupling the two together, back to back, took only a moment.

"Keep your mouths shut," said Tom, "and you'll be safe. I'm coming back inside a minute. If I find anything wrong, I'll start shooting to kill. Is that plain? Not a sound out of you!"

He stepped through the door into the cell room, carrying the bunch of keys and a pair of manacles from the deputy's drawer in one hand, and his revolver in the other. Instantly the guard whirled on his promenade.

"Hands up!" called Tom.

The shotgun crashed to the floor, and the hands went slowly into the air, but there was another effect upon which Tom had not counted. There was a deep, strong shout of joy from every cell on the big floor, and a cry of: "A break! A jail break! Don't forget me, pal. Don't forget me, for Heaven's sake!"

"Hush!" cried other voices. "You make a noise, and you gum the whole deal. Keep still!"

"Come down," said Tom to the guard, motioning with his gun. "Come down here, and keep your hands up while you're coming."

"Bat him on the napper," advised a savage whisper near by. "Curse him, I'd ram a knife down his throat if I had the chance, the swine!"

The guard climbed down from his walk and approached, trembling as though he anticipated some such treatment. But Tom merely faced him about, manacled him to the side bars of the main room, and then, with a final precautionary warning to keep silence, he started for the cell of young Ben Plummer.

It required priceless moments for him to find the right key, and, as he worked, he was conscious of faces pressed against the bars on all sides of him, and eager, tremulous whispers of joy and hope: "Me next, pal. Come along this way next, will you? I'll make you, pal. I'll set you up so's you don't need to do no worrying the rest of your days!"

Only Ben Plummer sat in the cell with his head still in his hands and not a stir of head or voice to indicate that he was aware of what was going on. Neither did he move until Tom Converse unlocked the door and, springing within, seized the youth by the shoulder and shook him.

The response was a tigerish leap in attack.

"Once more, eh? Curse you!" snarled Ben Plummer, and flung himself at the throat of Tom Converse.

As well as he could, Tom fenced him away with a straightened left arm and danced off at a secure distance.

"You idiot — you fool!" he groaned. "Don't you see I'm opening the door for you?"

"It's a trick," said Ben Plummer sullenly, stepping back from this big, patient man and eying the door with suspicion. "It's a trick. You ain't going to take me in again the way you have before — you and that hound Shriner!"

The occupants of other cells could hear, even if they could not see, the speakers. They raised their voices in pleading.

"He's nutty. Don't you waste no time on him! Come over this way, bud, and let that fool stay where he is!"

But this whisper, and then a cry from the adjoining cells, cleared the brain of Ben Plummer, stupefied by misery and despair. He jerked up his head and stepped to the door, wincing away as he passed Tom, as though in fear that he might receive a blow as soon as his back was turned.

Then he slipped through the door and into the open aisle. He was seen at once by other prisoners. A low controlled cry of joy broke from a score of throats, but Ben Plummer turned with a face pale with amazement and the dawn of joy.

"Good Lord!" he muttered. "You don't mean that I'm free to get out of this hole, partner — partner?" He repeated the word with a thrill of hope.

"Free to get out if we can," said Tom Converse, "but we need speed!"

At that moment a door toward the front of the jail was flung open, and a strong voice called: "Shriner! Joe Shriner! Hello, where are you!"

"In hell — or will be soon!" said Ben Plummer through his teeth.

But Tom, realizing that the way to the street might be blocked in ten seconds more, caught his companion by the arm and dragged him ahead.

"The other gun!" pleaded Plummer, reaching for the weapon.

"No, no," answered Tom. "We'll have no murder done! You follow me and do what I do!" And they broke into a run down the aisle.

The moment they were seen in motion, there arose a great wail, echoed and reëchoed through the length and breadth of the prison, filled and swelled by a score of wild voices: "They're breaking out without us. They're leaving us to rot here. Curse 'em!"

From the front of the jail there was a yell of alarm as the man seeking Shriner came to understand what was happening in the jail. The front door banged behind him as he fled to give the alarm.

Chapter Nineteen

Riding for Safety

Nor were these the only sources of clamor, for now the three guards, alarmed by the shouting of the prisoners, as though they feared that they might be attacked the next moment by the men over whom they had tyrannized so long, raised their voices in frantic calls for help.

"Fast!" cried Tom Converse to Plummer, and with that he plunged forward at full speed, but that speed was as nothing compared to the running of Ben Plummer.

Realizing that he was about to leave the prison and his tormentors, and eager beyond belief to work out some vengeance before he departed, Ben Plummer ran like a deer before Tom, looking for a chance to strike. He saw the third guard shackled against the heavy outer bars of the prison room, and with an animal shout of rage and exultation he flung himself at the throat of the man.

His lunging fist struck home. The guard crashed back against the bars with a yell and then hung limp as the other fist whacked against his head. Forgetful of all else, Ben Plummer would probably have stayed to finish his victim, but Tom Converse, sick with disgust, and wondering what sort of brute he had come to rescue, dragged the younger fellow away and thrust him on toward the office.

"Mind you," he shouted at the ear of young Plummer, "if I see you raise a hand against another gent that's helpless and down, I'll brain you myself. Don't forget!"

Ben Plummer flung a snarl at his rescuer, and they darted on side by side through the door of the office and into the presence of the guards. The pair shrank back as far as they could. On the floor lay the deputy, where he had writhed, and at length had managed to place himself in the exact center, twisting up his head and shoulders so that they rested against the lower part of the desk. In this cramped position, he stared at the fugitives with a convulsed, rage-swollen face which the size of the gag had already disfigured.

There was a stifled wail of regret from Ben Plummer as he saw these three whom he hated, so near at hand and yet so out of his reach; for behind and beside him ranged Tom Converse with a poised revolver and a stern face, warning him on. With a curse of rage, Ben Plummer dashed on into the narrow hall and so down the steps outside.

One glance at the street told Tom Converse that they had close work ahead of them. Men milled to and fro at a little distance, running out from the hotel. Just across the street from the jail he saw a newly arrived rancher, or cow-puncher, as though only just now apprised of what was up, fling himself from the back of a tall, powerful-limbed gray mare and rush on into a harness shop, drawing his gun as he ran.

Tom decided with lightning rapidity, as he ran on down the steps, that the first thing to do was to see that Ben Plummer was safely on the back of Captain and headed down the street. The next move was to get into the saddle on that tall mare himself.

"Onto that hoss!" he commanded Ben Plummer.

"Good Lord!" gasped the astonished boy. "Captain! And you are —"

"The Shadow, if that'll make you do what I tell you. Get onto that hoss and ride like the wind up the street. You hear?"

One look of mingled fright and worship was all that the youngster had a chance to throw to Tom Converse, and then, with a signal which seemed to indicate that he would ride to death in obedience to the commands of so great a hero, he turned and rushed for Captain.

Over his shoulder, as he reached the level of the street, Tom saw Ben Plummer swing into the saddle with a yell and then shake his balled fist in the direction of the hotel. As for himself, Tom rushed straight ahead. Through the window of the store he could see the rancher and the storekeeper raising rifles to draw a bead on him. He smashed one bullet through the top of the window, and the shivering of glass had not ended before he saw that both men had dived for shelter. This was not their day for standing up to the gunfire of The Shadow.

Other men, at a greater distance, to be sure, were ready to man the firing line. The hotel down the street began to pour forth fire and a hail of lead from the windows. Tom sent a shot plunging in that direction. It was a high shot, far too high to injure a soul, but it would serve to make them hug their cover and not take risks while they aimed shots at him.

In safety he reached the side of the gray. He whipped into the saddle at the same time that a wail of fury and grief burst from the inside of the harness shop, proclaiming clearly that the owner of the mare now realized the purpose of that charge across the street — for the first time knew what a loss was about to be his, and desired to die rather than submit.

"That shows," thought Tom Converse, "that she's as good as she looks — or better!"

He whirled the mare in a small cloud of dust and shot her up the street. At the same moment the owner exposed himself recklessly at the window of the shop and pumped after him shot after shot from a rifle which grief and rage kept in a hopeless state of tremor.

Luck, great luck, alone saved Tom Converse on that flight up the street — luck and promptitude of action; for, what has taken long to describe, occurred within the space of a few seconds.

Hardly had the men at the hotel and in the

154

few shops received the warning through the shouts of the man who first entered the jail and discovered the break, when down the steps from the building ran the stranger and the liberated man, followed by a dull roar of despair from the jail itself. A moment later Ben Plummer was flying up the street on the matchless dappled chestnut, with Tom Converse only a few seconds behind.

A swing in the street cut them off from danger in a few strides, and then Tom saw that Ben Plummer, instead of bolting for liberty at once, was drawing Captain back and waiting for Tom to overtake him. It was a gallant bit of cool-headed courage, and Tom ranged beside the youngster with the first warmth of heart which he had felt toward him.

Now for the first time Tom could view the action of Captain from a distance. He was almost as wonderful to look at as he was to ride, and even in the excitement of the chase Tom marveled at the bounding stride, frictionless and low-sweeping. The gray mare, with an advantage in height, was nevertheless falling far short of the elastic springs of Captain.

No wonder that on such a horse The Shadow had defied pursuit for many and many a day, and was like to have defied it still longer. Why he would have given up that horse, Tom Converse could not guess, for he did not know the story of the three men whom the outlaw had vowed he would destroy.

The town was now a riot of noise behind them as they swept into open country. They reached the top of the first hill, and behold, out of the end of the street rushed a cloud of pursuers, with a dense mist of white dust boiling up underfoot and rolling up thinner and thinner into the air.

They would never touch Captain, no matter how far he had already gone that day, and unless Tom was sadly mistaken, they would not seriously press the longlegged mare, fresh and keen for her day's work. A spirit of mischief came to Tom as he reined in the gray and turned back. Beside him, the face of Ben Plummer had paled until the freckles across his nose stood out boldly, but it was the pallor of excitement rather than fear, and the eyes of the youngster danced with joy. He dared not speak to so great a man as The Shadow until spoken to. So much was plain. But with all his heart he was aching to talk.

Tom drew out of its case the rifle which lay in the long holster in the saddle next to him. It was The Shadow's own gun, and, as Tom passed it through his hands and caught the balance of it, he could not refrain from an exclamation of pleasure and surprise. The weapon was plainly made to order for the sake of lightness and strength combined, so as to be most manageable on horseback, and in his two hands it was far lighter than a Colt in one. It was a .32, not at all short in barrel. The purpose was not to make a gun which one could uncase with extraordinary speed, but simply to create a weapon with which one could shoot with precision and comfort while sitting the saddle.

Tom dropped the butt into the hollow of his shoulder.

"As far off as that?" gasped Ben Plummer, and his words were clipped short by the explosion of the rifle.

Once, twice, and again the gun exploded, and in front of the racing posse — ten yards, perhaps from the leaders — there arose three little spurts of dust, one after another. The posse, warned by this skillful shooting that they were within range of a deadly weapon, drew their horses up short and milled around in confusion while the three echoes came crowding back swiftly from the neighboring hillsides.

"Good Lord!" cried Ben Plummer. "I've heard about some of the shooting that you've done, but I never dreamed that I'd see anything as good as that!"

Tom Converse laughed carelessly in response, as he reached over and jammed the rifle back into the case. That at least would keep them from pressing him too closely on this ride. They would give him elbowroom, and elbowroom was distinctly what he needed on a new horse in the midst of a new country.

He loosed the rein, and they rode on over the top of the hill. Behind them the noise of the pursuit began again, but already Tom was mentally putting that danger behind him. There remained to him, of all the action in Carlton and all the danger he had undergone, only a delightful sense of pleasant adventure, hardly less joyous than the peril and the escape from the hotel under the very nose of Sheriff Algie Thomas.

Chapter Twenty

Thomas Takes the Trail

A great silence had come over Sheriff Algie Thomas. When they asked him why he answered with his usual astonishing frankness and humility joined.

"It's going to be either him or me, and I think that in the end it's me that's going to go down with a bang! I can't help thinking that. He's the first one that ever I read all wrong. Mind you, the impudent hound had the nerve to come and stand right up in front of me over in Silver Tip and talk to me as cool as you please! Well, sir, when crooks feel that they can make as free as all that with old Algie Thomas, he's sure gone a long way past his prime; and I misread him entire.

"Sure, I seen that he was dangerous. I'd just watched him stand Alec McGregor and Timber Johnson on their heads right down the street from me. But who'd figure on The Shadow being quite so young, or so happy-looking, after the murders that he's done? Anyway, a laughing devil is the worst kind of devil, and The Shadow passed me by and made a plumb fool of me. After him there'll come another, I guess. Well, lads, I figure that this is going to be my last trail, but I'm going to work hard while I'm on it! Maybe I'm too old to've left Silver Tip for a saddle, but I'm going to do my best!"

And his best he had accordingly done. If he did not at once rush out of the town to hunt down the criminal, at any rate, after a long sleep that night, he rose early, saddled his horse, and started out by himself. But he had not gone far when he was overtaken by a great hue and cry.

Jess Sherman was gone from his house, and in front of his stable that morning his riderless, saddled horse had been found. Where could he be? He was known to have gone to bed that night immediately after the escape of The Shadow from the hotel.

Algie Thomas went directly to the ranch and took charge of the hunt down trail. It was not a difficult one to follow for a man of his experience. The ride had been made in the fresh mud, and the meeting place in the hollow was a mass of prints.

There lay Jess, face up, with the purple blotch in the center of his forehead. Most of the party turned back with the body, for what is a more fitting and conclusive end to a trail than a dead man? But Algie Thomas and a few others hung by the original work. If the body were found, the trail, nevertheless, continued on from that place, and that trail must be the trail of the murderer.

It went straight as an arrow for the house of

Plummer, and, where the horse had been left in covert, the sheriff dismounted from his nag and began to take a real interest in the problem. But he managed to discern the footmarks which left the spot where the horse had been placed, and which approached the house, coming straight to the side.

Here the sheriff paused and turned on his companions, who remained respectfully behind and a little to one side, unwilling to trouble or run the risk of disconcerting so great an artist as Algie Thomas.

"That room yonder — the one that window opens on — I'll bet you I can tell you who sleeps there!"

"Who?" asked the chorus. "Have you been inside the house?"

"Never been in Joe Plummer's house in my life, but I bet Sylvia Rann sleeps in that room!"

The murmur grew and subsided.

"Didn't The Shadow write back a letter after that night they laid for him? Didn't he write back a letter and tell 'em that he was going to live long enough to come again and do for the three gents that shot him? You got to admit that, any way a man can look at it, it was pretty cowardly work, that shooting when he come to see his girl! Well, sirs, he's come back, and Jess Sherman, that planned the lying in wait, is the man that's been killed first. And afterward, where does The Shadow go? He goes to the house of his girl to tell her he's back safe and had finished the first part of his vengeance — the most important third of it, in fact! Does that sound reasonable?"

They admitted that it did, and straightway they went into the house to verify his statements. The sheriff found Sylvia Rann in the kitchen at the unpoetic task of peeling potatoes for the noon meal. Before she had recovered from her surprise at seeing him, he asked in the most matter-of-fact tone in the world: "When did The Shadow come to see you last night, Miss Rann?"

"It was long after —" She stopped short; then, seeing that she had committed herself hopelessly, she flushed to the hair and stood up to face them.

There was a wail from Mrs. Plummer, a tired-faced woman at the stove.

"Sylvia! Sylvia! You ain't been letting him see you again, after all —"

"Hush!" said the girl, never wasting a glance for Mrs. Plummer, but reserving all of her strength and attention for the sheriff.

"He come to tell you what he'd done, I reckon?" asked the sheriff.

She would not answer. Her color had receded, save for a bright spot in the center of each cheek; but she kept a steady eye on the sheriff.

"Land sakes!" murmured that gentle old soul. "I ain't trying to drag no information out of you, girl. I'm simply telling you what the rest of us know. We was bound to find out, wasn't we? They missed Jess Sherman first thing this morning, and we're just after finding his body in the

162

hollow, right where Jess and —"

A shrill cry from the girl cut him short.

"Jess Sherman dead!"

There was no doubting her real astonishment. She shrank back toward the window as though the news had blighted her, and, pressing her face to her hands, she remained bowed and quivering for a moment.

He had come to her to talk of love and marriage after such a bit of work? He had come to her to talk of reform immediately after having slain? Had she not, after all, guessed what had happened? The little touch of horror, which from the first she had always felt in his presence, was with her last night when she heard his voice. It returned to her now, manifold. Slayer by night he had ever been, and slayer by night he would always be!

Algie Thomas stepped beside her.

"Honey," he said, "I've heard a pile about you, even if I ain't ever laid eyes on you before, and all I've heard goes to show that you're a good girl, and a kind and a true girl. What The Shadow means to you, it ain't my right to ask. But I'm going to ask you to take a look at things and say if it ain't a queer way for a girl to tie up her hands. Here you've been for two years refusin' to see any other young gents because you been keeping true to The Shadow. Now he comes back, and the first thing that he does by way of showing that he's glad to be near you again is to do a murder and —"

There was a stifled cry from the girl. Then

163

she turned and fled from the kitchen. Mrs. Plummer would have followed her, but the sheriff held the woman back.

"It don't no ways do no good after they get like that," he declared. "Words would just go in one ear and out the other, Mrs. Plummer. I've had a wife and a daughter many a year back, and I know. But I figure that she'll think a couple of times before she sees that gent again. She's started thinking on a new track, Mrs. Plummer."

He left the house, dismissed the companions who had followed him, and, with the statement that he was striking back toward the town, he went a little way down the road; but he took the first opportunity to drop behind, and at length, passing out of view of the others, he wheeled his horse and struck again for the house of Plummer.

Here he took up a new trail, and one which he wished to work out in quiet and silence by himself. He picked up the sign of The Shadow's horse where it was left last, at the covert near the Plummer house, and began to follow it slowly away.

It was not, as he had expected, easy work. The fugitive had taken the utmost pains in covering his track, going well out of his way to obliterate all sign of detours which passed over hard rock. Once, dropping into the bed of a stream, dry since the waters had been diverted, The Shadow had worked along for a full mile over hard-crusted gravel which left not a sign of a horse's hoofs.

But the sheriff found the place where the tracks disappeared near the bank of the stream, and he ran a course up and down the stream, a mile in each direction, until he found where the tracks left it again.

He was using up a great deal of time, of course, but the sheriff was in no great hurry. He had always found that The Shadow used as a center of operations the district which focused on the house of Plummer. Obviously, no matter how far he roamed from time to time, he would come back to the dwelling of the lady of his love.

Therefore, it occurred to the sheriff that The Shadow would not, without regret, pass far away from her now, especially since he had seen her only once during a space of two whole years. This was the meaning of the difficult trail which the fugitive was running. He wished to entangle any trailers, and eventually he might come to a stop at a point very close to the start. Time, therefore, was of no matter.

The sheriff went down the trail with his eyes as bright and as restless as the eyes of a ferret on a scent. It was long since he had been at such work, and he loved it for the sake of auld lang syne. Never had he worked better since his youth. It seemed to the sheriff that every tree beside which The Shadow had passed in his flight would, if he waited long enough, tell the secret of the outlaw's course.

Noon passed, and he was still at work, having covered a scant two miles. Midafternoon found him advanced hardly three miles more. Just as evening came on, and he was about to mark the end of that day's work and turn back to the town, the scent of wood smoke drifted keen and clear to his nostrils through the thicket ahead of him.

Chapter Twenty-One

The Meeting

The well-trained horse of the sheriff had been following him at a little distance all the day, grazing here and there on whatever appealed to its eye or its appetite. Now the horse raised its wise head at the smell of the smoke. To the horse, smoke meant two things — the most terrible of all dangers, most terrible because most fascinating, and the habitation of man, the end of the day's march.

Algie Thomas looked back at the intelligent animal, raised his hand in warning to be motionless while he was gone, and at once disappeared into the thicket before him.

No youthful woodsman, full of knowledge of how to make his way in stalking a deer, could have moved with more silent craft than did the sheriff. He simply dissolved noiselessly in the green foliage, and advanced in this manner until he came, some 50 yards farther away, to the edge of a small clearing.

Rather, it was not a clearing, but a natural opening in the woods, which seemed to have been planned by kindly nature for the greater convenience of man. A small stream — too small to attract attention with its noise, but large enough to bring a generous supply of drinking water — trickled into a basin formed by half a dozen large boulders, cupped out and cemented together in every crevice by a drift of fine white sand.

Over this basin rose an immense oak; the size of its protruding branches had thrust back the thicket of second-growth trees on all sides. Owing perhaps to the poverty of the soil, or to the presence of rocks very near the surface of the loam, there was an extensive open place on the side of the basin, an opening 20 paces or so in diameter. On the edges of the rude circle two horses had been tethered on ropes long enough to permit them to graze comfortably on the rich grass which grew everywhere on the surface of the clearing.

In the center, but conveniently close to the basin of water without endangering the water itself with ashes, was the fire, built in fine fashion between big rocks, and so arranged that the blaze rose to a good cooking point.

Over this, a frying pan was poised, and from the pan issued the sizzling noise of frying bacon, that inevitable accompaniment of the life of a camper in the far West. Beside this fire, partly veiled from time to time, as a gust of wind beat down and scattered the smoke in one direction or another, sat two men, one of them squat and grizzled, with three or four days' growth of whiskers on his broad face. This was the worthy directly facing the sheriff. He seemed more of a hobo than a wandering trapper or hunter or cow-puncher out of work. Opposite him was a slenderer, more erect fellow.

Instantly, the sheriff knew that the broad-faced man was the owner of the rawboned brown horse at the edge of the clearing, and the slenderer man was the possessor of the tall bay with all indications of speed in its build, and with legs which might well have made the long strides of The Shadow, or the presumptive Shadow whom he had been trailing. Quietly Algie Thomas went over the mechanism of his revolver, more by sense of touch than by sight, making sure that all was well with it. Then he stepped into the clearing.

There was a startled exclamation from the grizzled veteran, and a lowering, savage expression which told the sheriff more eloquently than words that the elder of the pair was by no means a friend to the law. If ever a look of stupid criminal brutality glared out of eyes, it looked at Thomas from under the fat brows of the other.

But the slender man did not so much as turn his head, for a moment. It was not until the sheriff spoke that he stirred.

"Gents," said Sheriff Thomas, without moving for his revolver, which he had restored to the holster before stepping into the clearing, "I'll have to ask you to keep your hands out in front of you and not to make no move for guns. I'm watching you tolerable close."

Here the slender man turned his head, and the sheriff caught sight of the profile of the sallow-faced man whom he had seen in Silver Tip some days before, one of those who drifted in and out of the village without particular reason for his goings and his comings.

"It's all right," said this individual at once. "That's Sheriff Algie Thomas, Scottie."

"Algie Thomas!" gasped the other, agape, and by no means sharing the quiet satisfaction of his leaner companion. "Thomas!"

If he had been confronted by the reflection of his own death mask in a mirror, he could not have been more disgruntled, more gray with horror.

"Sure," said the other, "that's the sheriff. He ain't apt to do no foolish mischief. Sit down, sheriff, and tell us what's wrong, will you?"

The smooth greeting made the sheriff smile until, stepping to one side, he obtained a fuller sight of the features of the lithe man of the sallow face. He had noticed the fellow before, in Silver Tip; but, because of his crippled condition, he had not given him so careful an examination as he usually gave to newcomers in the town.

Now he observed many things worth noting in the unhealthy skin, the dull, dark eyes, and the stern straightness of the month. It was a handsome face, a face that women would fear and love, and men would fear and distrust. There was no possibility of getting past the guard of those eyes and at the secrets of the mind behind them.

"I've seen you, son," said the sheriff, "but I disremember your name."

170

"Jim Cochrane."

"All right, Jim Cochrane, I'm going to ask you to go along with me."

"Is this an arrest?"

"Kind of looks that way."

The dark eyes flickered for the least fraction of a second, and in that tiny interval the sheriff knew that the fellow had seriously considered gun play and then dismissed the thought as Algie Thomas smoothly slipped his revolver out of the holster and let it hang quietly from his bony old fingers. In that flash the sheriff knew that the broad strength of Scottie was not to be compared to the deadly agility and quickness of mind of Jim Cochrane.

"What's the charge?" Jim Cochrane was asking.

"Murder," said the sheriff with equal calm, but ready now to fire two bullets, one after another, with the speed of light.

"Murder?" echoed Cochrane, and then whistled. "Murder! Well, who'd I kill, and where?"

"Jess Sherman, last night or early this morning, in the hollow about —"

The sallow-faced man shook his head. "It won't do, partner," he said. "It sure won't do a bit. I'd like to see you pick up the gent that done the killing, but you can't make a reputation on me. Scottie'll tell you where I was last night and this morning."

Was it to be an alibi? For a moment the sheriff hesitated. The trail he had followed had been a very hard one, and he certainly could not swear

171

that it led with surety and without interruption to this place. No, he certainly could not swear that.

"Jim was right here with me," said Scottie, "last night and early this morning."

"Right here?" exclaimed the sheriff suddenly. "You mean that you haven't traveled during the last day?"

"Just what I mean," said Scottie sullenly.

The sheriff pointed. "What's that saddle mark on the hoss over yonder?"

The mark was clearly outlined with sweat on the back of the bay.

"He ain't rolled," said Jim Cochrane calmly. "I guess that's a fairly good explanation, sheriff?"

"Fairly good — only fair. Scottie, will you swear to that lie?"

He brought the last word out with such a snap that Scottie jumped.

"Lie? It ain't a lie!" he declared. "It's gospel, Sheriff Thomas. I'll swear by —"

"Shut up," said the sheriff coldly. "It always riled me considerable to hear a gent swear his soul away."

He paused and looked the pair over thoughtfully. If he attempted to press the arrest further, he knew that he would have on his hands the hardest fight he had ever fought in his life. The sallow-faced man would in himself be a handful, and Scottie might well make a deadly flank attack when he had such help. No, it would be decidedly risky to press matters now.

And to what end should he press them? Even suppose that he captured Jim Cochrane, what absolute proof would he have? He had followed the dimmest of dim trails, that might have been crossed half a dozen times at least. On the strength of such evidence as this, he could not convict. He decided that he must back down. Yet it was unlucky, mighty unlucky, that Cochrane should have found a companion who would swear to an alibi.

He had come strongly convinced that that trail would lead to The Shadow and the dappled chestnut horse. He was strongly convinced that one of the watchers by that camp fire must be the boy who had given his name in Silver Tip as Tom Converse, but who was now hunted so fiercely through the hills as The Shadow. Even when the trail proved to have been laid by a bay horse instead of a chestnut, and ridden by this Jim Cochrane, the sheriff was still convinced that he stood before the man who had killed Jess Sherman.

It was very strange that two mortal enemies of Jess should have been abroad at the same time, but facts were greater than arguments. The Shadow was not here. He was far away, perhaps, and here was another malefactor to confront.

The sheriff stepped back and waved his left hand, at the same time sliding the revolver into the holster once more.

"So long, Scottie," he said. "Cochrane, I've got an idea that we're going to meet up again and see a good deal of each other!" And he melted at once into the thicket behind him.

He was hardly gone when Scottie turned with a sigh of relief and parted his lips to speak. A warning gesture from The Shadow halted him, and it was some time before Jim Cochran spoke.

"Thanks," he said. "You spoke up fine and loud for me, Scottie, but if you'd talked again so quick, you might have blowed everything. That old fox stopped inside the thicket for a minute or two after he got out of sight. He tried to listen in on what we said."

"I didn't hear a thing!"

"You need to get a file and sharpen up your ears, Scottie. They're sure all wrong!"

Scottie shrugged his thick shoulders. "Was it as much as that?" he murmured in an awed whisper. "Did you bump off some stiff?"

"Me?" answered Jim Cochrane, alias The Shadow. "Sure I didn't bump off anybody, but now that I've got that old devil after me, he'll make the ground hot. Why is he outside of Silver Tip? Ain't the town big enough for him any more?"

"I heard that he's got ambition," said the other. "I heard somebody telling that he'd left Silver Tip to hit the trail after The Shadow. I wonder how that brung him up to you?"

He dropped his elbows on his knees and leaned forward, staring at Jim with great cunning of insinuation as he spoke; but the latter shook his head.

"The Shadow?" he said, chuckling. "You'll be thinking I'm the King of England pretty soon, Scottie!"

"But who is The Shadow?"

"I dunno," said Jim. "But he's got neat ways about him, ain't he?"

Chapter Twenty-Two

Sylvia is Puzzled

It was some hours later that same night when Sylvia Rann, sitting wretched and alone in her room to brood over The Shadow and his ways of crime — shutting him out of her mind and her life with a greater and greater determination — heard a faint hooting sound which seemed to come from a great distance. It was that soft, weird call of the screech owl, the loneliest sound made by bird or beast; but, with the repetition of it, the girl started to her feet and ran swiftly to the window.

Long before, she remembered how Ben Plummer, in the manner of a foolish, imaginative boy, had practiced that call and had even attempted to teach it to her, though she had never been able to give it with his own uncanny skill.

She leaned far out of the window, so that the damp coolness of the night air blew around her face, and in that attitude she heard again, with a greater and more startling clearness, the same long, soft hoot.

It did not seem so far away. In fact, it must be given somewhere near the top of the hill, and there was something in the harshness with which the first of the call began, that made her think that it might be Ben Plummer, for he had always had difficulty with that part of the cry. Not until the first cry had been given, would his throat conform itself to the exigencies of the weird music.

But if it were Ben, why did he not come directly to the house? Was this a time for him to be playing jests and pranks? She remembered suddenly that there was a sad reason indeed for him to keep his comings and his goings secret. Not even in his own home could he appear because of information that might be given —

But what could he be doing free from the jail? Had it been possible that Jim, after all, had gone to Carlton and broken the jail to get Ben out? Her heart leaped, remembering her promise to the outlaw. Had she not pledged her word that, if he accomplished this much, she would leave her adopted home and go with him where he would?

The promise had been given in the first heat of sheer impulse, and now, as her mind wavered sadly, unable to believe what must have taken place, the cry was sent up for the third time. This time there was no mistake. Due either to a failure of breath or some other mishap, the cry broke exactly in the center. It was an imitation of the screech owl, and a very poor imitation at that. It must be Ben Plummer who stood out there calling to her.

No matter for reasons. Reasons told her that Ben was far off in the jail in Carlton. Perhaps

— oh, happy thought! — he had escaped by his own wit or prowess.

This hope gave her wings to hurry into a coat — for the night was turning cold — and steal out of her room, slipping softly down the hall through the sleeping house, out of the screen door which squeaked a little no matter how dexterous and slow one might be, and into the open.

Up the gentle slope of the hill she ran at full speed, only slackening her pace as she came toward the top, where she began to cry, half beneath her breath: "Ben! Oh, Ben!"

She had hardly called twice when a figure took shape, starting out from behind a shrub, and in another moment Ben Plummer, dancing with excitement and joy of seeing her, was wringing her hands and hugging her. She could have wept for joy, had it not been that a chill of fear stayed with her.

"You broke away yourself, Ben?" she said. "You did it all by yourself? Oh, I've been thinking of ten years of your life wasted — ruined — in prison, all because of that wild —" She broke off and added fiercely: "It was because of Jim. I know all that. It's his fault!"

"Don't say a word agin' The Shadow," said her foster brother sternly. "Of all the pals in the world, there ain't none to compare with him. If he started me wrong, at least he saved me from what might have happened to me on account of it. He busted the jail at Carlton wide open. He tied up Joe Shriner himself and three guards, and he got me clean off —"

The rest of his words went into a blur, so far as Sylvia Rann was concerned. Half of her joy disappeared. If The Shadow had paid in full the price she asked of him, how could she dare break the word she had given?

She asked gloomily: "How many men did he kill? How many, Ben?"

"Not one!" exclaimed the boy. "Nary a one! And he wouldn't let me act up the way I tried to act, neither! He wouldn't trust me with a gun, because he was afraid that I'd shoot. And I would have shot. If he'd let me have a gun, I would have been a murderer by this time, Sylvia!"

Wonder began to fill the mind of the girl. She had never allowed people to tell her tales of the terrible deeds of The Shadow, but she knew that he was a man to whom human life counted as nothing. Looking back to the beginning of their acquaintance, she wondered now at the girlish romanticism which had ever allowed her to think twice of such a ruffian.

That time was far gone. She saw him now as an enemy to society, a destroyer of life. Jess Sherman, she knew, had been in many respects an ugly character, but at least he had been a human being whom she had known in life, with good qualities mixed up with his bad. She knew that, when she next faced The Shadow, she would see beside his face the dead face of Jess. But what was this talk of the mercies which this dreaded slayer of man had shown in the jail at Carlton, and mercy shown to Joe Shriner, above all?

Dazed and bewildered by Ben's enthusiasm, she managed to say as quietly as possible: "Now tell me everything, Ben, from the time you — you —"

"From the time I cracked the safe? Well, I was a fool, Sylvia, and that's the long and the short of it. I thought that was the way to start out and make a name for myself, so that The Shadow would hear about me and take notice of me, and so that finally I could become a partner of his —"

"I know, Ben; I know all of that!"

"Well, afterward, they trapped me and got me and put me in that Carlton Jail. Sylvia, you've heard about gents being so hard that they were more like devils than men? Well, Joe Shriner, who runs that jail, is one of 'em! He did his best while I was in there to make me a crook for life, and he pretty near succeeded, I can tell you! He and his men hounded me — they hounded all the rest in that jail. After a while, what with getting the third degree and bad food and no chance to see the sun, I began to grow wrong in the head. I began to go mad, I think! When The Shadow come along, I was like a crazy man. I just wanted to kill one of them gents that had been pestering me when I wasn't able to hit back at 'em, but The Shadow wouldn't let me. He rushed me out of that jail, and he put me on the back of his own hoss, the dappled chestnut, Captain —"

"Did he do that!" breathed the girl, astonished again.

"Yes, and made me ride up the street, ahead. Then, when we got out of town and up on a hill, the posse was hot after us, and he dropped three shots — the prettiest you ever could see — right under their noses, with his rifle, and made 'em hold off so's we could have elbowroom, as The Shadow said. Just shooed 'em back the way you would chickens!"

He laughed joyously at the thought, and again the girl was puzzled. The terrible Shadow, of whom they had told her, was apt to shoot only to kill, never to warn.

"This afternoon we shook off the riders plumb easy, and we camped out in the trees along about evening time, and while he was sitting there, The Shadow takes hold of a note from you that he said you'd thrown into his room."

"Ah, he had that?"

"Yes. In a pocket right over his heart. He's sure fond of you, Sylvia. He says to me: 'How can a girl like that stick to a crook and a man-killer like — The Shadow?'

" 'You don't know her,' says I. 'She'd die rather than give you up while you're down and out, partner!'

" 'H'm,' says he, sort of thinking to himself. 'I tell you what, kid. You take Captain — so's they won't be any chance for you to get caught on the way — and you ride down to see Sylvia. Let her have a look at you so's she can see that

181

you're all safe. Then you come back here, and we'll find a way to get you out of the country. Understand?' "

Again the mind of Sylvia Rann turned over many possibilities. There was a rare delicacy in this message to her. Instead of brutally reminding her of the promise which she had made, and which she must not fulfill, he had simply sent down the boy without a shade of a direct speech to her. She could do as she chose to do. In fact, there was again in this delicacy a thoughtfulness so opposite to the acid directness of The Shadow she knew, that it was hard for her to reconcile what she knew with the facts as she saw and heard them.

While she felt her way toward the truth, she said slowly to Ben Plummer: "Tell me what he wants you to do? What's this about sending you out of the country?"

"He says that the long-rider game ain't a good game, Sylvia — which is what you've always told me. He says that to have to turn a gun on a man is fun — big fun — but that, if a gent is ever killed by that gun you're holding, it's murder, plain murder, no matter how you look at it, unless the law wants that man to be killed. Sort of funny talk to hear from The Shadow, eh?"

"Queer — yes!" breathed the girl.

And yet her heart sank. No doubt the robber-murderer had filled the ears of the impressionable boy with this sort of talk so that he would come to her and repeat what he had heard. But what was this?

"I asked him to show me some stunts about pulling a gun, Sylvia; but he wouldn't do it. He said that it was bad for a gent to be faster with a gun than other folks are. He said that the worst thing that could happen to a man would be to be a good shot and get cornered, because a good shot is apt to use his gun when he gets in a pinch. He told me just to forget all that I knew about guns. He said that, when I was mad at a gent, the best thing to do was to walk up and punch him on the chin so hard that he'd drop."

There was a truth about this that struck home in Sylvia, largely because it was phrased in a manner which she could never have expected from The Shadow, of all men.

"I asked him if it wasn't pretty hard for a gent that liked freedom, to have to work and slave all the rest of his life for money, when there was so much that was easy to get. But he says that, if a gent wants to get money, they's only one way, and that's to work for it!"

It was another shock to Sylvia, and suddenly she exclaimed indignantly: "Then how does he justify his own life?"

"He don't justify it. He says, though, that being free means so much to him that he doesn't see how he could ever go back to working ways and days."

"Go back to them?" cried the girl. "Has he

ever worked honestly one day in all his wasted life?"

"I dunno," said the boy. "He's mighty handy with a rope, and his hands are as hard as nails."

"Pshaw!" scoffed the girl. "His hands are hardly any harder than mine. You've been dreaming a lot of this, Ben. You've been hero-worshiping again! You've been blinded, and I guess you've heard some of the things he's said in the wrong way, too!"

Ben Plummer stamped. "You can't talk down to me like that, Sylvia," he said indignantly. "If The Shadow can afford to treat me like a man, I guess you can talk as if I was a man, too! I say his hands are hard."

The girl sighed. It was bitter to do, but now she must make the great sacrifice in order to save her honor. She had given The Shadow her solemn promise, and now she would redeem it, even if it meant the ruin of the rest of her life.

"Wait here," she said suddenly. "I'm coming back in a moment or two."

Chapter Twenty-Three

Hue and Cry

Back in the house once more, she cautiously lighted her lamp and moved a tall-backed chair next to it, so that the illumination might not attract attention in another room of the sleeping house. Then she placed writing paper on the bureau and quickly scratched a note:

Try to think of me kindly, as I shall think of you forever and ever with love. Why I am going with him, you would never be able to understand, so I must not attempt to explain. Please believe that I have thought long and hard before I take this step.

They call him The Shadow. I can only hope that he and I both may go so far away and pass into such a new life that you may never hear of either of us again. That is the happiest wish I can make, I'm afraid! Heaven bless you both for all the kind things you have said and done for me since you took me in.

She had to turn away for a moment, tears were running down her face so fast as she reached this point in her note. When she had dried them and looked back at the letter, she decided that there was no need to say any more. She simply shoved the slip of paper into the side of the mirror, where a flaw in the framing made it possible, and then turned to finish the rest of her preparations for departure.

They were quickly made. She took a coat, a slicker, a small case of toilet articles, and a little parcel of clothes. She tied the bundle, pressed the sombrero down over her hair and caught up her riding quirt. Then she paused, dismayed by the glimpse of the tearful face which she caught in the mirror.

Was this rain of tears a fit way in which to start the great adventure? She gritted her teeth until an expression of determination had come into her face, and then, as though that mock expression gave her real courage, she turned hastily and fairly fled from the room.

So great was her haste that she stumbled as she passed through the door, and instantly she heard the voice of Mrs. Plummer, ever wakeful, calling: "Who's that? Who's that? Joe, I think they's somebody in the house. Will you get up and have a look about?"

"It's I," answered the girl. "I haven't been able to sleep. I'm going out for a short walk and then I'll come in again and lie down."

"Out for a walk at this time of night!" exclaimed Mrs. Plummer. "Child, are you in your right senses? Have you got a mind to catch your death on a night like this in the damp and the cold?"

"Let her go, ma," rumbled honest Joe Plummer. "She's got such things on her mind that I don't wonder she's wakeful, poor girl. You go on out, Sylvia, if you're feelin' that way. You go out and have a walk, and maybe it'll do you good! Sh, ma. You stop talking!"

He had ever been her great ally, thought Sylvia, as she went on down the hall, weak with sadness. From the very first the big, clumsy-handed rancher had known a way to her heart and had seemed to possess clews to all that was going on inside her brain. Mrs. Plummer, though the height of kindness, had not understood so well. It was like leaving a second father and a second mother for her who had never known her real parents.

Just as she passed the front door and stood fairly outside under the stars — never to return, no doubt — Ben Plummer came up to her. He had waited until his patience was gone, and now he was about to pour out at her a flood of questions, when she stopped him with a gesture.

That gesture was hardly needed, for he had seen the sombrero and the bundle under her arm and the gleam of the oilcloth of the slicker and the slim length of the quirt in the darkness. She was prepared for riding, but where — and at this time of night?

"Sylvia?" he asked. "What's up? You're acting queer."

"Help me saddle a horse," she answered, "and

don't ask questions."

"You ain't leaving?"

"Don't bother me with questions, Ben. Just do what I ask, will you?"

As always, she had only to exert herself a little in order to establish unquestioned superiority over him. He sighed, then turned obediently toward the corral.

She leaned against the fence, too miserable to watch as he found a rope and went in quest of her favorite, cream-colored saddle pony, but when she saw his object, she called to him.

"Not that one, Ben. Catch the roan. Catch the blue roan."

"Old Bad Eye? Why, he's got a gait like a pile of bones rattling, Sylvia. You sure don't want him!"

"Get me Bad Eye," she insisted. "I know what I want. Get me Bad Eye."

There was a growl of protest, but presently she made out the snaky outshoot of the rope and its hawklike swoop over the head of Bad Eye. A few snorts, and then she saw the roan mastered, and a little later the horse was led to one side and the saddle flopped heavily into place. It was bucked off, thrown on again, and, at the end of five minutes of patient work, Bad Eye was outfitted for the world which lay ahead of him. The excitement of catching the blue roan was so great that Ben Plummer seemed to have lost all curiosity as to the ultimate purpose of the saddling until he led a champing, dancing Bad

Eye back to the girl outside the corral. There he prevented her from mounting.

"Here's the hoss," he said, "but before you climb into the stirrups, Sylvia, I sure got to know where you're going to ride on Bad Eye."

"I'm going to see The Shadow!"

She saw him start in the dimness. Then his hand fell on her shoulder.

"What's up, Sylvia?"

"I can't tell you, Ben."

"Then I can't let you go."

She peered at him through the darkness, amazed. He had not been wont to question or challenge her in this fashion.

"You don't trust him?" she queried. "You don't trust your own partner?"

"Look here!" explained Ben. "I'll tell you how I trust him, and how much I think of him. He's the squarest and the straightest gent that ever stepped. When I got out of Carlton and up in the hills, I was using all my time wondering how I could get at Joe Shriner and his bulldogs that work in the jail. I wanted to do four murders and get square with the world. Well, The Shadow put that out of my head mighty quick. He showed me why Joe Shriner had to be so hard. He went back and pointed out how many times the jail had been busted in Carlton. He showed me what a tough gang of crooks usually hung out in that town, crossing through from railroad to railroad. At length they got hold of Joe Shriner. They needed an extra hard man, and they put him in, and he picked out hard ones to help him. But, hard as Shriner is, The Shadow went right straight ahead and pointed out to me that it was better to have a deputy sheriff in a jail treating crooks bad, than it is to have a bunch of crooks free to run around the country treating law-abiding folks bad."

"He said those things?" gasped the girl.

"He sure did, and you can figure how much I trust a gent that can talk as plumb reasonable as all that. But just the same, Sylvia, I can't let you go up to him. It's bad enough for him to sneak down here and see you, but it's a pile worse for you to go up there to see him. He might lose his head and start trying to persuade you to run off with him and get married."

"You think that would be very bad, Ben?"

He snorted at the thought. "With about twenty murders on his head? Sylvia, you ain't talking serious?"

She saw that she could not carry her frankness too far. She must try a touch of mystery.

"I've given him a solemn promise, Ben. I've told him that I'd come to meet him."

"You better forget that promise, then."

"Ben, would you like to break a promise that you'd given to The Shadow?"

He was silent, and she guessed that he was shivering in the dark at the thought.

"Well," he stammered, and paused.

In that pause, she took the rein from his nerveless hand and swung into the saddle. There followed an exciting two minutes of struggle. Bad Eye had his own mind about submitting to any rider, let alone a rider wearing skirts, and he fought frantically against the disgrace.

Inside of two minutes, however, he had learned that it would be easier to buck from the saddle a feather glued in place, than the graceful, light form of the girl. He let his head come up and in, and dropped suddenly into a position of rest, with one hind foot pointed, as though he had never bucked in his entire life.

The girl, laughing and panting, slapped his neck lightly with her quirt.

"Why d'you want to ride that devil?" asked the boy.

"Because I want to make a quick trip both ways."

He had no answer, but turned silently and led the way to the place on the hill, among the shrubs, where he had left his mount. As he swung into place, they heard a far-off rattling.

"Somebody's coming!" cried the girl softly.

"Some dozen — they's as many as that, anyways!"

Ben, whose more distinguishing ear had made out a considerable group of galloping horses, raised his hand to silence her answer, and swung the mare squarely into the wind to listen, for the wind was blowing straight down the road along which the riders were traveling.

"They're coming straight down the main road, I think," said Ben. He waited a minute. "They've turned off onto the side road, and they're coming straight for our place!"

There was no need to follow the progress of the riders by the ear alone from this point onward. Now they could look down from the hill and see a black mass of horsemen pouring out of the obscure distance into view and thronging the narrow road which branched off from the highway and wound into the Plummer ranch.

"They've come for me!" exclaimed Ben Plummer. "Sylvia, go back, and I'll slip away."

As he spoke, the horsemen rushed up to the front of the Plummer house, halted, and loosed a volley of loud calls, in response to which a window was presently slammed up, and the two on the hill could distinguish the tones of Mr. Plummer accosting the band.

Chapter Twenty-Four

News for the Shadow

To understand the arrival of the horsemen, it is necessary to go back a few hours and return once more to the pleasant camp fire where Scottie and The Shadow, alias Jim Cochrane, had been interrupted in the evening by the formidable Sheriff Algie Thomas, and where, after that, there was no more disturbance than an occasional crackling as the fire reached a pitchy place in the burning wood.

This heavy silence was the result of the thoughtful mood of The Shadow, who rose from time to time and paced the clearing and again seated himself, never addressing a word to his companion. Although the burly Scottie several times opened his lips to speak, he always shut them again before a word had been uttered, abashed by the solemn expression of the outlaw's features. At length he turned his attention to making up his bunk for the night, and it was while he was engaged in this occupation that a third unit was added to the group.

A precautionary whistle was first heard in the offing, a whistle that made The Shadow lift his brows.

"Nothing to get leery of," Scottie assured him. "That's my old pal 'Limpy' Morris. He's got a lame gag that's good for a hand-out from a starving old maid. He could make a fat living battering doors in a town full of Scotchmen. That's how good Limpy is. He'll come in with some swag now. You watch if he don't!"

Limpy, accordingly, appeared a moment later, fairly bending under a great bundle. He cast it down by the fire and straightened again, wiping his brow clean of perspiration. He was a lean, sad-eyed rascal, of about the same age as Scottie, weak in appearance, but possessed of a lean and stringy quantity of muscle nearly as formidable as the more burly power of his comrade.

The face which he turned to Scottie was still slightly contorted into the expression of lugubrious woe into which he had twisted it all during the day while he was begging. Indeed, that expression was so firmly stamped upon his subconscious mind that, no matter where he might be, among what boon companions, the sad expression was apt to return to his face at any time and wither the mirth of the moment.

This hardy beggar now gave not a glance to The Shadow, but turned a wicked scowl in the direction of Scottie.

"Put the stuff away, will you," he asked, "and lead me to the mulligan? Soft for you, Scottie! Pretty soft, I guess. All you got to do is to sit out here in a jungle and fuss around all day long, while I go the rounds battering doors till my knuckles are skinned and whining until my head sings. Show me some eats, will you?"

Scottie obediently opened the bundle, exclaimed with profound pleasure at the sight of the contents, and, by way of answering the last question, pointed to the frying pan which The Shadow had contributed to the party. It was covered with a tin plate which Limpy now removed. He fell voraciously upon the provisions disclosed.

"They must've been easy to-day," remarked Scottie.

"They's a pile of things that looks easy after they been done," snarled Limpy. "Lemme see you step out and batter doors yourself and get the quarter part of as much as that!"

"And lemme see you," retorted Scottie, "live one month in the jungles without getting bumped off by some bo that you've given a bit of your lip to one time or other."

"I can take care of myself," answered Limpy. "Nobody don't need to worry about that. Start something yourself, you fat fool, if you got any doubts!"

"Don't go talking foolish, Limpy," said Scottie, raising a bull-like voice which he had hitherto masked, and which now rolled and rang through the forest. "Otherwise, I'll be taking a wallop at that skinny chin of yours and knock it around where the back of your head is now."

The answer was a torrent of profanity from Limpy, and both champions leaped to their feet. But here The Shadow interposed in a quiet voice.

"That's enough," he said. "Shut up and sit down, both of you."

Scottie instantly drew back, but Limpy turned in shrill derision on the intruder.

"What upstart gay cat is that?" he asked fiercely.

Scottie clapped a hand over the mouth of his partner. A whisper — a single word, it seemed — turned Limpy gray as dust and made his eyes bulge. He sat down at once, and until he had finished his food he did not once remove his fascinated eyes from the indifferent face of the outlaw, just as a thieving hawk, a petty, cunning miscreant, might cower and start at the lordly eagle which knows no fear.

With his dinner finished, however, the beggar regained some confidence and self-assurance with the first breath of smoke which he inhaled from his cigarette. He returned to the narrative of his day's adventures. He told what sympathy had come his way, how a sad eye melted one heart, and how a blow endured had melted another, and how a game taught to a child playing in the street was as good as a key to unlock the door of the child's house.

"But along about evening," he said, "when everything was going slick as a whistle, and the women was getting their stoves full blast, and when everybody was getting ripe for big handouts — well, just about that time, up comes the news from Carlton and busts everything flat!"

He shook his head sadly.

"That's my luck," he said. "That's the way things break for me. After I been working all day patiently and getting things ready — along comes a measly jail break down the country and spoils everything. Why, they wouldn't look at me, they was so busy talking about what had happened at Carlton."

Here The Shadow sat erect.

"And what happened down there?" he asked sharply.

"Nothing much. You've heard about The Shadow, I figure, if you're the gent that bumped off Garry West, the way Scottie says you did, when Garry was a pal of The Shadow."

The Shadow sent a keen glance at Scottie, under which the latter winced.

"I had to tell him something to shut him up," he said, "and that was what popped into my head."

His further explanation was silenced by the raising of the outlaw's hand.

"Go on," he said. "What has he to do with this jail break in Carlton?"

"He was the one that worked it," said the beggar, warming to his tale. "I got the yarn hot off the wire and it runs something like this: Early this afternoon The Shadow slips into Carlton on his hoss, with his face unmasked! They jumped him right off, but they couldn't believe that he was really The Shadow, in spite of Captain and everything. Didn't seem nacheral that any man would have that much nerve — to come into the town in broad daylight — did it?"

Here Scottie stood up, bewildered, and stared from Limpy to the sallow-faced man who sat frowning on the far side of the fire. He knew perfectly well that this was The Shadow, and that The Shadow had not been near Carlton that day.

"Well," said Scottie, "I'll be hanged!"

"Then he goes right up to the jail," went on Limpy, and shook his head with wonder. "He chats a while with the sheriff, Joe Shriner, and when he gets tired of talking, he bats Shriner on the jaw, ties up the three guards, walks inside, and sets loose the brother of his best girl — Ben Plummer!"

There was a short exclamation from The Shadow at this point. He had been following the narrative in a maze, but now he began to see the light.

"He put Ben on his own hoss, Captain, swiped the next best hoss in town, a gray mare fast as a streak of light, with no more give-out than the wind. Then him and Ben got clean out of town, with half the townfolk riding after 'em shooting their guns hot!"

He paused, heedless of the blank face of Scottie and the frowning face of the outlaw.

"Of all the things that The Shadow has ever done," asserted the beggar at length, "I figure this to lay over the lot. What say, Scottie?"

But Scottie was unable to speak. He could only stare helplessly at the outlaw.

The latter was deep in thought. It was tolerably

plain what had happened. The note which Sylvia had mentioned to him had been sent to the hotel and thrown into the room where his dupe, the stupid youth called Tom Converse, was sleeping. He had read the letter, accepted the difficult task suggested in it, and had straightway, out of a wild spirit of romance such as The Shadow himself could hardly conceive, started out for Carlton and accomplished the impossibility from which The Shadow himself had shrunk.

This much was undeniable. What would the results be? When, in the first place, The Shadow had shifted his identity adroitly to the shoulders of Tom Converse, it was in the perfect expectation that the latter would be filled full of bullets within a day or two at the most, and that the dappled chestnut, Captain, would then come back into his own hands through purchase or capture. But the day, and the two days, had passed; and not only was Tom Converse still alive, but he had just slipped away and performed a deed which would have been creditable to The Shadow himself in his fiercest moments. Such dare-deviltry was worth wonder, and The Shadow paid his share of astonishment.

There was, moreover, a certain chill of fear underlying his surprise. Was it not strange that the man to whom he had given his identity should have proved so gifted that he could live up to the name which he bore? The name, the horse, and the reputation of The Shadow were suddenly usurped by another.

Furthermore, now that Tom Converse had performed so great a service for the girl The Shadow loved, what would the result be there? What would Sylvia Rann feel and think and do when she met the rescuer of Ben Plummer — he who had dared so much simply on the bidding of an unknown woman?

That thought spurred The Shadow to his feet with an oath, and he made hastily for his bay horse. Scottie helped him saddle without a word, and still without a word the outlaw leaped onto the back of his horse and drove him crashing into the thicket.

Chapter Twenty-Five

The Thirteenth Man

Indeed, the more The Shadow dwelt on the thought of the girl and Tom Converse and their probable meeting, the more he winced. He had seen too many testimonies of her love of romance to be at ease now. Had it not been the same weakness which in the first place had made her open her heart to him? Simply because the rest of the world hated and feared The Shadow, she had seemed perversely determined to trust and love him. She had never been quite able to persuade herself that she could love him, but always The Shadow felt that that consummation was a thing which lay just around the corner of chance.

Now she would meet an entirely different man. She would meet a man who had been basely betrayed and thrown into terrible peril by the acts of the one to whom she had formerly devoted herself. She could not but believe the narrative as it would be told to her by the rescuer of her brother. What, then, would be the reaction on her mind?

There was only one thing to do, and that was to prevent the meeting between her and Tom Converse when the latter — as no doubt he would do — came up to receive his praise from the foster sister of Ben Plummer. The handsome face of Tom, his frank bearing, his dauntless courage, and his good nature — these things could not but prove the open sesame to the heart of the girl.

He could himself prevent that meeting; but if he stepped into the lists secretly, he would probably find himself opposed not only to Tom Converse — who seemed to be no mean foe — but also to Ben Plummer himself. The man who shot Ben Plummer could never expect to win a smile from the foster sister of Ben. It would be better, then, from every viewpoint, that he bring in the great authority of the law. At the thought a thrill passed through the heart of The Shadow. He, the prime offender, would strike by means of the legal arm!

Swiftly he cut across country to the town, following well-nigh an air line, until he dropped into the main street and dismounted before the hotel.

It was buzzing, as he had expected, with tales of the outrage in Carlton; but what astonished and hurt him was that for the first time he heard the name of The Shadow mentioned in kindly and even semi-approving fashion by law-abiding men.

"He could've killed Shriner and all three of his men," said the townsfolk. "He could've opened every cell in that jail. They was about thirty bad ones inside, and them thirty could've cleaned out

Carlton and then been ready to turn themselves loose on the whole length of the mountains."

But The Shadow had done none of these things. What might easily have been his most terrible crime, had turned out to be his cleanest. He had simply snatched one brand out of the fire, and, as every one said, Ben Plummer was more to be laughed at as a crack-brained child than sent to prison as a hardened offender. The Shadow had saved Ben Plummer, and, by refraining from setting the other prisoners free at the same time, he had turned every one of them into a mortal enemy. It was difficult to understand what had been going on in the brain of the great criminal.

The real Shadow listened and understood. By the very first act the difference between a criminal and an adventurer was made clear, and because the clean-handedness of Tom Converse made his own evil instincts more apparent to himself, he hated Tom and the whole world for it.

It was a revelation of himself to himself. He had always looked upon himself as a man fully as much sinned against as sinning. He had felt that he was the victim of circumstances, but now he saw placed on the stage where he had often walked, and in the role which he had so often performed, another actor who showed him the difference between himself and an honest man.

We hate those whom we wrong. The Shadow hated Tom Converse now with a consuming hatred greater than his love of Sylvia Rann, second only to his love of himself.

"Will they get him, d'you think?" The Shadow asked one of the bystanders.

"Get him? I dunno. Mostly they say that nobody can catch The Shadow, but I say, now, that his face has been seen, it'll be a different yarn. Besides, they's never been two such gents after him as the two that's taking up the trail now."

"No?"

"No, sir. Algie Thomas is running things, and Joe Shriner rode out of Carlton as soon as he got untied, rushed to the railroad line, and picked up a ride through the mountains. He dropped off in the pass and come down into town and went to Algie Thomas right off. They say that he didn't waste a word. He just asked Algie to let him work under him as a sort of lieutenant."

"Shriner taking orders from anybody else!"

"Sounds queer, don't it? But Shriner's plumb wild and green-eyed over what's happened. It's the first time he's ever failed, you see — the first time anybody ever got out of the jail, and the first time that he was ever beat in a fight. So he's going to get back The Shadow dead or alive. It'll sure be a dead Shadow before they tote him in!"

"Are they picking a posse?"

"Yep. A hand-picked one! They're taking gents that's got a hoss that can step, plenty of nerve, and a fast hand with a gun and a straight eye. If you figure to get inside that class, you might step over and apply, stranger!"

The Shadow shook his head modestly. "I'm

lame," he said, "and I ain't much good as a fighting man. But I figure that that posse'll get The
Shadow, all right!"

"You do?"

"Sure. All they got to do is to ride out and
wait around the house of Plummer. Pretty soon
you can bet that The Shadow will come up from
Carlton to boast to his girl about how he set
her brother free!"

"That's reasonable. But won't he know they'll
be watching for him there?"

"The Shadow ain't reasonable. He takes
chances. Besides he may figure that the posse
will start looking for him in hard places, not in
an easy one like Plummer's."

So saying, Jim Cochrane drifted away among
the talkers, but before he had been five minutes
in the room, he was greeted by his own plan,
which he had set afoot on the far side of the
same room, save that the matter of doubt was
now removed. It was taken for granted that, first
of all, the posse would look for The Shadow at
the Plummer place.

That rumor would reach the ear of the old
sheriff before long, and, if he had an ounce of
brains, he would act on the suggestion. What
pleased The Shadow was that he was so entirely
dissociated now from the rumor which he had
started. He went directly up the stairs and to
the room where the sheriff was keeping what
might be termed office hours, selecting the posse
with which he was to chase the greatest enemy

he had encountered.

A man was drifting out of the room, cursing softly, as Jim Cochrane approached.

"It's no use," said he. "They've made up their minds not to take no more. They want to get all the glory boiled down. They say that they don't like my hoss, but I figure it'll be something more'n that! Right low, I call it, of Algie Thomas!"

And he stormed on down the stairs, still swearing volubly. Was it not strange that all these men seemed to take it for granted that The Shadow was doomed to be captured on this expedition?

The outlaw opened the door and stepped inside. He found the little sheriff teetering back and forth in a chair near the window, with his hands locked behind his head, while the savage face of Joe Shriner peered with burning eyes from a farther corner of the room.

At sight of The Shadow the sheriff let his chair tilt down with a thud.

"Well, well," he said, "I suppose you've thought up a sure way of catching The Shadow?"

"A sort of way. But I ain't passing out ideas promiscuous to gents like you and Shriner. All I'd like to get is a place riding behind you. That'd do fine for me."

The sheriff smiled without mirth.

"What's in your mind, Cochrane?" he asked. "You know I was after you. D'you think you can worm your way into my posse to double cross me when I'm in a pinch — and get even?"

The other did not flinch from this direct attack.

206

"You think I'm some kind of crook. Ain't that true?" he said. "But what I want to do is to show you that I'm square. Give me a chance to work for you, and I'll show it. The reason is that I figure on living in these parts. I like the people, and I like the layout all around. That's why I want to get in solid with you, sheriff. If I got you behind me pretty strong, why, I guess I can manage to get along no matter what most of the other folks think about me. I've come here to ask for a chance to make good. Look me over; give me a try."

The sheriff, who was frankly amazed by this quiet-spoken outburst, now came out of his chair with an ease of movement and speed of foot which astonished The Shadow. He came straight to the outlaw and said to him softly: "Partner, I dunno what your game might be, but I'll tell you this, between you and me: If you should start on this trail, you'd be watched close every minute by my orders."

The Shadow nodded. "Look here," he said, "I don't pretend to be no angel. I just asked for a chance to make good. I want to settle down!"

The sheriff scratched his chin. "Gimme your gun," he said.

The revolver was summoned from the holster with a quick gesture and, flowing with liquid smoothness through the deft fingers toward the sheriff, was offered butt first to that worthy.

The man of the law accepted the weapon without comment, though he had noted with the eye of a connoisseur the frictionless speed of that draw. Now he examined the mechanism of the gun. It was faultlessly kept. It was clean — almost painfully clean. There was about it that indescribable look which is only acquired by patient, untold hours of care. It was not a new gun. It was a rather old make, and it showed signs of use, chiefly about the handles. All the working parts were covered with an infinitesimal film of oil. In a word, it was a weapon such as the sheriff himself would have loved to feel snuggled against the palm of his hand when he whipped it from the holster. He passed it back to The Shadow with a sigh.

"That hoss you got is the one I seen out in the clearing?"

"That's the one," said The Shadow.

"You talk to Joe Shriner, then, will you? I got to say that you suit me, but Joe has a younger eye than I have, and he's voting on every man with me. Hop into this, Joe."

The hopping consisted of a single stride out of the shadow, and Joe Shriner fixed upon the sallow face of Jim Cochrane his fiery glance. The torment of offended pride and vanity glowed in that glance. Only the death of him who had broken into the jail at Carlton could appease his hunger for revenge. In the interim he hated every man in the world, because every man in the world had heard of the indignity to which he had submitted.

There was only one reason why Joe Shriner had joined the forces of the sheriff. Joe himself felt that, alone, he could easily handle any man in the world, even if that man were the formidable Shadow. But Joe was not at all sure that he could get in striking distance of the criminal. The Shadow was one thing. Captain was another. How was he to reach Captain except with the aid of numbers? Hence he had joined forces, reluctantly, with the sheriff of Silver Tip.

"Did the gent we're after ever do you a wrong?" he asked.

It was the single question he had asked every man who applied for a place on the posse.

"Yes," said The Shadow.

"What sort of wrong?"

The eye of Jim Cochrane glinted. "They was a woman in it," he said.

Joe Shriner stared a moment at him and then drew back with a sigh of satisfaction.

"You'll do," he said. "Get your hoss ready. We start pronto. I think we'll be going out to the Plummer place. We hear talk that says The Shadow may head back that way, like a fox."

The Shadow grinned, nodded, and disappeared. How smooth his way had been into the heart of the enemy's councils!

Inside the room old Algie Thomas was shaking his head.

"What's the matter?" asked Shriner.

"I don't like that last gent."

"What's wrong?"

"I been adding up the list. He's the thirteenth man!"

Chapter Twenty-Six

At the Second Fence

Thirteen men, therefore, rode out of the town, thirteen hand-picked men, including the sheriff of Silver Tip and the deputy sheriff of Carlton. All agreed, who saw them leave, that there had never been a more choice group of man-hunters and man-fighters than this one. Besides The Shadow, who was naturally an unknown quantity, and the two leaders of the party, there were ten hardy fellows who knew every path and by-path of the mountains.

Most of them were youngsters, the oldest not more than 28, but every one of them had proved himself again and again. Not only were they chosen warriors, but they were choicely mounted, also, and they rushed out of the little village like a hurricane, followed by a ringing cheer.

Men felt, who saw them go, that The Shadow was taking his last trail, and the men in the posse had the same conviction. They rode in solemn mood, for the sheriff had gathered them together just before they started. They had been frantic to get to their work, but he had reminded them that time was the thing of which they had the most.

Then briefly he reviewed all the major crimes with which The Shadow had thrilled the mountains in the past, and he made each man stand out before his fellows and raise his right hand and swear to be faithful to the chase and faithful to one another until The Shadow was dead and buried beneath the sand.

"He's a strong man," said the sheriff. "He's a mighty strong man, and he's a clever gent, too; but I don't figure this brain is as strong as the brain of thirteen, and I don't figure he's as strong in the body as thirteen men. That's why I say, lads, that this trail ain't never going to end until we've beat The Shadow and put him under the sand. You hear? I swear to you, boys, that, if we hold together and ride hard, we got to win!"

The exhortation sent them somewhat more quietly to their horses, but once the spurs had been touched to the quivering flanks and the horses had bounded forward, caution and reserve were forgotten. Out along the road they thundered and paused at length, steaming and sweating, before the house of Plummer. There, in answer to the summons, Plummer himself cast up a window.

"This here is Algie Thomas," said the old man, jogging his horse through the press and coming to the front. "We've come out here to do you no harm, Plummer, but we've come to keep you from it."

"I know that, Thomas," said the rancher. "Just speak up and tell me what you want."

"First thing I want to find out if your girl Sylvia is safe in bed."

"I think she is. No — she just went out for a little walk. She couldn't sleep. Maybe she ain't got back yet."

"Will you take a look in her room?"

"Hey, Sylvia?" Plummer called, then: "No, she ain't here. But I'll give a look."

He disappeared into the house. Presently, they saw a match spurt behind the window of Sylvia's room, and then the lamp was ignited, filling the black windowpane with a soft yellow glow. Almost at once there was a loud cry of alarm from the rancher. He slammed the window up.

"Sheriff, she's gone! She's gone, and left a note behind that says — It says nothing I can make out. She's lost her mind. Heaven knows what's going on inside of her head!"

The sheriff issued a reply which was mingled with an order to his own men.

"We'll get her back. Scatter, boys!"

Joe Shriner had already set them a good example in the last capacity, for, when the halt was made, he had not been content to wait motionless before the house, but had been moving his horse about restlessly on the outskirts of the crowd. Just as the sheriff issued the order, it was the fortune of the deputy to see, very dimly behind the shrubbery on the top of the hill near the house, a slowly moving form.

Instantly his spurs were in the flanks of his snorting horse and he rushed like an arrow up the slope. He furnished his clew to no other man by sign or shout. If that were indeed a horseman, that cloudlike shape in the distance, he wanted the glory of discovery and battle to be his.

But hardly had he started when there was a muffled cry of a woman's voice from the top of the hill, and the slowly moving shape dissolved at once into two horses and riders breaking out of the shrubbery and tearing off down the slope at full gallop.

Joe Shriner measured the distance and decided to waste no time and energy in drawing a revolver. Instead, he flattened himself more closely to the neck of his horse to break the weight with which he cut against the wind, and pitched himself forward in the stirrups to give himself, as nearly as possible, the balance of a jockey, swinging from the withers of a horse to enable it to pitch forward at a sprinting stride. In response, the fine gelding he rode indeed sprinted like a racer on a track.

Behind, the bulk of the posse whirled and straightened after the two fugitives with incredulous shouts of joy. There was The Shadow before them, and The Shadow burdened with the care of the woman he was stealing from her home. What mattered the speed of Captain, now, when he was forced to keep back to the speed of the horse which the girl rode?

On the matchless Captain, poor Ben Plummer ground his teeth as he held back the bounding chestnut until the chin of the stallion was drawn almost back to his crest. Well did Captain know

213

that this was a race, and he was keen as the wind to be off and away, leaving the pursuers behind him farther and farther at every stride. But Ben could not let Captain take his head. He had to hold him back there with the blue roan, and how he groaned, now, to think that the stubborn girl had chosen this slow beginner in place of the quick-footed cream which she generally rode! Durable as steel was old Bad Eye, he knew; but where were his abilities as a sprinter?

Behind them a streak darted up the hillside, gaining at every leap. Bad Eye was not only losing ground because he had never had the speed to hold off such a burst as that of the leading pursuer, but also he was quitting. In vain the girl plied him with spurs and whip. In vain Ben quirted the rascal soundly. In spite of urging, the blue roan shook his stubborn head and dropped into a ragged hand gallop.

Ben Plummer stared wretchedly about him in the night. Now or never was the time to make his name and fame in the eyes of The Shadow; but, if he allowed the girl to be taken from him, he could never again expect to be called friend by the great man.

Sylvia Rann, too — Sylvia the dauntless — was giving up. She worked with quirt and spurs, but she worked only halfheartedly. How could Ben Plummer know that she wished to be overtaken and brought back to her home? Better to have to make explanations — far better — than to have to ride on to meet her fate in union with the outlaw! In the meantime, she told herself that she was doing her honest best; but she blessed the stubborn heart of the blue roan which made him sulk and quit under the punishment.

Ben cried: "Can't you get him going?"

"He won't budge," she answered. "Ride off for yourself, Ben. Save yourself. It doesn't matter about me. They won't dare to harm me!"

"I'll stay and be killed quicker! The Shadow would have no use for me if I let 'em catch up with you as quick as this. I'll stay and see the finish first. They'll have to get me before they get you!"

"No, no, Ben!"

"I say yes! I ain't going to run away, in spite of 'em!"

With a groan she realized that the stubborn boy would do as he threatened, and now she began to ride in earnest, but in spite of herself she could do nothing with the roan. When she turned her head, she saw Joe Shriner rushing up behind, and a little farther back she heard the roar of the hoofs of the dozen gallopers as they crossed a streak of crunching gravel. A minute more and the pursuers could begin shooting.

Then came the voice of Ben at her ear, a voice shrill and breaking with excitement:

"Turn downhill at the fences, Sylvia. Bad Eye'll jump. He can jump 'em like a bird if you're willing to risk it in the dark. Do you mind? Is your nerve up to that, Sylvia?"

Obediently she looked to her left. They had

come out on the shoulder of that hill, and below them the slope sheered down rapidly into a tangle of fences. An old lane had crossed there, with its two-board fence, still standing; and below the lane was a newly-fenced inclosure in barbed wire. That would have made a terrible ordeal in the dark of the night, but luckily there was a board in place of the top strand in both of the wire fences. Could Bad Eye see the obstacles which were barely perceptible to her own straining eyes?

She was growing desperate now, with the excitement of the race and the fear for the capture of Ben Plummer.

"What about your horse?" she asked.

"He ain't a hoss," panted the boy. "He's a bird. He flies a fence. This is Captain."

She remembered, then. It was Captain. She glanced aside, even in the fever of her fear, and noticed the long, raking action of the stallion. In spite of the moment, her heart jumped in admiration. But what would old Bad Eye do?

"Come on!" she called, and whirled him straight down the slope.

Bad Eye didn't like it. He braced his legs when he saw the fence, then became aware that his impetus was too great to check him in time, and attempted to jump. The result was that he crashed into the top board and snapped it as easily as though it were paper. He staggered as he struck on the far side. Then he tossed his head and caught a firm hold on the bit. He was what the old chroniclers call "wood wroth." He was not angry at the girl now, despite her spurring and whipping, but he was furious with that fence which had bumped his knees and legs so cruelly. He started up like a whirlwind, with Sylvia simply hanging on and gasping in amazement at the change which had come over her horse. How marvelous that so heavy a body should possess such buoyancy!

Right before her was another fence — the second fence of the lane. The leap over the first fence, considering the sweep which jumping downhill gave them, carried them well into the middle of the narrow passage, and beyond. Directly under the nose of Bad Eye rose the second fence. Even Captain snorted and grunted as he rose for it, but somehow he floated over.

Then Bad Eye. He reared, stretched his long neck, and jumped. The shock of the start was like the uncoiling of a spring. It flung the girl almost out of the saddle. Then there was the sail — a quick rattle and click as Bad Eye touched the board with every foot — and now they were flying through the clear beyond.

Right behind them came destruction. She saw that furious leading rider fly the first fence. But at the second fence of the lane there was a crash, and horse and man spun over through the air and landed with an audible thud, while the revolver which The Shadow — for it was he — had at length drawn, exploded as he fell.

Behind him the rest of the pursuit, marking his fall, swung their horses far to the left to make for a gate. The Shadow himself lay stunned for a moment and then staggered to his feet. He was erect, indeed, long before his head had cleared.

A wild necessity for action was driving him on. He must overtake them. He must get in at a death tonight. In front of him he thought Tom Converse was galloping with a girl who was already false to her old love and cleaving to a new.

He wanted to murder them both, but most of all he wanted to kill Tom Converse and have the girl watch her new lover die. She would denounce The Shadow for it. But who would believe her crazy tale that The Shadow himself was riding with the posse which hunted The Shadow?

That burning earnestness of mind at length enabled him to clear his brain of the fog which beset it. He was able to see the long-legged bay, which had failed him in the leap, standing trembling beside him with downcast head sniffing at the hand of the master as though imploring forgiveness.

In return for that attitude, The Shadow snarled a fierce curse and flung himself into the saddle. He would take that fall out of the brute before the night was over. He would ride the worthless nag to death.

He revised his full estimate of the catastrophe when, looking before him, he saw the two objects of the pursuit just in the act of vanishing over the crest of a hill not far away, and behind him the stream of the posse and the clamor of voices urging on their horses and one another.

The bay responded to the first loosening of the rein like a gentleman, and off they flew at a pace that promised to overtake the others in short order.

New hope burned high in the breast of Jim Cochrane. He had lost the first clash, but he would win the second. But why — why had he not fired when he was so near his target just before the fall? Why had he waited to make surety doubly sure?

Chapter Twenty-Seven

Tom Converse Intervenes

Once beyond the lane fences, the blue roan went better. He felt a sense of triumph in having shown his heels to one enemy of the same kind that had bruised him in the first attempt. Accordingly, when the first pasture fence jumped up before him out of the darkness, he skimmed it with a foot of open to spare, caught his bit again and dashed joyously at the fence on the opposite side of the clearing.

His exuberance lasted in a spurt which carried him to the top of the hill over which The Shadow saw him disappear. Now he began again to lose interest in his work and to play with the bit in his mouth; but though the roan dropped several degrees in speed, Ben Plummer was well-nigh hysterical with joy.

"Good old Bad Eye!" he chanted over and over again. "He ain't a hoss. He's a bird. Good old Bad Eye!"

And Bad Eye dropped back one ear as much as to say: "Little do you know me, youth!"

That renewed slackening in the gait was welcomed by the girl. It had been a sharp press up the hill, and they would soon wind their horses if they spurred too much at the beginning. At least, the roan might be worn out, and even the invincible Captain, with two long rides already behind him on this day, might weaken before the night was ended.

In the meantime, the roan was beginning to warm up and find his running legs. Never was there a horse born with the ability to run, in which there was not also born a love of running so long as it remained sound. Now the roan began to stretch his legs and make the ground shoot past beneath them as they took the next down slope.

"Keep him going his limit," said Ben Plummer. "He won't wear out. He's all iron; but they got a bunch of sprinters back there, and I doubt he'll be able to hold 'em until they get tired. Look at 'em come!"

Over the hilltop rushed the cluster of horsemen. Not one of them was so much better mounted than his companions that he could draw away more than a few lengths into the lead. Only The Shadow possessed a truly superior animal, and The Shadow's horse now had a big handicap to make up.

"Shoot into the air — anything to make them hold back!" urged the girl.

"Shoot into the air?" echoed the boy quietly. "Nope! I can't do that. If The Shadow was here on Captain, he'd shoot a couple of hats off their heads and make 'em slow up a bit, but I ain't The Shadow. Them fools behind think I am, though, and I ain't going to spoil The Shadow's reputation by some fool gun play now. You know what he says about gun work?"

"What?" She asked the question carelessly, more mindful of that dangerous cluster of horsemen bursting down the slope behind.

"When in doubt, leave your gat in the holster. I'll take that advice now!"

He resolutely persisted in that course, even when the posse, coming up the next slope, uncased two or three guns and began snap-shooting at Ben. But such was their care to avoid striking the girl, and such was their deliberation in making their shots bear well off toward the left, which was Ben's side, that all their bullets flew wild.

They ducked over the next rise and saw before them a long straightaway, unbroken by tree, fence, or hill for miles, so it seemed in the darkness. Here the blue roan began to give of his best. Well it was for the fugitives that he did, for the posse, though somewhat worn by the additional distance which it had traveled in coming out from the village, and by the detours which it had been forced to make around the fences, now was gaining gradually with every 100 yards.

Off that open stretch and into the trees they darted, with a scant margin dividing them from the horsemen behind. Once in the forest, Ben's perfect knowledge of the country stood him in good stead. He could veer off to the right as they entered the trees, and so lay the horses after a brief space of time, in a narrow footpath.

They had to run in single file, here, with the blue roan, of course, in the lead, and the riders flat along the necks of the horses on account of the low branches whipping overhead. But the solid footing and the clear path gave them a priceless 100 yards handicap on the posse before the men of the law discovered the trick and followed by the same route.

Undoubtedly, that 100 yards saved, was the saving of their lives as well. When they entered the next clear stretch, Ben Plummer leaned over the neck of Captain and listened carefully to his breathing; by the lightness of his gallop one would never have guessed that the gallant stallion was far gone, but the threefold labors of that day had exhausted even his strength.

"Captain's near to wabbling," announced Ben huskily. "Now for the straightest course to The Shadow. He's the only one that can save us — and how he can do it, beats me!"

"Is he far off?" panted the girl.

"No, thank Heaven!"

They worked on in grim silence for another half mile until the pursuit began to draw close once more. Then Ben Plummer drew his revolver and fired in the air three times in quick succession.

Behind them a chorus of shouts was raised. The beat of the hoofs was redoubled.

"They know it's a signal!" cried the girl. "They'll catch us, Ben!"

His answer was another flash of the revolver's blue barrel as he swung it up and fired again three times. After that he refused to speak, but silently reloaded the weapon from his cartridge belt.

Then he looked back through the scattering of trees. At length he announced his determination firmly to the girl.

"If The Shadow don't come inside the next five minutes, I'm going to begin shooting — to kill," he said. "And when I start that —"

"No, no, Ben!" she cried in horror. "You can't do that! No matter why you shoot, it's murder, and —"

"You've talked enough," said the boy with a calm and dignity that made it impossible for her to continue her argument. "This is man work, I guess!"

He resolutely reined Captain back and drew out his freshly loaded weapon.

She waited, after that, with breathless horror, for the explosion of the gun. Something told her that when he fired he would not miss; but second after second went past, and still the weapon did not explode.

They burst into another clearing, a wide stretch of half a mile, where the forest thinned out to a mere scattering of knee-high seedlings here and there. Halfway across, the girl turned her head. Just as she had anticipated, the flight of the posse had grown swifter as they entered the clearing, and now Ben Plummer had turned in the saddle and poised his gun to fire at one of the dim, bouncing forms behind them.

But, as he turned, there was the explosion of a rifle straight ahead of them — that unmistakable sound which comes with a ring of metal in it, so different from the short bark of a revolver. She saw the gun, raised in the hand of the boy, waver and then fall. Looking ahead, she saw a rider on a gray horse burst out of the woods and rush toward them — a rider on a tall gray horse.

"Steady, Ben!" cried the rider. "Steady up!"

It was not the voice which she had expected to come from the lips of The Shadow, but this must unquestionably be he. He passed her with a rush like the swift sweep of a hawk through the air, and she could not but admire that fierce courage which carried him so confidently into the very teeth of a dozen hard riders and fierce fighters.

She heard the rifle explode again and again, but now she broke into the forest once more and kept on, with the leaves and breaking twigs crashing beneath her, until she heard the voice of Ben calling to her from behind.

"Pull up. Pull up!" he was crying.

She obeyed, wondering, and in another moment he was reining a fuming, sweating Captain beside her and had actually flung himself from the saddle to the ground. There he busied himself at the cinches and suddenly drew off the saddle and threw it, also, aside.

"Are you mad, Ben?" she cried.

"I hope not. But Captain can't run no more

tonight — not unless he runs himself to death. And I wouldn't do that — not for the sake of my head and the heads of all them behind!"

"But, Ben, are you going to throw yourself away? What can we —"

"We can't do nothing but stay here and hope that The Shadow'll turn 'em away from us. He's back there fighting. Listen!"

They could hear the ringing explosions of the rifle, mixed with the short, choppy barking of the revolvers of the posse, and then the clarion voices of more rifles as they uncased their heavier weapons.

How many were falling in the posse? She bowed her head and shivered. But how wonderful it was that one man should dare to go back and fight so many!

"What can he be doing?" she asked.

"I dunno!" cried Ben joyously. "But listen. You hear the shooting work farther off to the north? They're following him. They're shooting at him and the hoss. The fools! They can't ever hit him! Maybe he's slipping along from tree to tree. He gave 'em a flash of himself when he went past me, shooting!"

"Did — did any one of the posse fall?"

"Fall? Why, he ain't shooting to kill, Sylvia. That ain't his way. I'm sure of it. But he's shooting so close to 'em that they'll think he is, and they'll all take after him. They thought I was The Shadow, but the minute they run into the real article they know the difference. Listen!"

226

Farther and farther away rolled the shooting.

"They'll be pulling down the trees, pretty soon, they'll be that rattled!" Ben remarked, with a chuckle.

Chapter Twenty-Eight

The Face in the Flame

Sylvia was amazed, and with reason; for Ben Plummer, who had been in a semipanic throughout the flight, was now perfectly at his ease — as much so as though he had found refuge on a cloud and were smiling at the petty concerns of men so far below. He went about rubbing down the dappled chestnut carefully and briskly, while the noble stallion stood with head outstretched to make his breathing easier, and drew in the life-giving air with heaving sides.

"It's terrible, Ben!" she murmured. "It's perfectly terrible!"

"Captain? Oh, he'll come around all right. Another mile of that running, and he might've been done for, but now he'll come around. The Shadow says they ain't no killing this hoss, and I reckon he's about right. Look at him coming around now and sticking his head up higher! Good old Captain!"

"I don't mean the horse, but the men, Ben, the men! How many honest fellows have been killed already by The Shadow? That's why they're holding back!"

"You wait till the fuss is over. If they want

to have sound skins with no scratches, they ought to take other trails besides the trail of The Shadow. He ain't no old lady to be chased through the woods all night. Hark at that! They've lost him!"

In fact, the firing, which not only had passed to some distance but had grown more and more broken and light in volume, now stopped altogether.

"Or else they've killed him!" cried the girl.

In spite of herself her heart leaped with relief. For how could she have faced the outlaw if he had come back victorious?

"I guess not killed," answered Ben Plummer slowly. "I got an idea that it'll take broad daylight before they'll see well and shoot close enough to kill The Shadow. Listen!"

There was nothing to be heard, however, in spite of the cautioning hand which he raised. He returned to his work with the stallion.

"They'll come back and find us," insisted the girl.

"Not while The Shadow's around," answered Ben, in such perfect confidence that he did not even raise his head. "The Shadow'll take 'em off on a wrong trail. That's where they're riding now. They think that he was playing sort of rear guard to us. They don't know that we've gone one way and him another. Pretty soon he'll pop up here as calm as you please. Then —"

He stopped again.

"Listen!"

This time they heard, thin and soft, the sound of a whistled air coming through the forest.

The girl gasped: "It can't be he!"

"It's him, right enough," said Ben Plummer. "Look at the hoss if you don't believe. Him and Captain spend hours talking together. Captain knows that whistle as well as I know my name!"

That faint, weird whistling, in fact, caused the stallion to throw up his head and neigh softly in response, and, before Sylvia Rann had recovered from her amazement, she saw a dim form of a horseman come through the trees and trot toward them.

"Hello!" said a voice, stronger and more musical than she recalled the voice of The Shadow. "Ben, what do you mean by bringing her out here?"

"It wasn't me. She made me let her come. I couldn't stop her. They jumped us and gave us a run just as we were getting away from the house. That's the straight of it."

"You know," broke in the girl hotly, "that you made me promise to come to you if you got Ben out of jail in Carlton. You know you made me give you that promise! Aren't you ashamed now to pretend to be surprised?"

There was a cry from Ben Plummer. "Good Lord! Is that the way I was brought out of jail? Is that why you had to come with me, Sylvia?"

"Wait," said Tom Converse. "There's a queer little mix-up here, and I think I can show the lady the way out of it in a minute."

He rode the gray mare closer, scratched a

match, and, by the bluish spurt of flame that shone from between his cupped hands, she looked into a face far other than the face she had expected to see. She saw a man larger, heavier, stronger, in every way, and she cried out: "Ben, Ben! It's not Jim Cochrane! Someone from the posse —"

"Steady up!" cried Ben. "This is the gent that got me out of Carlton jail. This is The Shadow. Why, Sylvia, what's happened to your head? Don't you recognize him?"

"I must be going mad!" answered the bewildered girl.

"Give me a moment to explain," said Tom Converse. "I'd have told Ben long before, if I had thought there was any danger of you coming here with him."

He went back to the beginning and told quickly how he had walked into Silver Tip, and how he had encountered there the man of the sallow face; how he had gone from one strange adventure to another, until, that day in the hotel, he had found her note on the floor of his room; and how, for her sake, and for the sake of the very danger, he had ridden to Carlton and brought Ben Plummer away.

They listened, spellbound, the whole narrative being punctured by exclamations of Ben Plummer as he saw the terrible Shadow dissolve into a law-abiding citizen.

"The reason I didn't tell Ben at once," confessed Tom Converse, "and the reason I wouldn't tell him now, is simply because I was afraid he wouldn't do what I wanted him to do unless he thought I was The Shadow. I wanted to get him out of this part of the country and off to another place where he'd have a fighting chance to make a new name for himself. In order to do that I had to play The Shadow up to the very last. I'd still be playing it, Miss Rann, but here you've come out and taken my mask off; and that leaves me just a plain, ordinary gent — Tom Converse, which is my name. The only time I ever run afoul of the law in my life was when I broke into the jail at Carlton."

"You did all that simply because a woman you'd never heard of, a woman you thought loved a murderer, an outlaw, asked you to?"

"Partner!" cried Ben Plummer suddenly. "You're a greater man than The Shadow ever dreamed of being!"

"Lady," said Tom Converse, "I'll tell you how it was. It wasn't entirely on account of what was in your letter. I'm ashamed to say that I sort of liked playing the part of The Shadow and seeing what I could do with it. The good news I'm going to take back to the world is that a gent can break into a jail and lead a posse off of the trail without ever sending a single bullet into a man!"

"There was no one hurt tonight?" breathed Sylvia.

"Not a soul. They figured that I was covering your trail — the trail of you and Ben, you see. So they kept smashing away at me. All I had to do was to drift along ahead of 'em among the trees and fire once in a while over their heads. They couldn't see clear enough, in the dark and in the shade of the trees, to hit a house and barn painted white. So they didn't spot me and the old gray except just by little glimpses; and here we are, safe and sound!"

"Easy, ain't it?" remarked Ben Plummer ironically. "But I don't have any hankering to play that sort of game. Understand?"

An incredible relief had come over Sylvia Rann. She felt weak with gratitude and thanksgiving.

"Heaven sent you to us," she said at length. "Heaven sent you to save us, Tom Converse, and I'm going back now to tell the posse the truth about you."

"They wouldn't believe you."

"Yes, they would believe me. I'm the only person they would believe. They'd believe me because they know I'm the only one who knows the face of the real Shadow — the real murderer!"

The quiver of horror in her voice brought Tom close to her.

"Do you figure him to be that?" he asked.

"Murderer?" she said. "Yes, yes! I can see now that he would never have gone to risk himself for the sake of poor Ben. I asked him myself — I begged him to try, but he wouldn't promise; and all the time another man, one who had never seen me, was planning to ride to Carlton, and today you did ride and do the thing Jim Cochrane didn't dare to do!"

"Wait a minute," protested Tom. "Maybe something held him back, or maybe he got to Carlton after me."

She shook her head. "I know him too well. At least, I begin to know him for the first time. He wouldn't have gone. Mr. Converse, you've done a fine thing in giving Ben a chance to work out a new life for himself, and you've done a wonderful thing for me in opening my eyes to Jim Cochrane. I'll never forget you for either of those gifts to us, and the first small way in which I can repay you, is to go back to the posse and tell them the truth."

Ben Plummer agreed, with a clamor; but Converse himself was doubtful. They would not believe her, he said. They would think it some scheme on the part of The Shadow to send her in to call them off the trail; but if they once caught sight of him, they would shoot, and shoot to kill.

She insisted. It was burning in her, this desire to get at work in some manner to repay him, and, while he was still arguing, she turned the head of the blue roan away. Tom Converse rode beside her for a few paces.

"It sort of gets under my skin," he admitted, "to think of you going away, and me not yet having a chance to see you. But it's like a lot of other things worth while — keeping won't spoil you."

She swung Bad Eye closer and wrung the hand of Tom Converse.

"In an hour I'll have found them," she said eagerly, "and I'll be back with the good news to you. Wait here and keep your heart high. They can't refuse to believe me!"

Then she was gone, fading quickly in the darkness; and he had not yet seen her face.

Chapter Twenty-Nine

Sylvia Talks

It was some time after the disappearance of Tom Converse and the gray horse that Sheriff Algie Thomas called to his men to stop firing. He brought them into a small open space where, inside of a minute or two, a small fire was kindled.

"Because," said the sheriff, "they ain't nothing in the world that's half so helpful to a gent's thoughts as being able to see himself and see other gents when they're a-talking."

Over and around that fire they held their conversation. Joe Shriner was for beating on through the woods, shooting at whatever looked like a living creature. But others agreed with the sheriff that they'd shot enough bullets already to have cut down a thick oak tree, and that this blind pursuit was folly. The Shadow had slipped away from them, and they must cast about slowly until daybreak before they started seriously to attempt to pick up the trail once more.

"He started shooting, even when he knew it was too dark for him to hit anything," commented Algie Thomas, "because he knew that, when we heard them bullets of his whining anywhere near our heads, we'd start shooting back. The racket

236

we set up with our shooting was so much that he was able to slip away under cover of it. Otherwise, we'd have heard him go. Listen, now! Seems like you can hear every heart beating within a mile of us!"

In fact, that heavy silence of the forest surrounded them, a silence which is composed of a thousand half-heard whispers as the wind moves among the leaves. The scent of wet wood, also, was thick in the air — that scent which is ever in the woods after rain, and the firelight was only keen enough to bring into relief the great blackened forms of the trees behind and above them. Each face that listened at the bidding of the sheriff was painted rudely in splotches of red firelight and sweeps of shadow, and always there showed the uneasily glittering eyes.

Such was the assemblage on which the real Shadow, standing habitually on the outskirts, looked with doubt and dismay. He had thought that they must certainly have run down the two fugitives, but here they were, with their winded, spirit-broken horses, standing in a loose circle behind them, and neither Tom Converse nor the girl was their prisoner! His own bay, just behind him, was trembling with weakness. The poor beast, after having made up the distance which the fall had cost it, had been exhausted by the speed of its sprint across country. It would not be capable of another run before the morning.

All was failure with Jim Cochrane. A curse had fallen upon him since that unlucky hour when he tricked Tom Converse, and saddled death and his own crimes on the shoulders of the other. For it seemed that he had given his own luck to the man to whom he had given his own danger. His lady, his horse, and his fortune and fame had all passed into the possession of the stranger!

As for the others in the posse, they looked upon him as an outsider, a stranger whom the old sheriff had chosen to be among them by a freak of an old man's whim. His word was not regarded by them. His advice was passed over. All in all, he was in the position of a man who had to prove his worth.

He heard them bickering back and forth, but chiefly his glances hung on the features of two men. One of them was short, wide-shouldered, rosy of cheek, and yellow of hair. That was Harry Lang. The other was one of those thin-faced men who, by some involuntary contraction of the cheek muscles, appear to smile continually, and it was only by studying his black, intense eyes that it could be seen that he was serious or merry. This was Chuck Parker, and it seemed to The Shadow that the two men who completed the trio of those whose death he had vowed, and who had been included in the posse by a trick of fortune, were devoted by fate to his avenging hand!

From all the members of the posse The Shadow held aloof, but particularly he made it a point to direct all of his pleasant speeches to these two men. Sooner or later he would inveigle them, one after the other, into battle, and kill them as they deserved to be killed. So fiercely did this prospect prey upon his mind, and so greatly did he rejoice in it, that he forgot to follow the drift of the talk as the argument swayed to and fro.

At length it was he who saw, in the offing, the form of a rider approaching, and saw it grow and develop until he made out that it was a woman — a woman! — and therefore Sylvia Rann!

He saw in a flash what had happened. Ben Plummer had come for her. The terrible horseman on the gray had been Tom Converse. And now, having seen for the first time that the rescuer of Ben was not the real Shadow, she was riding back to the posse to announce her discovery and claim freedom for Converse. What would happen if she saw him among them so soon? Who could tell what her fierce denunciation — and denounce him he knew she would — would effect in the posse?

Quickly he stepped back into the shadow of his tall horse, and, by tipping his broad-brimmed sombrero forward, he effectually masked the upper part of his face. A moment more and the girl was in sight. The sound of her galloping horse made all the heads in the posse swing toward her. A murmur of astonishment, and then of pleasure, ran from throat to throat. Algie Thomas himself came out to greet her as she drew rein with a suddenness that cast up a shower of gravel clear to the fire, and set the blaze sputtering and snapping.

"Gentlemen," she said, "I've come back with

good news. The man you're chasing isn't The Shadow!"

They merely blinked. If she had said "The sun will never rise again!" they would have stared at her in the same manner. Then old Algie Thomas came beside her.

"You tell me all about it," he said, and turning his head a little, he winked broadly to the others as though to assure them that he was not quite so simple as the tone of this speech might lead them to believe. "Tell us first of all whatever was in your head, honey, to be gallivanting around the country at this hour of the night!"

She swung down from the saddle, disdaining the proffered assistance of the sheriff, and walked straight into the inner circle of the firelight.

There she paused and looked swiftly around upon the stern faces of the men. But only two of them smiled at her, and those two were Harry Lang, of the yellow hair, and Chuck Parker, who was forever smiling, anyway. To the rest, she was something forbidden. For years they had never dared to think of her as other than a danger sign, for she was The Shadow's lady. Lang and Chuck Parker had dared death to come courting her. The others had greater discretion than love of beauty.

"You talk right out, Miss Rann," said the sheriff. "We're all friends of yours and Mr. Plummer. We're all hoping for the best. You talk right out and explain how it comes that the gent we're after ain't The Shadow. We all know that you're the only one that's ever seen his face."

"It's — it's a queer story," she said, stumbling a little as she realized just how strange that story was. "But I'll tell it to you. You have to believe!"

She sketched in, swiftly and firmly as she could, the tale which had been told to her, not many minutes before, by Tom Converse. But it was not until she began speaking that she realized how absurd it was.

A man walks into a small cattle town, has a fist fight, falls into a gambling game, is stripped of his money and his watch, and then plays cards for an absurd stake — a ride to a mountaintop where he is to light a bonfire! He rides to the mountaintop, lights the fire, is attacked by many men, flees from them, rides into the next town on the horse the outlaw has provided for him, and then, being recognized by the horse, is attacked, escapes, and proceeds, having found a note on the floor of his room, to go to another town at the request of the unknown writer of the note and rescue her foster brother from jail at the infinite peril of his own life.

Such was the prodigious story which the girl rehearsed, and, as she finished, a hot flush began to steal over her face, for she knew that the tale had been ridiculous. Her own faith wavered for a moment; but, then, as she remembered the steady voice of Tom Converse, and the honest, manly face which the spurt of light from the match had revealed to her, her faith returned. He could not have lied so smoothly to her. He simply could not! She doubled her fists and looked defiantly back at the faces which were watching her with poorly concealed smiles.

Even the sheriff was smiling, and he should have known better.

"It's true!" she cried. "I know it sounds like a silly dream, but it's true! He's not The Shadow!"

There was no direct answer. Not a man there was anxious to give her the lie save Joe Shriner only. His own vanity had been so rent and tortured by the work of The Shadow that he had no feeling for others.

"This gent that's out yonder in the woods," asked the deputy from Carlton, "is he the one that took Ben Plummer out of my jail by a dirty trick?"

"He's the one that took Ben Plummer out of your jail," said the girl, "without spilling a drop of blood — though he had a great many lives at his mercy!"

It was an admission, but it was also an answer; in boxing parlance, it would have been termed a hard counter, and the deputy sheriff was shaken. He stood blinking. Then he shook his head.

"It sounds pretty," he said, "but it won't quite do."

"Why not?" asked the girl.

"Because there ain't two men alive who could do that same thing. The Shadow might trick me once, but no other gent could do it, any more'n The Shadow can do it twice!"

In the darkness, how infinitely it tickled the

242

ear of Jim Cochrane to hear the respect with which his name and fame were handled!

"Do the rest of you agree?" asked the girl, and she turned about toward them all with her hands outstretched.

"Don't you see, honey," said Algie Thomas kindly, taking her hands in his, "that the very fact that you're here among us pleading for him, is proof enough that he is The Shadow? We all know that you been true to him these two years, and now that you've found him, no wonder you want to keep him safe! But it can't be worked that way. A gent has to pay for his fun, and the fun The Shadow has had, has lasted a good many years — all on credit! Lady, we've come to collect, and if it spoils his happiness — still, we've come to collect!"

He ceased talking pleasantly. His voice had a harsh rasp to it as he ended, and the girl shrank from him.

"Will you make me one promise?" she said.

"In return for what?"

"In return for getting him to come in here and surrender — in return for getting this innocent man to come in here and surrender."

"What return can we make?"

"You can give me your solemn word of honor, every one of you, that, if he comes in, you'll keep him quiet until he's had a chance to prove his identity."

Algie Thomas shook his head. "They's no place to keep The Shadow safe except in a jail, and they's no jail except in a town, and they's no town in these parts where he could be given a very safe guarantee! No, sir! It couldn't be done. Folks are like wolves when you just mention the name of The Shadow, let alone having him as close as the thickness of a wall."

The wind touched the fire and blew it high, fluttering the girl's hat at the same time, so that she turned half away; and, turning, by the aid of that flare of the firelight she found herself looking straight into the eyes of Jim Cochrane.

Chapter Thirty

The Battle Signal

If there had been needed one more touch to prove to Sylvia that her affection, her foolish and romantic affection for The Shadow, was gone forever, it was afforded now by her first glance at that thin, sallow face and the dull, cynical eyes. Her whole reaction was one of horror and fear, and she shrank back from him.

"What will you do," she cried suddenly, "if I give you the real Shadow in place of the man you think is The Shadow? There he is — there stands Jim Cochrane! Take him! Don't let him go!"

It was like putting the very wail of the ghost in the lips of the teller of the ghost story. The posse shrank, and, so realistic was her expression of face, her ring of voice, that every hand jerked up and took out a gun. All turned — to see no desperado, but him who had been taken into their midst as an extra member, and taken by the special approval of Sheriff Algie Thomas. So the guns were reluctantly lowered as the men turned back to the girl, frowning.

"Ah, you won't believe that he has the courage to do it!" she cried. "But I tell you he'd dare anything, simply for the sake of the pleasure he gets out of danger! Oh, seize him and hold him!"

In fact, the men nearest The Shadow now moved back a little, so that they might more easily bar an attempt at escape, but escape by sudden flight was not in the mind of the outlaw. He deliberately doffed his hat and advanced into the full flare of the firelight, where he bowed to the girl.

"Lady," he said with the utmost gravity, and as he straightened from his bow it was noted that his dead black eyes were fixed without emotion upon the face of his accuser, "I'm a stranger to these parts, and it may be that you've mistook me for somebody else. It may be that I've got kind of a look like The Shadow — which I'm right sorry to hear! But now look me over, and I guess you'll see that I ain't the man!"

He stood there so quietly, with such a matchless effrontery, that her breath was taken.

"Here's a scar along the side of my head," he said. "That ought to be enough to identify me as Jim Cochrane and not The Shadow!"

"How did you get that scar?" she asked.

"When I was a youngster, playing tag with some other kids. I was climbing through a barbed-wire fence just as one of the other kids come up behind. I turned my face sidewise quick, to look at him, and at the same time I jumped to get through the fence. Well, a prong of that barbed wire caught me and sliced my head open to the bone."

"It's not true," answered Sylvia Rann. "That scar, and you know it, was clipped there by a bullet from the gun of Harvey Canby. You told me that three years ago! Harvey Canby's bullet clipped past your head there, and your bullet went through his heart!"

Evidence pro and con was flowing so fast from the lips of each of the contestants that the others drew close, all save Deputy Sheriff Joe Shriner, who walked away, kicking at twigs and cursing softly, as though wondering how grown men could come to waste so much time over nonsense.

"Don't you blockheads see?" he roared at length. "She's been sent back here to make a fuss and hold us up. That's all the meaning of this play. She's to come back here and accuse somebody in the posse, simply because she knows that nobody else has seen the face of The Shadow — nobody except herself, unless the gent that raised the devil in Silver Tip, and Carlton is the gent. And I say he is the gent. I ask you all — is it likely that there could be two gents like that living at the same time?"

No matter what Sylvia Rann said, it was hard to make headway against such an argument as that. She saw heads shaken around her. Besides, The Shadow never once lost his calmness.

"I remember Harvey Canby's death," said Sheriff Algie Thomas. "There was a bullet fired out of his revolver, and Harvey was as good a shot as most anybody I ever seen. If he fired that shot, he must've come close to The Shadow with it."

He stepped up and stared at the long scar which seamed the side of the outlaw's head.

"Looks like a tolerable broad scar for a barbed-wire prong to cut."

If Sheriff Thomas took the matter seriously, it was high time for others to grow serious, also. The shaking of heads stopped.

"Sure it's broad," and Jim Cochrane smiled. "I'll tell you why. That cut got infected and swelled up something terrible. Doctor had it all bandaged up for pretty nigh a month, seems to me."

"Where was it that it happened?" asked Algie.

"Down at Calsuon."

"Calsuon? That's a dead town, eh?"

It was an old cattle crossroads town, long since deserted and deceased.

"I reckon it's dead," said The Shadow. "But still, there might be a couple of folks still around it, that would be able to tell you who Jim Cochrane is, and about how he cut his head that time. But, say, gents, does it sound likely, if I was The Shadow, that I'd be here talking about this scar and pointing it out to you?"

That argument was a hard one to overcome. Sylvia Rann looked desperately about her.

"Will no one help me?" she said. "Isn't there someone here with a brain as clever as the brain of this devilish fox of a man? Oh, it's maddening! There he is right before your eyes, and you let him —"

Deputy Sheriff Joe Shriner, who had listened to all that he could endure, strode through the circle again and confronted the girl with outstretched arm.

"Gents," he said, "you must be plumb nutty to listen to her and think for a minute that they's anything in what she says. D'you think that she'd be down here accusing a gent that she's been keeping company with all these years? Why, it's common talk all through the mountains about how Sylvia Rann is keeping true to The Shadow. Lord knows why. But the Lord only knows how the brains of a lot of womenfolk work! She's throwing up a false alarm to save time for the real Shadow, and that's him off in the woods!"

He turned a little farther and strode up to Jim Cochrane.

"The Shadow?" he said. "Huh! I could handle a dozen gents like him without no trouble. No trouble at all!"

Some of the color deserted the sallow cheeks of The Shadow. He had been subjected to a bitter torment by the girl. He saw all his hopes of her disappearing, and yet he had to stand among these men and assume an appearance of indifference while his heart was breaking within him. The new blow, delivered by the deputy sheriff, was almost too much for his forbearance, and for a small part of a second he hesitated.

He might draw, kill the deputy with a shot, and plunge straight across the circle, scattering the small fire with his foot as he passed. In another moment he would be among the horses. In another moment beyond that, he would be into some random saddle.

Then, with a faint sigh, he gave up that tempting thought. No, he would stay here among the men of the posse. He would stay here and help them to trail down the pseudo-Shadow whom he himself had created, and to whom the strange girl had transferred her interest and her affection.

But what devil, from the first, had hounded him into this grim affair? What fiend had prompted him to choose Tom Converse for his dupe?

"Shriner," he said slowly to the insulting man of Carlton, "you sure have a name for a fighter. But, after you and me and the rest of us get back from this trail, we'll have a little talk. We'd have that talk right now, but I figure that I'm Sheriff Algie Thomas' man. I've come along to prove to the sheriff that I'm an honest man, and I'm going to prove it. When this trail is ended, why, you and me can have a little chat. I'll have a couple of words to say that won't take very long!"

There was such a mixture of perfect self-control and quivering rage in the voice of Jim Cochrane that respect for him mounted at once in every breast in the party, and even Joe Shriner fell back and blinked. His own courage was so well established, and the offense which he had offered was so terribly broad, that he even went so far as to offer an apology.

"I talked quick and without thinking," he said. "I'm sorry for what I've said, Cochrane. I ain't got any manner of doubt that you're a good man in a pinch. Here's my hand, if you feel like shaking and forgetting what I've said."

The Shadow would sooner have driven his fist into the complacent face of the deputy sheriff, yet there was nothing he could do but submit. He took the hand and shook it heartily.

"I don't hold malice," he said.

"Malice?" echoed the girl. "Mr. Shriner, you'll live to be sorry for the day when you first saw his face." She turned. "Chuck Parker! Harry Lang! Do you believe that I'd lie? Are you going to let him —"

Algie Thomas raised his hand and interrupted her. "We've heard enough," he said, "to make up our minds. We figure that you couldn't do this if he was really The Shadow and —"

"I'll tell you why I can do it — because I've never before believed all the terrible and cruel things that I've heard about him, but now I believe them all — all! I wouldn't trust what others said until I heard Tom Converse speak!"

"And why do you trust this Tom Converse, as you call him?

"Because he dared go to Carlton and get Ben Plummer free from the jail where they were turning him into an animal with their brutality!"

"That's one for you, Shriner," said The Shadow, bowing in mock courtesy to the deputy sheriff. "If we stand around long enough, the

251

lady will have some hard things to say about all of us, I guess."

Shriner flashed him a glance of savage agreement. Even the patience of Algie Thomas was exhausted.

"The best we can do for you, Miss Rann," he said at length, "is to keep you here with us so that you can't get back to The Shadow and get filled up with a lot more queer talk to come back and give us."

She drew away, but, at a signal from the sheriff, two of the men fell in behind her.

"Let me at least go back and try to identify him before it's too late," pleaded the girl. "You haven't made any effort to make sure that there is a Tom Converse who corresponds with this man you think is The Shadow."

Thomas, a little thoughtful at the memory of the frantic appeal which he had heard through the door of the hotel when Converse was hemmed in, regarded the girl closely for a moment, and then shook his head.

"We can't take no chances," he said. "All that a crook needs to fool a thousand men is an outside agent that'll work with him. I'm afraid that The Shadow has it fixed up for you to be that sort of outside agent for him, Miss Rann. No, you'll have to stay with us tonight. In the morning —"

His words were cut short by the sight of her revolver flashing out of the small holster which she wore. It was a little nickel steel weapon which she pointed toward the sky.

"Stop her!" cried the sheriff.

But he was too late. Three times the gun quivered and barked before Deputy Sheriff Shriner beat it out of her hands.

She stood nursing the fingers which he had bruised in his brutal method of disarming her, but still she was able to smile defiance at them.

"That," she said, "will tell him that it's to be a battle to the death."

Chapter Thirty-One

The Woman Who Believed

In the interim, Ben and Tom Converse had not been idle. At the suggestion of the former — for Tom Converse seemed to be in a waking dream — they began to move slowly forward, making the horses walk so that they might not cool off too rapidly, and at the same time, in this manner, putting behind them what might prove to be an invaluable bit of ground if the pursuers were to come on their traces again.

They went forward in silence until Tom Converse asked quietly:

"You ain't told me much about her, Ben. What sort is she?"

"The best that ever stepped," said the boy instantly. "Her and me have always been pals. If she'd only been a man, she'd have been a wonder! She rides like a man, she can shoot like a man, and she's got all the nerve that a man needs. Only trouble is that she ain't a man!" He added sadly: "Just nacherally hard luck, that's all!"

"Hard luck," agreed Tom Converse absently, and then corrected himself with a start. "Hard luck? Why, Ben, you sure talk foolish. That girl, so far's I could judge, is sure a great beauty —"

"You couldn't judge," insisted Ben. "It was dark, wasn't it?"

Converse growled. "I lighted a match, I guess," he suggested sternly.

"H'm! That match you lighted to show that you wasn't The Shadow, and it shone right plumb in your own eyes. Besides, she was a lot too far away for you to've seen her."

"Was she?" said Tom fiercely. "Well, kid, I'll tell you this: You can judge a girl by her voice. Never seen one yet that you couldn't draw a picture of after you've heard 'em talk once."

"Go ahead," answered Ben. "Just go ahead and lemme see the sort of picture that you make of her. That's all that I ask."

"Don't be so darned hostile, will you?" protested Tom Converse.

He sighed. The sound of that voice was still a-tremble at his ear. Indeed, it seemed to him that he had almost seen her face behind a veil.

"She's tall," said Tom. "I could make that out easy."

"How tall?"

"Why, about five feet eight, I'd say."

"You're wrong. She ain't more'n five feet five."

"That's about the right height," remarked Tom Converse. "I always noticed that one of these tall girls was hard to dance with. You can't steer 'em through a crowd, because you can't see past 'em very easy."

"Go on," chuckled Ben Plummer, who seemed to obtain great amusement from this description.

"She's got blue eyes. I could almost see 'em sparkle. Blue eyes, and sort of yaller hair. Ain't I right, Ben?"

There was a note of pleading in his voice as he pronounced this last.

"Wrong," said the inexorable Ben. "Her eyes ain't blue at all, and her hair ain't yaller. Her eyes are brown — the brownest brown you ever seen — and her hair is bluish-black, sort of."

"Good!" said Tom. "That sure is a fine combination, in particular when it goes along with a fine white skin."

"Look here, her skin ain't white at all. It's all tanned from being out in the sun so much — she likes to ride, you see; and she's got freckles across the nose."

"The devil!" exploded Tom.

"Don't blame me for spoiling the picture," said the boy. "If you want to see in the dark, you ought to be a cat, not a man. I can't help it if she ain't the way you want her to be!"

"Who said she wasn't?"

"And if she is, what difference does that make to you? Ain't you going to go on with me? Are you ever likely to see her more'n a couple of times in the next few years?"

This observation was greeted with a sigh.

"Some folks," said Tom at length, "are just plumb pessimistic by nature, and you're one of 'em, Ben."

"How come?"

"Well, don't you suppose, when we get all settled down some place and maybe have a house started — of our own — we might be able to send for her and she'd come out and keep house for us?"

"By Jiminy!" exclaimed Ben Plummer. "Wouldn't that be slick?"

"Better'n safe cracking, eh, Ben?"

"Out of sight better! But —" he paused "— it wouldn't work."

"Why not?"

"She'll be married before that happens."

"Confound you, Ben! You got a hankering for spoiling plans. Why'll she get married?"

"Well, wasn't she pretty fond of The Shadow?"

"That's all over and done with."

"That's over and done with," and the boy nodded with a marked emphasis. "You've showed him up to be such a skunk that she'll never look at him again. But that don't make no difference. My pa says that, when a girl gets to the marrying age, it don't make much difference to her. She falls in love with one gent, but, if he turns out wrong or moves away or breaks his leg, or if something like that happens, she cries for a couple of days, and pretty soon she's smiling at some other gent."

Here he was astonished to hear a stream of subdued but violent profanity.

"What's the matter, Tom?" he asked.

"Shut up," said Tom with asperity. "I never heard such a fool kid as you in all my life!"

"It ain't me, it's what my pa said; and he knows

all about women. I've heard him tell ma so a pile of times. He says that, when the time comes, a girl can't help marrying, no more'n the grass can help getting green when the spring comes along. I guess that's pretty reasonable, partner?"

"Reasonable? They ain't nothing reasonable about it."

"Well, you go argue with pa about it. I don't know nothing about girls, and I don't want to know nothing about 'em. They don't interest me none, and they never will interest me none. That is — all of 'em except Sylvia. She's different."

Tom Converse agreed with this idea with enthusiasm.

"She sure is different. A gent can tell that just by the first sound of her voice. Ain't that right, Ben?"

"Maybe. But I ain't got the kind of imagination that you got. What makes you so dog-gone interested in her, anyway, Tom? A gent might think that you was getting her for a Christmas present, or something, and wanted to know how much she cost!"

"Son," said the other heavily, "I've heard you chatter for quite a while about things that you're a pile too young to understand, and you want to hark to me sing when I tell you to change your tune, Ben. Don't go talking about ladies and Christmas presents to me, but —"

Ben Plummer had listened with commendable patience during this irritable outburst. Now he broke out laughing softly.

"I'll tell you another thing that pa is always saying. He says: 'If they's ever any trouble between two men, the first thing to look for as the cause of it is a woman. You'll find a woman somewhere at the bottom of it.' "

"You're bright, kid," said Tom Converse presently; "but I don't foller your drift."

Silence enveloped them; but presently Tom spoke again in such an absent manner that it was plain he had quite forgotten all about the sharp words which they had recently interchanged.

"It's a queer thing," he said, "how a gent can go along for years and years and never pay no attention to important things, and then all at once wake up sudden and find out that he's been overlooking the finest things in life and —"

"What you talking about, Tom?"

"H'm!" said Tom. "Well, I wonder if they's anything in what your pa says."

"What's that?"

"Why, hang it, ain't you just finished telling me that, when a girl once gets interested in the marrying idea, she keeps right on until she's finally all tied up with a ring and a husband and everything like that?"

"I dunno; my ideas don't seem to be worth nothing much to you. So you make up your mind to suit yourself."

This retort drew another grunt from Tom Converse, but, before he could continue his further conjectures, the air was broken by the discharge of a revolver in the distance — three explosions

259

in rapid succession.

"It's her!" cried Tom Converse. "They've got her, and they're holding her. They've got her, and they won't let her get away and come back to us again, curse 'em!"

So saying, he flung himself into the saddle on the gray and would have dashed off in the direction from which the shots had seemed to come, but the boy threw himself in front of the mare and, at the imminent risk of being trampled underfoot, managed to grasp one of the reins and check her progress.

"Let go, Ben!" cried the rider. "Let go! You're crazy to try to stop me!"

"And you're crazy to try to go!" panted Ben.

"Didn't you hear?" shouted Converse. "They've got her. That's her signal!"

"I dunno. All I know is that, if they're holding her, you can't help."

"They's only a dozen of 'em." cried Tom.

"Only a dozen?" echoed the boy in tones of shrill dismay.

That tone cleared the brain of Tom Converse so that he stopped wrenching at the rein to clear it from Ben's persistent grasp.

"Besides," said Ben, still holding the rein tight and not trusting the impulses of his companion, "maybe it's more a signal to us that she's failed, and for us to be getting along on our way, than it is a call for us to come help her . . . That ain't her style. She wouldn't be calling for help like that if she knew that her call would bring us along and get us into a pile of trouble. I know her!"

There was no resisting the logic of this argument, and Tom Converse lowered his head suddenly and struck his forehead with his fist.

"I was a plumb fool ever to let her go. That yarn about me is too queer to be believed."

"I dunno. I believed it," said the boy loyally, "and she sure believed it."

"That's because she knows that I'm not The Shadow, and she's about the only one in the world that does know I'm not The Shadow, I guess! But you're right, Ben; we got to get on. I dunno where, but somewhere that'll be hardest for 'em to find us. What you suggest? You know this country."

The importance of this problem staggered Ben Plummer. To think that this mighty warrior of horse and revolver should be appealing to him for direction!

"Best thing we can do," he decided at length, "is for us to stay right here and let the hosses rest. Am I right?"

"Right," agreed Tom sullenly. "Give Captain five hours' rest, and he'll break the hearts of any of the rest of 'em when it comes to running. Where'll we camp?"

"I know a place. It's back here in the woods. We can strike over through the trees and hit it pretty close inside of a mile. Had we better try that far?"

"Sure. The farther the better, if we can hit

a good camping place with the right kind of water."

"This place is made to order. You wait till you see. Running water, clear as spring water, too; and grass enough to feed a herd."

"Start along, then."

They started, winding slowly and cautiously among the trees, for the loud crackling, as twigs broke under the feet of the horses from time to time, might very well reach to the ears of some spies of the posse scouting beyond the rest of the party.

Chapter Thirty-Two

Scottie is Amazed

Once or twice, as they proceeded on their way, Ben Plummer heard his formidable rear guard muttering, and on one occasion he lingered behind and made out: "Just as sure as the spring brings the grass? Hey, Ben!"

"Well?" answered Ben, inspired with awe by the reckless freedom with which this hunted companion of his raised his voice.

"That idea of your pa's ain't any good. When I see him, I'm going to tell him what I think of it. A girl like that would wait ten years to find the right man."

"All right," answered Ben. "I ain't arguing, if you know as much as all that. But here we are!"

With that they dipped into a sandy bottom, and, coming up on the farther side, they made out a glimmer of firelight among the trees.

"It's taken!" groaned Ben Plummer. "Dog-gone it, partner, ain't that our luck — to have my pet camping ground taken?"

"Go see who's there," said the other. "If it's only one man, we'll camp there, anyway. Won't do any harm to be seen by one. Besides, I want to rest, and that fire is made to order for me. Go ahead and see how many are around that clearing."

Ben cast a glance of wonder at Tom Converse, and then made off among the shrubbery, stealthy of foot, like the good woodsman that he was.

When he reappeared, after a few minutes, he slipped to the side of Tom Converse saying: "They's two bad ones inside the clearing, Tom. Never seen much worse in all my life. Look like murder, both of 'em!"

Tom shrugged his shoulders. "There's a fire in yonder," he remarked; "and there's most likely food in there, too. We'll go in and help ourselves. Two men? I guess they can be handled!"

He turned toward the horses.

"You stay here with these. When I whistle, you can come on, not minding how much noise you make."

He left the gasping Ben Plummer and entered the shrubbery in turn. Presently, the firelight grew brighter, the trunks of the trees more and more black; eventually, he stepped behind a trunk, around which he could view the camp scene of Scottie and Limpy — whom The Shadow had left a few hours before — taking their ease by the warmth of their prodigal fire and playing blackjack with considerable gusto.

He eyed them for only a moment, surprised by the reactions which were going on in his brain, for he found himself looking on the two quite impersonally. They possessed food and warmth.

He was determined to have both. Would they give what they had to him, or must he take it by force? To be sure, they seemed of the kind who would ruthlessly take for themselves when the occasion proffered. But, had they been most harmless and gentle in appearance, Tom Converse knew that he would, nevertheless, have felt no scruple in taking what he needed from them.

No wonder, then, that he shook his head. He had gone farther along the path of The Shadow than he had dreamed. He had gone along that path not only with horse and name, but in spirit, also, he found. It was useless to attempt to justify himself by pretending that he had a right to take what he needed because the powers of the law were now pursuing him without justice. It was not true. Justice was on their side. He had stolen a man from the grip of the law, and therefore he must pay for it in full, or more than in full! But no matter for such moralizing; there was work to be done. He must not leave Ben Plummer shivering in the dark. He stepped from behind the tree.

"Gents," he said, "I sure hate to bother you, but —"

Here he paused. They had whirled at him of one accord, covering their stakes of money with one hand and reaching for weapons with the other hand; but they found themselves covered by a revolver held in a hand which dangled carelessly at the hip of the stranger. That negligence meant more to them than if the newcomer had had ten armed men beside him. They pocketed their money deftly and stowed their guns once more. Still, they studied the face of Tom Converse with fierce eyes.

"Well?" they growled together.

"I got a pal back in the woods," said Tom. "He's holding our hosses. I thought I'd come along first and find out if we could get a place by your fire and chow with you tonight?"

They stared at him; they stared at his gun.

"Ain't nobody to keep you away from the fire," said Limpy glumly.

Tom raised his head and whistled sharply. He could hear the call of Ben in answer, and presently made out the crashing through the underbrush as the two horses were led toward the fire in the clearing. Then they came in view, with their reins in the hands of Ben Plummer.

No sooner did the chestnut appear than Scottie leaped to his feet.

"How come you by that hoss?" he asked in great excitement.

"It's a gift," said Tom truthfully.

"A gift!" Scottie choked. "A gift!"

It was plain that he recognized Captain.

"Don't you figure that that hoss is mine?" asked Tom carelessly.

"I don't do no figuring," said the grizzled tramp. "I don't do no figuring at all. If you got that hoss from the gent that used to own him — well, you can have anything of mine that you want without asking for it!" In fact, a smile was quivering on his lips. "The Shadow!" he breathed. "Did you get him?"

"Why d'you ask?" said Tom, made deeply curious by the strange actions and words of the other.

"Shut up, pal," said Limpy. "You're talking too fast."

"You fool, that's Captain," said Scottie. He added to Tom: "You don't need to fear me, pal. I can keep my mouth closed. I'm wise to what The Shadow is. Didn't the skunk once run into me when I was down and out and hadn't nothing but one rag of a blanket between me and a blizzard? And didn't he take that blanket away from me and kick me out of my place? Curse him, if I'd of had a gun that time —"

He paused, writhing with rage at the memory.

"But I'm no fast hand with a gat, and when I've met him a dozen times since, I've had to talk pleasant to him when I've been wanting to tear his head off his neck! So talk out, son, and —"

Tom raised his hand. "You're talking a bit too much," he warned the tramp not unkindly. "The Shadow may get wind of what you've said and —"

"You mean to say he's alive and some other gent has his hoss? You mean to say that that gangling bay he's riding now, he's riding because he's lost Captain and —"

Scottie stopped, his mind apparently whirling. He shook his head.

"It beats me! But go on, general. Tell me what's

happened. Bunk in here by the fire. Limpy, start some chow. There's stuff for the hosses. Boys, make yourselves at home. So The Shadow's lost his hoss!"

The news seemed as incredible to him as though he had heard of the sun rising in the west. In the meantime, he showed his interest in the presumptive conqueror of The Shadow by opening to him his home and board, such as it was.

Chapter Thirty-Three

Jim Learns the Truth

The second camp fire in the woods had by this time grown into a considerable blaze, for, by the last decision of the sheriff, they were to camp here until the first light of the dawn and then start their excursion after the fugitive. So they skirmished through the woods and collected a great pile of deadwood and pitch pine, and from this supply they built two separate circles of fire. In that high altitude the night was becoming sharp with cold, and the arrangement of two fires, which merely touched at one point in their circles, enabled every member of the group to keep warm.

There were only a few hours remaining until morning, but, even so, some of the cow-punchers who rode in the posse prepared themselves to sleep, well knowing that an hour or two of complete repose might redouble their strength for the coming day. It seemed to be the common opinion everywhere among them that this would be a trail such as no man had ever ridden before.

Half a dozen, therefore, were soon asleep. The others sat about in positions of the most complete relaxation, all save the fire guard; and the man who kept the fire watch, self-appointed to this

269

irksome duty, was no other than Jim Cochrane.

He felt that, if he had to sit still among these prostrate or partially recumbent figures, he would go mad. He wanted to be riding at full speed through the forest, or fighting — singing — anything to occupy his mind and his body fully, so that in a moment of stillness the realization of what he had lost might not steal into his thoughts.

Busily he worked, then, limping back and forth from the piles of deadwood, or going far afield to renew the supply of these larger stacks themselves, or stirring the fire from the bottom, or heaping fresh fuel upon the top.

Never once did he allow his eyes to stray to the face and form of Sylvia Rann where she sat in an obscure outer corner of the circle with no one near her — for she had given her word to the sheriff that she would not attempt to escape from them — her chin resting on her clenched fist, her eyes liquid with the rapid play of the firelight.

Yet, no matter how resolutely he kept his glances away from her, he could not help seeing her even the more continually in his mind's eye, with the shadows awash across her, and with the light tangled from time to time in the hair that fluffed out beneath her sombrero. She was so close to him, but so many miles away. Never since he first knew her had she been so far.

If he should go to accost her now, would she even answer, unless it were to denounce him? And, if she did not denounce him but sat in silence, what would the other men think of him? How utterly would they despise him if they watched him attempting to speak to her after she had assailed him so fiercely that night!

But he could not help it. The impulse was stronger urging him forward than was his will power holding him back. Something snapped in him during that struggle. Suddenly he was standing before her, leaning on a stout branch covered with twigs, a branch which effectually cut off sight of her from the others near by. But, having turned his own back on the rest, The Shadow did not see the little old sheriff raise his head of a sudden and flash toward him a penetrating and unfriendly glance.

Indeed, all that The Shadow saw in the world at that moment was the gloomy face before him. Sylvia did not waste an upward glance at him.

He pitched his voice so that it would reach her ear, but be cut off from the ear of the nearest of the others by the steady crackling of the fires.

"Sylvia," he said, "will you exchange a word with me, a single word, Sylvia?"

She did not stir.

"Will you even listen when I talk? If you've sworn to yourself that you'll never speak to me, just raise your hand to give me a sign that you're willing to listen, anyway!"

She looked up at him, at that. "Jim," she said, "do you remember that dog of mine — that Charlie dog?"

He quivered from head to foot at the sound

271

of her voice, so great was his joy. It did not matter that her tone was hard as iron ringing on iron.

"I mind him well — the shepherd."

"You may remember that when he died I grieved for him a long time, and you used to say that finally I'd get over it and forget him. But I never did until we found out — a long time after Charlie had died — that he once was a sheep killer, and that he would have been a sheep killer still, if he had lived. When I heard that, it killed all my kind thoughts of Charlie. I could never think of him again, except as in the act of sinking his teeth in the throat of a poor, helpless, silly sheep. And that's true of you, also, Jim. When I heard of what you had done to Tom Converse, it killed every good hope I had ever had for you, because suddenly I could look back into your past, as I have known it, and see that it pointed out and confirmed a hundred things I had seen before, but never allowed myself to take too seriously. I see them now. I believe in them; and there is nothing about you that I wish to remember, Jim. Not a thing. You are dead to me!"

If she had spoken with more passion and less certainty of expression, it might well have been that he would have found comfort in the very fact that she would say so much. But, as it was, he shrank back a little, and his head, his very shoulders, bowed as though a great weight had been placed upon them.

In spite of herself, a little exclamation of surprise and pain came from her lips at the sight of his anguish — as though it were a perpetual astonishment to her that a man with so much evil in him could feel in this respect an emotion so clean and strong.

He answered that brief exclamation rather than her speech.

"If you'll listen, Sylvia, for a couple of minutes, I think —"

"Don't you see that there's no way in which you can twist out of this?" she answered quickly, as though she felt it would be an act of compassion to prevent him from opening the subject.

"I'm not going to lie," said The Shadow slowly, gradually lifting his head and seeming to recover his pride and self-possession at the same instant. "Even if lying would get back your good opinion, Sylvia, I wouldn't do it! What I've done to Tom Converse may be bad. I dunno. I suppose it is. I'm not asking you to think that it ain't, and if you go back over the story of what I've done in my life, I figure that you'll find a pile of other things that ain't been of the best. But, Sylvia, there's one thing that's still true, and that'll always be true — I love you! No matter what I may be in other ways, they's nothing wrong about me in that way. I've kept the thought of you clean, Sylvia, and I've never left you out of my mind. Does that count with you?"

"I have to tell you the truth when I admit that it does. It counts so much that during all these years I've fought against my own common sense in trying to believe only the best about you and as little as possible of the bad. But the story of Tom Converse is the final blow. It wrecks everything!"

"Curse Tom Converse!" said the outlaw through his teeth. "If that blockhead didn't have brains enough to —"

"Don't say any more," interrupted Sylvia. "Oh, Jim, what a lot I can read between words in what you say! You hate him, and you hate him because you know he's the better man."

"Better man?" cried The Shadow. "Ay, better for a picnic. But when I meet him —"

"When you meet him face to face," said the girl hotly, "he'll break you!"

"Never in a thousand lives!"

"Because he's a stronger man than you are, Jim!"

"Stronger? What's strength? It's speed and accuracy that count!"

"He's quick and accurate. Look inside your own mind, Jim, and you'll be forced to admit you dread him. The thought of him haunts you!"

"What devil told you that?" gasped The Shadow, recoiling a little.

"I can see it in your face, Jim," said the girl more relentlessly than ever. "You don't stand with your head as high. You look at the ground when people speak to you. You're nervous. Your hand shakes —"

"It's steady as a rock on the butt of a gun."

"Until you face him —"

"Sylvia, I think you want him to murder me! Is that it?"

"I want him to crush you," she answered. "And he will. I want him to crush you, because I know that, until he does, you'll follow him, you'll trail him, until you have found a chance to kill him by stealth!"

He had lost all color, and he was shaking with combined rage and anguish.

"I reckon," he said, "that a blow at him would be a blow at you, Sylvia. Is that right?"

"Yes," she answered hotly.

"You're tolerable fond of him already, eh?"

"Fond of him? I — I think I love him!"

"After seeing him once?"

"How many times do you think are required? I saw you a hundred times, and always there was a barrier between us. I saw him once, and suddenly we knew each other. I could trust him; he could believe me. Oh, Jim, if you had one spark of his generosity, of his kindness, what a man you could be! He rode across country and broke open a jail to save a man at the request of a woman he had never seen —"

"He's a romantic fool — that's what!"

"And you were afraid to attempt that task, even for the woman you said you loved — even when she had made it the price of her love. Ah, Jim, what a comparison is in that!"

He waited a long moment.

"Suppose I was to kill him?" he asked at length

in a ghastly voice.

"I'd find a man to strike back at you for it. I'd help strike myself!"

And by the ring in her voice he knew that words would not help him. He turned away.

Chapter Thirty-Four

The Trap

Unable to meet the eyes of others in that time of agony and humiliation, Jim Cochrane strode into the darkness blindly, until he struck against a tree and leaned with his face pressed against the wet bark, his mind in a delirium of grief and shame.

When he could control his expression and fitly veil the torment of anger and hatred which boiled in him, he returned to the fire. There he busied himself for a time, heaping fresh boughs on the fires until the blaze, which had fallen low during his conversation with Sylvia Rann, leaped up again to an unprecedented height, snapping arms of flame above the boughs of the trees around him. That increased heat made the sleepers around the fires wince and draw away, and those who merely drowsed in the heat, turned their heads.

The Shadow looked at them with a bitter scowl. If they guessed his identity, how swiftly would they be at his throat! But now he stayed there and ministered to their comforts!

He turned from one to the other. It seemed to him that old Algie Thomas, sitting with his head supported on arms that were crossed upon his knees, had recently moved, and there was a rigidity of his limbs little fitted to the attitude of profound sleep in which he had composed himself.

The Shadow showed his teeth beneath a tightened upper lip. He recognized an enemy in the sheriff, an enemy in sheer difference of type, just as the wolf hates the dog with a profound and instinctive hatred. He half guessed that the sheriff was awake; he half suspected that the sheriff had been watching him from the first, and had been listening as hard as he could listen in the vain hope of catching some of the conversation between him and the girl. So for an instant Jim Cochrane stared malignantly at Thomas and then turned, deciding that the old man could not be awake.

He turned, and the moment he presented his back, the head of Thomas stirred just enough to expose one eye. Peering through his bush of eyebrows, the sheriff looked keenly at the criminal. He saw Jim Cochrane again move toward the girl in the shadow, and this time she was asleep. Yes, in spite of all the storm of the words which she had directed against The Shadow, she now slept. Perhaps that outburst had exhausted her; but at any rate she now lay back against the tree with her left arm loose in her lap — her right arm fallen limp at her side, with the palm of her hand turned up.

The Shadow picked up the folds of the girl's long coat, which had fallen apart in her sleep, and drew them cautiously together. So much the sheriff could make out, and, shaking his head in astonishment, he once more covered his eyes and bowed his head before The Shadow turned, with a movement as quick and unheralded as the turn of a cat.

He shivered from head to foot, and his dull black eyes filled with uneasy lights as he ran his glance from face to face. He had felt watching eyes behind him; he could have sworn to them. He felt them as acutely as he would have felt a light playing upon closed eyelids.

But there was nothing to be seen, nothing to be feared. He turned again, and this time directed his attention to the rest of those who slept soundly or drowsed beside the fire.

Had he himself been the pursued, would he not have crept close up to the fire, cuddled his rifle against his shoulder — that matchless, light rifle of his — and picked off two or three of the sleepers with quick shots? Then he'd be away before they could stir to overtake him.

At least he could have done that with perfect security, had it not been for the old sheriff sitting there with his rifle leaning against the tree which supported his back. Was the old rascal asleep, or was he shamming?

He dismissed the problem of the sheriff for a moment and turned to regard the others. First of all, of course, his glance found out the forms of two of the sleepers — Harry Lang, with his yellow hair glinting in the firelight beneath the brim of his sombrero, and Chuck Parker, smiling sourly in his sleep.

Here were the two he had sworn to slay. Suppose he were to go to the edge of the clearing, shoot them both, and disappear into the night on the best of the horses? No, that would be a confession of his identity. The girl's strange story would be believed, then, and Tom Converse would return to society, a welcomed member — most of all welcomed by the girl.

But would it not be the most perfect touch if he could continue with the posse, a great power threatening to strike down The Shadow, and one at a time find ways of destroying these two? By infinite care he might be able to do it and win the bitter satisfaction, at length, of breaking the heart of the girl as she had broken his heart.

He went to the pair and leaned over them. Did they recognize, subconsciously, the danger which was near them in this man hunt? Was that why they were so close together? But which one should he choose?

The less formidable should be first. That would save the better for the last. He touched Harry Lang with the toe of his riding boot, and the latter, waking with a start, bounded to his feet with an agility surprising for a man of his squat bulk. He stood panting as he confronted the other with eyes that sparkled with fear, and his hand gripped the handle of his revolver.

"I've had the worst dream that ever a man had!" panted Lang. "I thought — I thought —"

"Well, let's hear about it," said The Shadow

with a good-humored smile. "That'll get it out of your system, and you won't be so apt to dream it again."

"It was about you, Cochrane," said Lang, flushing with embarrassment. "Dreamed that I'd gotten into a fight with you, and somehow all at once I was paralyzed, hand and foot. I couldn't stir, and there were you standing beside me, grinning.

"Pretty soon you said: 'Listen!' and held up your hand. I listened, and I heard a rumbling off in the distance.

" 'A landslide's started up the hill,' you said. 'So long, Lang!'

"You disappeared, and then above me I heard the noise growing. It hit the forest with a roar. I heard the trees going down with cracks like cannon being shot, and just as it was about to sweep over me and polish me off into grease — well, just then I wake up, and darned if I don't see your face right here above me the way it was in the dream — grinning!"

He finished the narration with an apologetic laugh, but plainly he was much perturbed by his dream.

"Come along with me," said The Shadow, "and I'll show you some things that'll make you forget all about your dream. Come off and take a walk with me, Lang, I've got some ideas."

"Ideas — at this time of night?"

"Time of night doesn't keep a man from thinking, does it?"

"Well, what's up?" The irritation in the voice of The Shadow found an echo in the tone of Harry Lang.

"I'll tell you," said The Shadow, instantly making his manner more amiable. "I've been lying here and wondering what could be done by a couple of gents who were willing to tramp off in the forest here and find what they could find?"

"Such as what?" growled Lang, totally unreceptive.

"Such as The Shadow."

"Eh?"

"That's what I said, The Shadow!"

"Find him by night?"

"Listen," said Jim Cochrane, "I know that's what you think; I know that's what all the rest are thinking — that it's no good chasing him any more till day comes. But did you ever think that probably The Shadow has known the way we'd think? He'd know that we wouldn't chase him the minute we lost sight of him. We'd sit and wait for daylight, and so would he. He ain't the kind to waste his strength blundering around in the woods in the dark."

"Go on," said Lang, frowning with curiosity now. "I begin to get your drift, partner. You mean he'd just outguess us and do exactly the same thing that we're doing? He'd camp here and rest himself and his hoss and wait till the morning?"

"Now you're reading my mind," agreed Cochrane.

"That sounds pretty risky, though."

"Ain't The Shadow always been known to be one to take risks?"

"That's true."

It was all Cochrane could do to keep himself from smiling when he saw that his victim was walking into the trap. His plan was perfectly simple. He would persuade Lang to go out with him on a still hunt for the marauder through the night, and, when they were at a distance sufficient to muffle the sounds, he would turn on his companion and with a few brief words tear the veil from his eyes and let him know the truth about The Shadow. Then a second forty-five-caliber slug planted squarely in the center of his forehead as the slug was planted in the center of the forehead of the first of the three — Jess Sherman. That would square the long account.

"Come along," urged The Shadow.

"Hadn't we better take another along?"

"Why?"

"To tackle The Shadow."

Cochrane groaned. "Are we going to give up all the fun and all the glory by getting a whole gang along?" he asked. "Besides, where two might be able to sneak up on him, three would never be able to get near a fox like him."

"That's logic," admitted the other, but he shivered at the thought of what work lay before them.

Then he gathered his courage about him like a cloak. "We'll make the try. I'm game for it if you are, partner. Here we go. But before we start, here's my hand! I'll stick by you to the finish, Cochrane. Will you do the same by me if we should run into him?"

The Shadow brushed the hand aside playfully. "No use starting out as solemn as all that," he declared. "This is a game, not a funeral!"

He whistled softly as he stepped into the night with his man beside him.

Chapter Thirty-Five

Sure Shooting

"How simple it was!" thought The Shadow, as he conducted his dupe through the woods, never once dreaming that what he proposed as a mere false inducement was entirely true.

In the meantime, he maintained a quiet under-current of talk with which to keep up the spirit of his companion, detailing over and over how great a glory would be theirs when they had struck down the notorious outlaw. To all of which Harry Lang listened with growing discontent as they increased their distance from the camp.

That distance The Shadow kept constantly es-timating, for he wished to go only so far that the noise of the exploding revolver might not carry to their own camp fires. By this time those fires were dying down for lack of fuel, and the men about it might begin to waken.

"I figure it's a wild-goose chase," said Harry Lang for the tenth time, and now he came to a pause. He was brave enough, but he had never figured himself a single-handed match for the fa-mous desperado. He had joined the posse and been accepted by the sheriff simply because he was known for courage, and because he would do his best in all situations — also because he was very well mounted.

Now The Shadow looked about him. It was barely possible that they were out of earshot of the camp, and he might well say that here he and Lang sighted The Shadow in the night, exchanged shots, and the outlaw escaped while Harry Lang fell. He turned to Lang, therefore, with a word of hate forming on his lips, when an excited whisper came from Lang:

"Look yonder! Ain't that a camp?"

The Shadow turned, and far off he made out the glimmer of a fire. He immediately recognized the direction. It was the same fire by which he had sat with Scottie and Limpy. At the thought of Scottie, he shrugged his shoulders. Suppose the vagabond should tell what he knew — but there was little fear of that. Scottie's dread of the outlaw was too complete. In the meantime, though he could have sworn that Tom Converse would never be so rash as to sit by any fire that night, the light might be an excuse to lead Harry still farther away.

"Ain't that what I said we'd find?" he asked. "Come on!"

"It's someone else," muttered Harry. "The Shadow wouldn't be fool enough to —"

"But he might be dare-devil enough to. And think of the easy shot we'll have! The Shadow against the light of his own fire! Who could ask for a better target than that?"

There was no resisting such a temptation. The

fire of the hunter entered the veins of Harry Lang at once.

"Take the near side, and I'll take the far side," he whispered, and with a wave of his hand he glided away beyond the trunk of a huge tree.

The Shadow cursed softly. He by no means wanted that separation from his victim-to-be.

"Wait!" he called.

But, as he hurried around the tree in pursuit, he was stopped by an impenetrable wall of thicket. He sprang back and ran down to the opening which he thought Lang had taken.

When, after a moment, he did not overtake his former companion, he stopped to listen. There was no sound. The double veils of shrubbery and darkness walled him away from Lang. What a devilish trick of fate this was!

He called aloud. There was no answer. There was nothing left for him but to continue even as he had planned with Lang and bag in their net — two hobos!

At the thought of this wasted effort he ground his teeth in rage. However, on their way back to the other camp fire something might be done.

In the meantime, the gray of the early morning was growing. It was not distinguishable when one looked straight ahead beneath the trees, but was barely noticeable when, looking up, the black treetops were found more distinctly outlined against the sky.

In a little while he found himself at the edge of the clearing where the fire threw up a narrow tongue of flame. About it on the ground were stretched the two forms of the tramps, and he could make out the grizzled features of Scottie, the leaner face of Limpy.

Looking to the side, he saw the horse of Scottie — for the lame man always made his journeys on loot — and still farther away were the forms of two other horses.

Here his heart sprang into his throat. Unless he dreamed, yonder was Captain, his sleek coat of darkly dappled chestnut shining faintly by the firelight. Twice the outlaw rubbed his hand heavily across his eyes, but the vision would not fade. It was Captain beyond doubt.

Realizing now that his vague guess had been the truth, after all, he swept the ground with a more careful scrutiny. Beyond the gray and the chestnut horses he saw two other forms prostrate. Ben Plummer and Tom Converse, beyond question.

But how should he tell?

In his joy a certain humility entered. There they lay in his power. With one whistle he would bring Captain back to him and Tom Converse sitting stupidly erect, sleepily awaiting the bullet which would end his life.

For that shot he made himself ready by kneeling, drawing the rifle butt carefully to his shoulder and holding the weapon ready for a quick sight and shot. He could not miss at that distance!

In the meantime, Harry Lang must be somewhere beyond.

He whistled — the light, sharp note to which he had trained Captain to respond. There was instant response from the beautiful chestnut. It threw up its head, whirled, broke the rotten rope end that held it, and came trotting toward the place where The Shadow knelt.

Indeed, so instant was that response that it hurried the second and more important part of The Shadow's plan. As Tom Converse started erect from his blankets, the stallion trotted straight into the line between him and the rifle of the outlaw.

Jim Cochrane, cursing through his teeth, jumped to the side and aimed again, but the golden opportunity was tarnished. Tom Converse, with incredible speed taking in the whole situation, had flung himself on his side and rolled over and over the half dozen feet which separated him from the timber at the edge of the circle.

The outlaw fired twice in quick succession, but Tom Converse was out of sight and out of harm's way among the trees.

Cochrane swung his rifle back as he himself drew close behind a thick trunk. In the center of the circle, near the fire, lay the two tramps, with their two pairs of hands thrust up into the air, neither of them daring to stir from this attitude of surrender. There was a devilish impulse in Cochrane to send a bullet crashing through one of those arms, snapping the bone like a pipe-stem.

Instead, he turned it on a broader object. Young Ben Plummer had come to his feet and was plunging toward safety. It was half a stride away from him when The Shadow jerked his gun-butt back into the hollow of his shoulder and fired. Ben whirled with a scream of pain, faced The Shadow with arms outstretched, pitched forward, and lay writhing.

"Head him off!" shouted The Shadow. "Head him off, Lang!"

"I'm here!" yelled Lang's excited, panting voice in answer.

And then came a call: "Captain!"

The chestnut checked his trot toward The Shadow which he had maintained in spite of the shooting.

"Steady, boy!" cried The Shadow and stretched out his arm and showed the upper part of his shoulder to attract the horse. Instantly his own rifle — how well he recognized the ring of the explosion! — went off among the trees on the far side of the clearing, and a bullet clipped past that exposed shoulder, just slicing the skin as though with a razor edge.

He drew back in astonishment. This was marksmanship worthy of himself — worthy of the gun which was being used! No carelessness hereafter.

"You dog," cried the strong voice of Tom Converse, "I'll kill you by inches for dropping the kid! Captain!"

This time Captain turned toward the voice which called. Sweat broke out on the face of the outlaw. Had his own horse been taught, so soon, another signal to which he responded more readily than to the whistle?

He whistled again, the sound cutting through the voice of Converse as the latter called for the third time. But now the stallion merely shook his head in defiance of the summons of his old master and trotted toward the far side of the clearing.

Madness stormed up into the brain of Cochrane. In his fury he caught up the gun and trained it on the head of the horse. If he could not mount the animal, no other man should. Besides, mounted on that horse, Tom Converse would ride to safety — which meant that eventually he would ride back into good terms with the powers of the law.

And then, just as the rifle was trained on the head of the galloping chestnut, just as the sight caught a dead center and his forefinger curled around the trigger, the gun of Tom Converse exploded, and the heavy slug struck the barrel of The Shadow's weapon and knocked it shivering to one side.

Here was shooting indeed! Before the outlaw could recover his poise, the stallion had hurtled out of the clearing and plunged into the thicket on the farther side to safety and to Tom Converse!

There was only one hope to stop him, now that horse and man were united, and that was through the efforts of Harry Lang. But at the thought of Lang beating down such a man as Tom Converse had this night proved himself to be, The Shadow groaned, and in his desperation, he left cover and raced across the clearing in pursuit, exposed to death.

Chapter Thirty-Six

Black Looks

No bullet greeted him, and he well knew why! The fugitive had flung himself on the back of the chestnut and, believing that the entire posse was gathering to surround him, had galloped off through the night, bareback, guiding Captain with touches of his hands.

Following that sound of crashing through the shrubbery, Jim Cochrane dashed on, only praying that he might be able to gain a fleeting glimpse by which to send a bullet home, for now the quickening dawn gave a ghostly light which might be sufficient.

But, as he swerved down a natural path in the shrubbery, he turned a corner at a blind speed and crashed into Harry Lang, running in the opposite direction. The impact of the squat, compact bulk of Lang cast him reeling until he lay flat on his back.

He recovered to a sitting position with the speed of a spring coiling, and there stood honest Harry Lang, whose death he had vowed, gasping and panting and staring at him in the gray of the morning.

"Lord!" cried Lang. "For a minute I thought

you was The Shadow —"

"You fool!" snarled The Shadow, bringing his rifle around so that it covered his man squarely. "I'm the man!"

"The what?"

"The Shadow! I brought you out here to tell you that I've come back to get even for that time you and Sherman and Chuck Parker waited in the hollow —"

Harry Lang drew back, agape with horror.

"You rat!" The Shadow went on relentlessly. "Now, I'm going to finish you, and Tom Converse will get the blame of it! A fool to kill a fool!"

He touched the trigger, and Harry Lang slumped heavily to one side and lay moveless in the path. There was an inert bulk to his fall that reminded the outlaw of the fall of a steer under the butcher's mallet.

Then, remembering, he listened. There was noise in the clearing, but noise of many noises, not of two. What had happened? The sleepless sheriff — that suspicious cat of a man!

He stood looking down at the body in the path. Then he caught the hair of Harry's head and jerked up his face. Even in the dim light he could see the gash of the bullet where it had struck his man squarely in the center of the forehead.

Instant death it must have been, he decided; but the man must not lie here, even if his death were to be attributed to the work of The Shadow. With amazing strength, considering his slightness of body, he lifted Harry Lang, carted him a few steps aside from the path, and cast him down heavily on some rocks among the trees.

He heard the bone of one of the dangling arms snap — a muffled, ugly sound which was disagreeable even to the ear of The Shadow; but he shrugged his shoulders at the thought and turned back toward the clearing.

He found it a mass of milling horses. In the firelight knelt Sylvia Rann, at the side of her foster brother. Was the young rat dead? Had Scottie or Limpy told who did the shooting? No, they would not have told, even had they known. Their dread of The Shadow was too complete for that. Yet Cochrane would have given ten thousand dollars to have rubbed their knowledge about him out of their minds.

He broke through the little crowd. There was the quiet sheriff, still on horseback.

"What's happened?"

"We came out, Harry Lang and me," said Cochrane, "to try to hunt up The Shadow, because we had an idea that he might be somewhere around. We found him here just the way I thought we'd find him, though I didn't have no idea that we could ever catch the fool taking chances with a camp fire. Here we found him, and Captain along with him, also Ben Plummer. We missed The Shadow when he rolled into the woods, but Lang shot Plummer while he was trying to get away. The Shadow called Captain to him and broke off through the woods, with Lang and me after him. Lang got close enough to get in a shot.

I heard it. But he didn't let out no yell, so I guess he didn't get The Shadow; but he kept right on running. I came back."

"That accounts for the last shot we heard," said the sheriff, though still his burning eyes would not leave The Shadow. "That accounts for it, I guess."

"One lie was told there," said a voice which seemed to speak from the ground — a weak and broken voice.

The Shadow turned on his heel. It was Ben Plummer who had spoken.

"The lie that was told," said Ben, "is that Harry Lang shot me. I heard Lang's voice. It was straight ahead of me. It was him that spoke just now, that shot me from behind!"

So saying, he heaved himself up with great difficulty, half breaking away from the hands of his foster sister and Chuck Parker, who attended him. Having cast a wild glance around him, he was able to pick out The Shadow; he pointed a trembling arm toward the latter.

"Him!" he said and dropped back, fainting.

Sylvia Rann cast at the outlaw one glance of horror and anguish and then leaned with a groan over Ben Plummer, but Chuck Parker cheered her.

"He was born lucky," he said. "That slug hit him on the ribs, and, instead of going plumb through him the way it ought to've gone, it skidded around his ribs and come out in front. He's losing strength pretty fast, but, if that wound

296

is plugged up and they ain't no dirt in it, he'd ought to come along pretty smart!"

She gave him brief thanks for that news.

In the meantime, the others were gathering about the sheriff at his command. He gave swift directions. Two of the men were to stay behind to take care of Sylvia Rann and her wounded foster brother, while Scottie and Limpy were to be sent into town to get help for them. The horse of Harry Lang would be left in the clearing, where he was sure to return for it after he had tired of his mad run after the mounted Shadow.

With the ten remaining, including himself, the sheriff would push instantly on in pursuit of the fugitive. He gave the command; The Shadow leaped into the saddle of his bay, which they had brought up for him, and was off with the cluster of hard riders, smashing through the shrubbery. But the sheriff himself lingered for an instant and reined his horse close to the white-faced girl.

She sprang up and caught both his hands.

"You'll give him a chance — a good fighting chance?" she begged.

"As good a chance as any man ever had," the sheriff assured her.

"And you'll try to believe what I've told you about The Shadow?"

He shook his head. "If Cochrane is The Shadow — then he ain't The Shadow. He's the devil! But I know this much, that he's a slippery customer. I'm watching him as close as I can. Will you rest happy with that?"

"I'll try to. Heaven bless you, sheriff!"

He waved his hat to her, whirling his mount at the same time, and so he was gone catapulting among the trees, and then out of sight at once in the shadows of the young dawn.

In that group of hard-riding men, The Shadow kept somewhat to the rear and to one side, though the bay had proved sufficient of foot to keep well ahead of the fastest sprinter of the lot. But, fast as the bay was, it could not live for a minute against the terrific pace which The Shadow well knew Tom Converse could establish and maintain on the back of the chestnut. He could only hope for one thing, so far as the immediate capture of the fugitive was concerned, and that was that, through his ignorance of the ground over which he was riding, he would make some blunder which would cost him a fatal amount of space and time. In the meantime, he kept this rather rearward position, not only because, through his adventure of the night, he had proved himself of sufficient courage, but because he wanted to study the faces of his companions.

It had seemed to him, in the clearing, that they had been strangely backward in their manner with him. Now, as he glanced them over one by one and directed the bay so that he came up to them one after another, he saw unmistakable signs of aversion on their part.

They swerved away from him almost instinctively, and he knew that someone had been spreading a bad opinion about him among them. Could it have been the work of the clever old sheriff himself? Or had the stormy words of the girl had an effect? Or was this all because they penetrated through the mask and on their own account recognized him as a foe and detested him for what they guessed him to be?

At any rate, the feeling which he sensed in them made him hate them with an intense hatred. He hated them as we are too apt to hate persons whom we have wronged. Let them feel as they might on suspicion, he would give them all ample cause to lament the day they had ever laid eyes on him.

He was beginning to see that this was the end of his masked career. Before this adventure was a thing of the past, the world would know the face and features of the true Shadow.

It was the crisp, early time of the dawn when they broke out of the wood and came onto the brow of a pleasant hill. There, by common assent, they reduced the pace and let their horses fall into a rolling canter which they could maintain endlessly.

"We can't expect to outrun him," the sheriff said. "We can only hope to keep within some sort of striking distance."

While they cantered on in this manner, The Shadow spoke to the deputy sheriff.

"Shriner," he said, pulling his bay alongside the grim-faced jail keeper, "what started you and the rest of the boys out of the camp tonight?"

"Why d'you ask?" commented the uncommunicative deputy.

"Because when I left the camp everybody was snoozing sound and dead to the world."

"Go ask the sheriff," said the deputy. "It was his idea. If I'd been in his place, I'd have kept 'em stirring around all night. We nearly caught The Shadow with two men — we'd sure've bagged him with a dozen!"

Accordingly, the outlaw swung over beside the sheriff himself.

"Well," he said, "what's the news, sheriff? What started you out on the road tonight?"

"D'you want to know?"

"That's why I asked."

"Well, Cochrane, I scented something. You see?"

And he turned on the outlaw a face wrinkled with the faintest of smiles.

Jim Cochrane pondered over that remark for a moment in silence. At length he remarked: "But what's the matter with the rest of the boys, Thomas? They look at me as if I was poison or something. What's been at them that they give me so many black looks?"

"I'll tell you how it is," said the sheriff with perfect good nature. "You see, all of us have figured, right from the start, that Ben Plummer was only a kid, and that there would be no need of handling him particular rough. It sort of rode the boys a bit to see that you'd shot to kill when you shot him down. But maybe you didn't know about Ben being just a fool kid?"

"I didn't," said The Shadow shortly.

"That explains. Matter of fact, soon as he stands his trial, there won't be nothing to it. He was getting all of his bad time in jail, by agreement; and when he comes to trial he'll be let off easy. All he needs is a lesson — you see?"

"I see," answered The Shadow.

He dropped back and rode apart from the rest. It was easy to tell that in a crisis all hands would be against him.

Chapter Thirty-Seven

Deadly Ground

The hills broke into a pleasant little valley. Twice against the distant sky, sweeping over the hills, they had made out the form of the fugitive on Captain.

"Funny that he keeps this way," said the sheriff, more and more concerned as the flight continued. "They ain't no good hole-in-the-wall country ahead here, so far as I know about, unless he plumb disappears into the sand! No, sir, he seems to be heading right down the valley for Curtin! Darned if he don't! And why he wants to come near a town — who can tell? He's sure a queer boy, that Shadow! Seems to me almost like he lacks sense in some ways!"

But the real Shadow, listening, chuckled softly with pleasure. He began to realize what he had surmised before — that this was a strange country to Tom Converse; and, if that were so, he was indubitably lost!

His pleasure increased with every mile that they put behind them. Still Tom Converse headed straight down the valley, running his head into trouble with every stride. Curtin was a town which would respond to the alarm of The Shadow

302

like a swarming nest of hornets.

Now the valley narrowed, with a range of hills growing higher on either hand, and still the fugitive did not turn, until at length, letting out a few links on Captain, he sent that matchless horse out of view into the distance.

The posse, in the meantime, quickened its pace also to keep as near to the rider of the chestnut as possible. Soon, flinging over the top of a rise of ground, they came full in view of the town of Curtin in the distance.

Here the fugitive must have turned. They rode to the first house on their right, and there they made their inquiries. The answer was better than their fondest dreams. Yes, the rider of the chestnut had passed that way. He had passed that way, turned to the right as he viewed the town, and then galloped over the hill toward Curtin River.

There was a shout of triumph from the posse. Even old Sheriff Thomas, white with excitement as he saw ahead of him victory in this, the greatest effort of his long life, cried out and struck his gloved hands together.

Then he turned hastily, picked out the rider of a fast-stepping young brown mare, and sent him down the road to Curtin to call out every man and boy who could ride a horse and carry a gun.

"Tell 'em I want 'em all!" roared the sheriff. "We've got him bagged, I think — the greatest catch that was ever made. But the Lord knows why he's riding that way unless he's gone crazy! Ride, ride, ride! We need speed!"

The man on the brown mare darted off, leaning far over the neck of his mount and flogging with his quirt at every jump. The sheriff changed the direction of the others with a sweep of his hand, and they tore off up the long slope to the right.

"But he ain't going to take to the timber," said Deputy Sheriff Shriner through his teeth as he galloped at the side of Algie Thomas.

"I dunno," groaned Algie Thomas. "I don't dare do no thinking. I don't dare!"

And so they swept up over the brow of the hill. Below them lay, far down the hillside, a considerable grove of trees, chiefly willows, and beyond the willows rolled up other hills.

Why this should be a trap was not at first apparent to a stranger. It seemed a simple matter to ride down through those trees and up over the easy slopes of the hills beyond; but the posse paid no heed to the trees or the hills beyond them. It paid no heed, but every man looked eagerly up and down the valley. There was no horseman in view, though they could look for miles in either direction, where the trees thinned out on each side, and the narrow waters of a creek were visible.

"He's in!" shouted the sheriff.

"He's in!" whispered the deputy sheriff, his lips curling.

Without a word, The Shadow simply took out his rifle and began to clean and reload it.

"Here's nine of us!" cried the sheriff. "We'd ought to be able to cover this side of the trap pretty well. Spread out! Spread out! Each gent get an equal distance from the gents on each side of him. Then take to some kind of cover, leave your hosses, and lie down. Every man lie down."

The injunction was obeyed quickly, and the nine strung out — with wide spaces between them, to be sure — all along the side of the hill, a hundred yards to each man, so that they spread in a loose arc clear across the face of the wood — or, rather, along the hills commanding the wood and commanding, also, each end, where the trees tapered off and disappeared.

The trap was closed; at least it was closed as well as nine men could close it. But, though every man had a hundred yards on either side of him to sweep with his rifle, they were no ordinary shots, and lucky indeed would Tom Converse be if ever he got out of that danger.

What made the place a trap was simply that the waters of Curtin River, flowing harmlessly through the rolling hills, here dipped into a depression. In an ordinary depression, of course, a lake would have been formed, with trees growing about its banks, a pleasant place to rest the eye. But this hollow was made strange by the nature of the thin, loose soil; and in place of a lake there existed a famous and hideous bog known far and wide through the mountains as Curtin quicksands.

Beyond those trees it lay, and before one could

pass through the forest and gain the pleasant hills beyond, there had to be passed a flat, deadly stretch of ground which was neither solid nor liquid, but a horrible mixture, too treacherously thin to sustain a weight, and too terribly thick for swimming.

Many a man and many a horse had been claimed by those sands in bursting suddenly out of the rim of the willows and striking, almost without warning from the moisture of the soil, the deadly bog. Once it laid its grip on the unfortunate, no bulldog could be more tenacious; mere struggling only served to send the condemned deeper and deeper until the quicksand reached the lips, bubbled once — and then death in its most horrible form.

That was why the watchers on the hillside, though their eyes shone in the anticipation of victory, had compressed their lips. It seemed unmanly to call in the assistance of such a horror in defeating even so terrible a criminal as The Shadow.

But the great question remained: Why had The Shadow, knowing the country like the pages of a book, chosen this direction? The deputy sheriff, Joe Shriner, gave the only possible solution.

"He was in a daydream, curse him!" said Joe. "That must've been it. He was planning some deviltry. Pray Heaven he won't wake up to where he is until he feels the sands sucking him down!"

Chapter Thirty-Eight

Into the Quicksands

There was at least one great truth in what Shriner said, for, when Tom Converse rode over the hill, he had no concern in his mind save for poor Ben Plummer. That the boy was killed by the shot of The Shadow, he had not the slightest doubt. His own anger and regret rose when he thought that he had seen the face of his arch-enemy again and yet allowed the man to escape alive.

If only that shot, when he had fired at The Shadow in the shelter of the tree, had passed a couple of inches farther in and crashed through the bones of the shoulder joint! That wound would at least have ruined the outlaw's cruel activities with weapons for the rest of his life.

Such were the thoughts of the fugitive when he came down the valley in sight of the town of Curtin. He pulled up Captain, and then, shrugging his shoulders at the realization that he knew practically nothing of the country through which he was riding, he swung to the right and went up the long slope.

From the crest he saw a cheering prospect. The trees were green beneath the hillside, and, beyond the trees, easier hills rolled in the distance, hills up whose sides Captain could trot or gallop at ease.

So he loosed the reins, and down the hillside went the stallion like the wind, a pace so smoothly flowing that the heart of the rider leaped, and for the moment he forgot all about the troubles of Ben Plummer in sheer rejoicing that he was alive in such a joyous world.

Through the trees he plunged and rushed on, singing, though the presence of the thickening willows should have warned him that he was approaching water, at least.

But what did he care for water? Had he not seen the river farther up the valley and farther down, and was it not a mere glint of water? Indeed, all men wondered how such a stream could have supplied the water which made Curtin quicksands, but until they were drained it would never be known whether or not there were springs which contributed.

Such a petty stream as Tom Converse expected to meet could be cleared with ridiculous ease by Captain, and that was the reason he touched the good horse with his heel when he saw the trees thin out in front of him, and the brightness of daylight just beyond.

Through the last row of the willows they burst. Too late he saw the flat, shining horror before him. Too late gallant Captain flung back. They went crashing down the slope and into the midst of that glimmering slime.

Tom had time merely to clear his feet from the stirrups, and then he swung up his heels so that they rested above the surface of the sands into which Captain, struggling with terror, was sinking, and sinking the more rapidly with the violence of his struggles.

Swiftly Tom tore the heavy, coiled rope from beside the saddle. Then he made the rope-end taut around the horse and leaped for the safe shore. It gave under his feet, and he went down halfway to his knees in the deadly sands; but he threw himself forward on his face and so dragged himself to safety, still carrying the rope.

At that desertion, as he felt it to be, Captain neighed his agony — a cry in fear of death; and his struggles became so furious that now the shining shoulders sank out of sight in the black stuff. All around him, small, heavy waves of oil-filmed quicksand moved away from him and returned, drawing him deeper and deeper.

Tom Converse, with a sick heart, found the first strong willow and turned the rope around it with all his strength. Too much strength it was, for it merely forced the stallion an inch forward and two inches down.

Captain's struggles would quickly kill him, and Tom called frantically to him to be still.

"Steady!" he called, the order which always transferred the stallion to a rock of stillness. "Steady, Captain!"

And behold the struggles ceased, and the brave ears pricked. There was only the panting breath which whistled in and out of the shining, red-rimmed nostrils.

Tom ran back, loosened the rope, and, carrying it swiftly down the bank, he managed to make it pass under the chin of the horse before he tied it again around another trunk.

On that line, therefore, Captain could support his head, unless, in the frenzy of new struggles, he should throw his head entirely clear of the rope. Still, something must be done to keep him from sinking, in spite of the pull of the rope.

Sitting with his heels sunk in, and registering every gain he made by turning a half hitch around a stump, Tom commenced tugging with all his might. Inch by inch he saw the bulk of the stallion turned inland, until at length his head was faced directly ashore.

But now, with despair in his heart, and agony making him beat his hands together, Tom saw that he could never draw Captain in to safety. Already the quicksand had reached up nearly to those quivering nostrils, and, once the nostrils were touched, nothing could keep Captain from falling into another paroxysm of effort, which would surely send his head under the surface.

The hands of Tom had been torn raw by the rope, but, though he looked down at the lacerated palms, he did not feel the pain. The horrible certainty swept over him that Captain had come to the end of his glorious life, and the noble animal was dying with his own matchless courage, his eyes still bright with pleading and trust rather than terror, his ears pricking in a calm hope that the master would find some method of saving him.

Tom Converse closed his eyes. It seemed an eternity that he stood there, but, when he looked again, with the sweat pouring down his face, the head had sunk only a fraction of an inch, and he knew that his eternity of time had been, as a matter of fact, only a few seconds.

Suppose he were to run back and give himself up to the posse which by this time must have come close to the wood. Suppose he were to give himself up, and only ask as the price of his life that they come back with him and help him to save Captain?

He would have made that sacrifice gladly, had it not been for the knowledge that, long before he returned from such a quest, Captain's beautiful head would be beneath the surface, never to rise again.

Looking about him with helplessly moving hands, he saw near by a great dead trunk. Lightning might partly have blasted it, for surely no storm could have had the strength needed to uproot it.

Tom ran to it and tugged, hopeless of stirring it, but moved to action merely because it was impossible to stand quietly by while Captain died.

He seized it, tugged, and, to his consummate astonishment, the trunk was budged. No doubt the core of that trunk was rotted by time and long weathering. But now, in a frenzy of sudden hope, he called: "Steady, Captain! We'll win out yet!"

Then he laid hold of the trunk and put his might into the labor. It rolled toward him. He got behind it again, lifting with his arms, driving at it with his shoulders; and again it stirred. Into the work of moving that trunk those five desperate feet to where the shore toward the quicksand began to slope, Tom Converse gave his entire power.

In great moments we can use our strength in that manner. Stored in us and static, it can be loosed in some moments like a flash of electricity. Such was the strength which Tom Converse now gave like a prodigal. In thirty seconds he wearied himself. During that half of a minute he had poured out of every hidden recess in his being the last scruple of hoarded strength, and now, as he labored, he turned his head over his shoulder and saw that it was too late.

The head was down, far down in the slime, and the deadly stuff had even encroached on the straining red nostrils. Tom Converse staggered and groaned, and, as he gritted his teeth in that agony of hopelessness, a faint whinny came from the horse, not in mere terror, but as a sort of conversational expression of sympathy for the immense labors of the master.

That low call sent a thrill of new strength through Tom. He leaped back to his work, prying up the trunk with might and main, until, as his heart was nearly breaking with the struggle, the edge of the bank crumbled, and the mass of the trunk rolled by its own weight and impetus down toward the sands.

It struck the yielding edge of the slime. It cast a heavy splash a short distance on either side, and then it lurched down, threatening to strike the stallion and send him under.

Its weight, however, was too great for that. It passed beneath Captain's body, striking his forelegs and bringing him into sudden action.

That struggle, which would have ruined him before, saved him now. The hammering blows of his forehoofs drove the log slowly down, while at the same time those blows forced his own head and entire forehead above the ooze.

Battering his way, he came in, drawing his fine body inches out of the tenacious slime; and now his progress became quicker and quicker.

Tom Converse, lying in a state of collapse on the bank, saw the gallant horse winning his way little by little, saw his head raised higher, heard his loud snorts of effort; and at length he won in until his feet were on the firm ground. A moment more, and a convulsive effort had drawn him in, and he was shoving his muddy, dripping muzzle in the face of the master.

Chapter Thirty-Nine

The Impulse to Kill

It is strangely true that men, after great efforts in which they have won large rewards by their own unaided powers, become suddenly weak and simple and look about them for another being to whom they can render thanks.

While the trembling stallion nuzzled the face and hands of Tom Converse in grateful recognition of that salvation, poor Tom humbled his heart as he had never humbled it before and gave thanks to God.

He sat up, at length, and, when the buzzing had passed from his ears, he stood up on shaking legs. It was strange how completely he had spent his entire powers in the labor of moving that giant log. But it was stranger still that he could have moved the log at all. Looking down at the forest of branches and the huge, thick stump which thrust out from the black quicksands, it seemed to Tom that a giant must have stood on the shore the moment before and been at work.

He took a small, stout willow twig, then, and with quick strokes whipped the slime from the body of Captain. He picked up a few handfuls of dead grass and rubbed him down so that, except for the stains on the saddle — which Tom had carried when he dashed away from the posse, and which he had placed upon Captain when he had ridden to temporary safety — the noble chestnut was nearly as well off as he had ever been, save for the weariness caused by his work to get free. Even the rifle, secured by the tight case in which it lay, had sustained no injury.

The sight of that rifle, as he drew it forth, brought home to Tom the situation in which he stood there. He had no time to waste.

How long he had been struggling to get the stallion from the sands, he had no way of guessing. It might all have passed in the space of a single minute; it might have been an hour. To judge by his own feelings, it had been weary years, for he felt greatly aged. But, no matter what the elapsed time had been, the thing for him now was to get out of the trees at once and string across the country in a straight line toward safety.

Even then he must be in doubt as to the ability of the chestnut to stand a long run. It was impossible to tell how much the good horse had been exhausted by the efforts it made in the marsh, but, with the aid of a few long-range shots from his rifle, he should be able to keep the posse at arm's length, so to speak.

He gave the stallion a chance to regain his wind, at least, by letting him go unridden toward the outer rim of the trees. Running on ahead to recover the possession of his own nerves, Tom found that Captain trotted at his heels like a dog!

Nearing the edge of the trees, he felt his heart jump with relief, for, so far as he could see in any direction, looking past the trunks, there was no sign or sound of the horsemen approaching. Might it not be that they had missed the trail?

He came to the limits of the wood and received instant announcement of where that posse was. Though the hillside seemed swept clean of all living things; yet the bare rocks spurted fire, and two bullets chipped past the head of Tom with a wicked singing.

He leaped backward and sidewise to the shelter of a stout trunk as two more bullets followed. There was a yell of triumph from the marksmen up the slope.

Apparently, they thought that they had hit their mark at the second fire, for now one of them started to his feet. Tom jerked up the rifle which he had carried slung under his arm. It was so simple a shot that he almost fired automatically, but he checked himself in time.

Instead, he gave them a shrewd warning. He raised the rifle and fired twice, as quickly as his finger could press the trigger. The first shot smashed to pieces the pipe which the fellow carried between his teeth — turned to the side so that it offered a fair mark — and the second shot splashed on a rock at the very feet of the man. If he were not a fool, he would know that one who could plant two shots so accurately at head and feet, could easily split the difference and drive a slug through his heart.

Indeed, as the man toppled back into his shelter with a yell, Tom felt like registering in his life account: One man saved from death, for never in his life had he been so close to shooting to kill.

In the meantime, his fire was answered by others up and down the hill. They had scattered along its entire length, he could see, and now he understood fully, as the bullets crashed through the branches above him or thudded into the trunks around him, that the trap which they had closed on him was very nearly sealed tight.

To make sure, having sent Captain back a little distance, he himself retired a few ranges of trees and then picked out a tree a little taller than the others. He ventured to climb among the branches.

He did not go high — certainly not high enough to expose himself to easy view of the posse, but he at least reached such a height that he secured a viewpoint which allowed his eye to plunge down at an angle on the hill. In this fashion he could distinguish the posse in their places of concealment.

Of the nine men, he could see the five most immediately opposed to him. As a rule they had simply dropped down behind the first large stones which they found, and here they waited, rather securely sheltered from breast-high fire, but quite exposed to the angling bullets which Tom Converse, wedged between trunk and bough on his tree, was able to send at them.

317

He poised his rifle, thoughtful. If he were to start shooting, he could kill a man with every shot. Two shots would destroy the two men directly opposite him, and then, when they saw what was being done, the others in view would probably jump up and take to their heels to find stronger shelter. Or, if they dared to stand their ground, it would be a simple matter to drop them in quick succession — the magazine of his gun was full! Then, calling Captain directly under the tree, he himself could swing down swiftly through the branches, drop into the saddle, and spur like a bullet through the gap which only dead men guarded — and so again safety. The chances were hard to take, to be sure, but they were at least one to three in his favor.

He turned and whistled softly, so that the sound could reach the horse but not the men who watched on the outside. Presently he saw Captain coming, and at length the chestnut stood beneath the tree and whinnied softly, very softly, when he looked up and saw the master.

After that, Tom raised his rifle, and down the shining barrel he looked full into the face of Deputy Sheriff Joe Shriner behind the rocks directly opposite!

Of all men in the world, there was only one whose life he would sooner take in this manner, striking unseen. He looked to the right, and there he beheld the meager, swarthy face of The Shadow!

Surely fate had placed these two before him!

He could see the outlaw twisting a little this way and that. It was Shriner who had, in the first place, jumped up, and from whose mouth the pipe had been knocked. How sore his teeth must be now!

Tom Converse chuckled softly at the thought, and, having laughed even at so small a jest, his humor was suddenly softened throughout. Again he looked down the sights, training the weapon full on the head of The Shadow — him first, and then the burly form of Shriner to follow.

But his forefinger was cold and numb. It would not operate, so it seemed, in response to his will. How could he press that trigger and send the spirit out of the body of a living man? No matter if those two out yonder were now hungering with all their hearts to do to him what he now had in his power to do so easily to them. The fact remained that these were human creatures, and that to destroy one of them was to put a curse on his own head.

Never was that greatest of all great moral lessons learned with more difficulty. He lowered the rifle, and, in lowering it, he knew that he was giving up practically all hope for his life. That seemed the one gate through which he could possibly escape, and, with that gate closed, a wretched death at the hands of the posse awaited him.

There would be no trial. Even when he was in the hotel, the sheriff had been unable definitely to promise him the right of a trial in the face of the enraged mob. Now that they had ridden so far and so long in the pursuit, there would be no holding them when they found in their power the man they thought to be The Shadow.

As he lowered the rifle, he saw his last hope shut off, indeed, for there was roaring in the distance like the roaring of the wind, far off, and now over the top of the hill came a mingled rout of men, old and young, even boys. They came on every sort of horse imaginable. They came with every species of gun; also shotguns, rifles of every age, revolvers of every make; and this horde spread down the hillside, scattering out like water from the sprinkler-nozzle of a hose.

They came shouting and throwing up their hands, and the nine men in hiding behind the rocks, as though realizing that the death of one or two could now be no object to The Shadow except to whet the appetite of the avengers, also sprang up exposing themselves recklessly, and greeted the crowd from Curtin with a wild dance of joy.

It was the end of The Shadow. Every one could feel that; and Tom Converse, crouched among the branches of the tree, sighed and bowed his head.

There was only one great question remaining to be answered, so it seemed, and that was: How long could he hold out in the wood without food?

Chapter Forty

Harry Lang's Courage

It was toward noon of that day when, on the rocks where The Shadow had dropped him, Harry Lang stirred, groaned, and then sat up, spurred into activity by the stabbing pangs which darted through him from his broken arm.

As for his head, there was at first no feeling in it whatever. By the aid of his left arm, he managed to drag himself erect, grasping at the bushes around him. He then pulled his right arm around and stared at it, fascinated.

What had happened, he could not remember. His mind worked not on the past at all, but was fully occupied with the present. At first all he noted, besides the exquisite agony of that arm, was that his right hand lay in his lap in a strange position — a twisted and singular position such as he had never seen it assume before.

This was odd, exceedingly. Moreover, a mask seemed to be glued to his face. He raised his hand. His face was covered with scales. It was like dried mud. He lowered his hand, and on his fingertips adhered some of the scales, a deep red. Red mud? No. Then he knew what it was.

He leaned back against the tree, sick at heart

with the pain, and gradually he began to remember how he and Jim Cochrane had left the camp; how they had stalked through the wood hunting for The Shadow; how they had come at length on the camp fire with the dappled chestnut in sight; how the shots had been fired; how The Shadow, so it seemed, had escaped; and how, as he ran through the woods in pursuit, hoping to get in a shot by the dawn light, he had crashed into Cochrane.

That speech of Cochrane had burned into his memory. He was the real Shadow, and he had come to repay the bullet which Harry Lang had sent into his body that night, two years before, when the three lay in wait in the hollow.

Then the rifle had exploded. There had been a blow on his head — darkness. He raised his hand and felt a great welt in the center of his forehead and, above it, a gash extending across the top of his head, concealed by the hair, which was matted with crimson. Then he could understand.

The bullet had glanced up from his forehead and plowed across the top of his head, but The Shadow, looking at him, had seen what seemed the beginning of a wound that passed straight through the head of his victim.

Jess Sherman had been found dead with exactly such a wound.

Then surety came to the injured man. Jim Cochrane was indeed The Shadow, and he lived and rode with the posse under the guise of a law-abiding citizen, hunting down an innocent man who would die for his crimes! With his death The Shadow would be washed clean of guilt!

With that thought, the sweat started out on the face of honest Harry Lang. He sprang to his feet, and for a time he was able to well-nigh run through the woods, until he came to the clearing where Scottie and Limpy had built the camp fire around which so much had happened. But now no one was there. The surface of the ground was cut up by the trampling of many horses, but there was no sign of a human being.

How recently they had left — that was attested by the fact that the little stream of water which had been so crystal clear was still running muddy. At the sight of it, Harry Lang dropped down to the ground with a groan. He had realized in a flash how far he had to walk before he would reach a house, and the realization sickened him.

Never could he do it, he felt. Not only was there the agony of that arm dangling at his side, but also his head was light, and there was a sound as though a seashell had been pressed to his ear. Sooner or later the waves of blackness which surged in his brain would overwhelm him, and he would lose consciousness.

He might fall, then, and never waken; he might fall and die there in the forest. But that was not the thing which haunted him with fear. The great horror was that an innocent man might die in the place of the doubly guilty Shadow, with The Shadow himself officiating in a leading rôle in the destruction.

Men on the verge of delirium are most apt to receive obsessions, and this became the delirious dread of Harry Lang.

He managed to construct a sling, tearing his silken bandanna to pieces with his left hand and his teeth. That sling he passed around his neck and under his right forearm, so that it might support the weight and make the agony more endurable. Then he stumbled to his feet and started to walk.

The first 100 yards were the hardest, for every step was now a hot thrust of pain, and in his brain the waves of blackness swept to and fro, threatening to cover his senses. He fought a double battle — against sheer pain and against sheer weakness.

After the first 100 yards the problem was simplified. He consigned the physical agony to his subconscious mind. He was so desperately set on reaching men and making them understand that The Shadow they hunted was not the real Shadow that he could have walked through fire without feeling the flames.

If only he could draw out of the air, by prayer, strength enough to carry him to the house of a man! He knew the path, and he knew the man who lived nearest. It was Jerry Loftus in his red-roofed house. From any of the surrounding hills one could always see the bright red of that house among the trees.

The dizzy mind of the wounded man carried him off to other days when he had ridden the ridges of those hills and looked down on the splotch of bright, cheerful color, but he fought off that dreamy feeling with a sudden touch of terror. That dreaminess was his greatest enemy. He must not allow it to gain on him; but gain it would, in spite of himself.

Once he wakened with a start, to find that he had been walking in his sleep, and that he had wandered to a strange road. It cost him half an hour of traveling in a circle before he was able to locate the right way again.

Worst of all was the feeling that often swept over him, always with that delirious horror, that he was on the wrong path even when he was on the right one; and always he had to stop and lean against a tree and so convince himself by degrees, as he forced his mind to clear, that it was actually the correct, the familiar path.

Then he would stumble on again, but every mile was costing him terribly. Alternate waves of heat and cold began to rush over him, shaking him to the heart. His throat was incredibly parched, and when he knelt and leaned over to satisfy his burning thirst at a little stream that crossed the way, he nearly dropped senseless as the pulses pounded in his head.

As he staggered on, he became possessed with the dreadful certainty that it was not life fluid which flowed in his veins, but a liquid fire cunningly placed there by the devil for his torment on earth.

He went on, forcing himself each step of the way. It was not for himself. It was for that innocent man who was pursued by the hounds of the law, and he kept muttering to himself, as he staggered on, that unless he hurried with great speed, it would be too late.

Then, wakening from one of his walking sleeps, he saw that it was sunset, and against the sunset there was a house with a red roof. Or was that the color of the sunset and not the roof? Vaguely it dawned on him that, no matter whose house, this was a place where he would find a man, and that man would help him to get to the rest of the world the news that Jim Cochrane was The Shadow!

He almost ran the last few steps. He reached the little house. He beat on the door. He yelled.

There was no answer save only the echo of the noise as it passed through the interior of the building. He reeled to a window, dragged it open, thrust in his head, and shouted again. Still no answer came; and then, going back to the front door, he found a card thrust under one of the little moldings with which it was trimmed. On the card was written a sentence which danced under his darkening eyes. At length he made it out: "Back Wednesday."

Harry Lang collapsed on the veranda and lay in a faint. When he recovered, it was cool of night, and that coolness brought him to; yet it was not quite dark. He could see the road wandering past the house, a white streak through the evening, and that reminded him of the work which lay before him.

Of course, another man would long since have fallen into a swoon from which there would have been no waking, but Harry Lang had the natural strength of a bull. He got onto that road, walked half a mile, and pitched onto his face.

Half an hour later he wakened again, and again he went on. All was black before him now, and he stretched out his hands. Only luck kept him on the road in his delirium, and it was in this whirling state of mind that he heard behind him a brief rumbling sound. He listened to it with a curious and puzzled interest.

Then he recognized it. It was the sound of a buggy rolling across a wooden culvert which had been built into the winding forest road. The thought of help again carried through his mind the reason that he was struggling on to find human beings. It was not for his own sake, but for the sake of him who was being hunted as The Shadow.

He ran down the road — it was a staggering run no faster than an ordinary man's walk. His arms were outstretched, and he thought he was shouting for them to pull up and wait for him. In reality, he was uttering a hideous, thick-throated scream.

Sturdy Jefferson Lander drew up his nag with an exclamation of dismay and reached for his revolver. Strange things had happened on that road, and many a man had been the victim of a holdup within the space of this last half mile. He poised the weapon just as he was able to make out a figure running toward him, the figure of a man!

He drew down on the target, setting his teeth. He had never before pointed his weapon at a human being, but now he would shoot and shoot to kill. In his pocket was fifty dollars. He would risk his life for the sake of it; but, with his forefinger curling around the trigger, he saw that the figure wavered from side to side.

The horrible sound came again, not a threat, but a scream of despair and pain, a thick sound in which there was an attempt at syllabification, but the words could not be distinguished.

It was enough to make Jeff Lander lower his gun; and then to his utter amazement, he saw the figure collide with his horse, and, while the latter snorted, the man dropped back and lay inert in the dust, groaning.

Here was an adventure which would hold his wife and all his family breathless. The good man climbed down from his seat, still carrying his revolver tightly gripped.

The man did not stir when he leaned over him and called. He lighted a match, and as the light flared, it showed a face covered with dried crimson, with a ghastly, gaping wound in the forehead, the eyes open and staring. It was like a mask of death in its most grisly form.

The thick lips, swollen out of shape, were moving, and, as the farmer leaned lower with a gasp of horror, he was seized by a trembling hand while he made out the faint whisper: "The Shadow ain't The Shadow! For Heaven's sake go tell 'em! The Shadow ain't The Shadow!"

"The shadow ain't the shadow?" echoed the farmer. "Plumb delirious and probably dying! Lord spare him till I get him home!"

He gathered the ponderous body, lifting Lang in his strong arms, and carried him toward the buggy.

Chapter Forty-One

With the Besiegers

The long watch of the guards who had gathered along the hillside was not spent altogether in discomfort. As the time drew on toward evening, women came out from the town of Curtin and from neighboring farms, bringing with them whole buggies full of cooked food and sandwiches. Every woman in the countryside was as interested in the fall of The Shadow as were the men.

So they feasted and actually sang aloud songs in chorus within hearing of the supposed outlaw who was starving in the wood below them. But they took care, now, not to expose themselves unnecessarily, for sooner or later, like a mad dog, The Shadow would rush out at them and take what lives he could.

They were simply ranged behind the very crest of the hill. By this time there were fully 250 men lying out with revolvers and rifles, waiting for the end of the famous outlaw, every one of them feeling that there was an element of the heroic in their work, for crowds of the very bravest and kindest men are a little cowardly, a little cruel, and vastly apt to have the attitude of a power-swollen bully.

In their consciousness that The Shadow could not escape them, they exulted. There was absolutely no loop-hole, so far as could be seen. From one end of the forest to the other stretched the solid cordon. Upstream and downstream from the wood, men watched on improvised rafts. Neither by water nor land could he budge without encountering at least a score of determined enemies, with 200 more at a short distance away.

They waited with their horses kept in readiness for the impossible, if The Shadow should by a miracle succeed in breaking their lines. A plentiful supply of hay was brought out for the animals. In fact, a little impromptu city had sprung up for the sake of watching the outlaw.

It was just before sunset of that day that a ripple of excited comment broke out at one end of the semicircular line and ran all the way to the other end in a few moments.

The girl in the case had come. Sylvia Rann had arrived at Curtin quicksands to witness the death of her outlaw lover, said the rumor, and a quiver of excitement followed the tidings. They could not help pitying her, no matter how foolishly she might have placed her affections. Indeed, they could not help reverencing her, for she had remained loyal to The Shadow during the two years of his absence.

As very often happens, she received her applause for a thing deserving none. A foolish, romantic emotion had kept her so faithful to The Shadow, and had closed her ears and her mind to the truth about him. But now she was ready to fight and die for that man in the wood — that man who had never ever seen her face, but who had risked neck and all at her bidding.

The crowd, of course, could not read what was going on in her mind, and when she rode up to Sheriff Algie Thomas, there was a murmur of sympathy and admiration around her. Yet never had she looked less attractive. The wild night, the labor of the day, had told on her. Her eyes were sunken and deeply shadowed. Her face was drawn and colorless, and there was about her an expression of haunting sadness and despair. Now, behind her, rode her foster father, Plummer, as she made her way, after the first eager inquiry, straight to the side of the sheriff.

It was Plummer himself who spoke first. "Thomas," he said, "I've come here on what I feel to be a sort of wild-goose chase. But I had to come to keep the gal from plumb breaking her heart — or pretending to break it, which seems to work on her just about as much! Thomas, she swears to me that the gent you been chasing ain't The Shadow, and that the man you call Jim — Jim Cochrane I think it is — is the man you'd ought to be after!"

Algie Thomas looked mildly at the girl, mildly at her father. Then he pointed.

"There's Jim Cochrane," he said.

Of course that was no answer — simply to point out a man; yet it strangely silenced Plummer. He rubbed his big knuckles across his chin and shook his head.

"I just nacherally had to come," he said, "she was that set on it!"

The girl broke in: "Sheriff Thomas, if I swear to —"

He raised his hand and prevented her. "Swearing won't do no good. When a woman gets all worked up, she'll do anything to save a man. Some folks might hold it against you, Sylvia Rann, to be trying to shift the blame off The Shadow and putting it on an innocent man, but I don't. I've seen good women do too many queer things before, but I advise you now that you just turn around and ride back home and try your best to forget him. He ain't no more!"

He uttered the last sentence with a fitting solemnity; it seemed as though Tom Converse were already dead. Turning her eyes away, the girl encountered, among the other faces, the hard, triumphant, but joyless eyes of The Shadow himself.

"Will you let me go to him, then?" she asked.

"With food so's he can hold out longer? Is it good sense to ask me to do that?"

"I have no food with me. I want to see him for the last time to say good-by. Will you let me go, sheriff?"

She made an impulsive gesture of appeal as she spoke, and, if the sheriff had ventured to oppose her at that moment, every man in the crowd would have helped her through.

"If you want to do a hard thing and a thing

333

that'll hurt you bad, Sylvia, go ahead," said the sheriff. "I ain't going to stop you. All I ask is your word of honor that you'll come right back. Will you do that?"

"Yes."

"Then go on down to him!"

She tried to thank him; her voice broke; and then they saw her hurry on down the slope and presently disappear inside the rim of the trees. There was not a stir in the crowd. Then a breath of wind blew faintly up to them the thin sound of her calling: "Tom! Oh, Tom!"

It brought a gasp from every listener, that dim voice.

"Sheriff," cried the big rancher, Plummer, "they's something wrong about all this! They's something that had ought to be done!"

"You figure the way I'd like to figure," said the sheriff. "But I can't quite make it out. No, sir, I can't quite make out that the gent that rode Captain into them trees is anything else than The Shadow. It ain't common sense, somehow. I've tried to put myself in the boots of the girl. I've tried, honest, to see this her way, but I can't. Down yonder is a man that's got to die. That's final!"

"Couldn't this be held up until we've sent off and found out for sure if he's what he calls himself?"

"Send away some place that'll take a couple of days?"

"Why not? Ain't it worth while making sure?"

"Sure it is," agreed old Algie Thomas; "and I'd do it if I had the power to, but I'm only one man in two hundred here. On the trail I could run things, but here they vote me down. Look around you, Plummer! They's gents here that have been riding all day with their hosses in a foam they've hurried so hard. They've come miles and miles. They've dropped everything in order to get here.

"Why d'you think they've come? Because every one of 'em has had a cousin or a brother or a friend that's been held up or hurt or killed dead by The Shadow! They want a killing, Plummer, a killing! If I was an orator, I'd sure try to swing 'em around so's we could give that poor devil a last chance — though he never took no trouble to give last chances to gents that he had backed agin' the wall; but I can't talk good enough for that. I don't think that nobody could!"

Plummer looked around him. So far as he could see up and down that long line, there were only stern faces. A little farther back was a scattering of the women, putting up their lunch baskets or laying down fresh supplies for any who chanced to be hungry or thirsty. Even the women moved quietly about their work — a stern quiet in which voices were seldom raised.

"I guess you're right," said the rancher. "I guess they ain't no chance for the poor devil! But what's that?"

The same question was repeated by a score of voices, for behind the greenery flashed the form of a horse. Then, as they pitched up their rifles, ready to fire if it proved to be the fugitive making a dash for liberty, they saw Sylvia Rann riding out on the back of Captain.

Chapter Forty-Two

The Shadow Strikes Again

The stallion seemed to come with greater pride than he would have shown in carrying a mere man. Up the hillside in the sun he came like a dancer, throwing his head and playing with the bit, while his arched neck and his gleaming eyes seemed to indicate his desire to break away at full speed and dart across the hills.

The murmur of admiration swelled to a deep humming sound of voices as Sylvia Rann brought the horse to a standstill on the top of the hill.

"He fell into the quicksand and got out. Look!" they pointed to the marks of the deadly marsh where it had well-nigh covered the head of the horse. Before long they began to pack thickly around her.

It was then that the girl chose her time for addressing to the sheriff the plea which her foster father had already made.

"Sheriff Thomas," she said, "the man you claim is The Shadow has given me his horse and asked me to ride for his own homeland and his own people to get means of identifying him. Will you let me go?"

"No!" shouted a voice, and Deputy Sheriff Joe

Shriner shouldered his way forward in the crowd. But he was received with a growl.

"Let the lady talk," they warned him. "Let her talk. Words don't do no harm."

And Thomas added tersely: "I'll try to handle my end of this deal, Shriner. Miss Rann is talking to me, I think."

He turned to the girl as Shriner ground his teeth and subsided.

"If I had the power to do it," he said, "I'd sure let you have the time. But these men here — you see them? They won't wait. They want action!"

A deep-throated murmur ominously confirmed what he said.

"But you'll have to wait that long, at least," said the girl, "unless you set fire to the wood. The Lord knows there is no one among you willing to do a thing as terrible as that. You won't burn him out, and, unless you do, it will take you several days. In two days I can be back."

She threw out her arms to them.

"All of you who have a brother or a father you love," she said, "give me your help now. Not whether you think I am right or wrong, but simply because I love him. Tell me I may have that time! Two short days — is that a great request?"

It seemed to those who heard her that the appeal was made directly to each one of them. She seemed to have sorted each one out and asked for his influence. A quick muttering followed.

Then Jim Cochrane, in a panic lest she should succeed, called: "Are you going to let her get through with that hoss? Are you going to let that happen?"

"Is it your horse?" asked the girl fiercely. "Is it your horse, that you ask about it?"

The hostile sentiment toward The Shadow, which had been growing among all the members of the posse with whom he had ridden, now broke out in noisy protest from half a dozen of them who were near the sheriff, and who had heard the appeal and The Shadow's comment on it.

"Back up!" they called to The Shadow. "Back up and give the lady room. What call have you got to start barking here?"

Cochrane turned away, not daring to face them lest the murderous anger show in his face. Yet it was maddening to him to think that, when the man had been brought to the very verge of destruction, he should be saved by this appeal of the girl to the generosity of the men who surrounded Tom Converse. Moreover, here was Captain almost within reach of his hand, but barred from him as by a great distance.

He heard the murmur in favor of the girl growing.

"We'll wait," they were saying. "What's two days in a matter of life and death?"

If she had waited, they might have changed their sentiment. But she put her question to them suddenly:

"Friends," she said, "will you give me the two

days I want? Two small days?"

They answered her as Westerners by generations of habit had learned to answer the request of a woman. They said "Yes," and they said it with a shout.

Before they could change their minds, she was down the slope on Captain and racing across the smoother surface beyond. The Shadow, watching her depart, felt that she had torn from his grip the prize of victory for which he had fought, for which he had schemed so deftly.

She would strike for the railroad beyond Carlton, no doubt, and from that point send volleys of telegrams to the home town of Tom Converse. She would return long before the two days elapsed, with a thousand proofs of the identity of her man. Once that identity was proved, might not her statements concerning him, the real Shadow, begin to be believed?

Far off, she disappeared as she swung onto the road and straightened off toward the west, riding hard. In this fashion she dipped behind the shoulder of a hill. Then, as the others settled down to their former positions, The Shadow walked away to think and to be by himself.

For one thing, he did not wish to be too close to those who had so quickly resented his ungenerous attack on the girl's proposal. The best way to induce them to forget their resentment against him was to be far from those who disliked him most. Those rough men would be very apt to try bullying tactics with him, and such tactics

340

would be, he knew, too much for his temper.

He was like a tiger who could be identified by his claws, and wished to avoid danger which would make him show them. So he strolled down the hillside, elaborately failing to take notice of the slighting comments which were made on all sides as he passed.

It was strange how keenly they disliked him, he decided. Or had his life apart from other men during so many years changed him, until he was offensive to law-abiders? At any rate, those hostile murmurs irked him so that he began to see red, and, had he not quickly passed beyond the range of the angered cow-punchers who had overheard his attack on Sylvia, matters would have been quickly brought to a crisis.

He journeyed on down the line until he reached the narrow reach of Curtin River. It was not more than 20 yards across at this point, and extremely shallow; so much so that it was hardly more than a yard deep. It made up for its shallowness by flowing with extreme swiftness. Through the crystal water the watchers could look down to the sand from one side to the other; and yet a raft had been hastily thrown together and anchored with lariats in midstream.

"Suppose he was to try to get out by swimming?" they explained to The Shadow.

"Agin' that current?"

"Why not? I've seen gents do it, and what other folks can do at all, The Shadow can do well. Wouldn't be much surprised to see him come swimming right up agin' that current like a fish!"

"If he did, he'd sure get a hook before he was through," and The Shadow smiled again.

It pleased him to hear of this belief in his greatness. As a matter of fact, he could not swim a stroke, and now with his lameness, he could never again figure as an athlete. He could do one thing well — and that was handle guns of all kinds. But, so long as he lived, no doubt men would believe him to be invincible in everything to which he cared to give his attention.

His informant dropped a burning cigarette while he was speaking, and in a moment the steady, freshening wind fanned the coal to a bright orange-yellow. Then the dried grass smoked and took fire. The late smoker instantly started stamping out the blaze, but so quickly did it spread through the grass that two other bystanders had to come to his help.

"If it got into that tall grass, they wouldn't be any help for it," they explained to The Shadow. "The woods would catch, and The Shadow would be roasted out of 'em. Well, I figure he'd ought to die, but I don't figure that no man in the world is so bad that he'd ought to die by burning!"

"Don't you?" said Cochrane, catching at a glint of hope. "Well, I don't know. I've heard of some things that The Shadow's done that have took all of my sympathy out of me. I'd see him die in one way or another, and it doesn't seem to me that it makes much difference whether he dies by water or fire or rope. Does it to you?"

But the other stiffened at once. What perverse devil made men disagree with every syllable he uttered?

"You got a right to your own opinions," said the fellow. "It ain't my opinion, that's all!"

The Shadow turned away again, but, before he left that eastern end of the wood, he examined it carefully and thoughtfully. There was, as has been said, a tall growth of dead grasses near the point of the wood where it tapered off against the creek.

Just behind this grass was a group of young pine trees, seedlings and saplings, which had been killed by some recent change in the soil in which they grew — perhaps an infusion of alkali. Once a wave of fire started in that tall grass, it would strike those tinder-dry little pines in almost the first wave, and after that, with this east wind fanning it, the fire would be out of control in ten seconds, and Tom Converse would roast or be driven out to die by the guns of the posse.

That thought the outlaw carried away with him as he strolled on by himself, his mind made up. He had no longer any hesitation. The girl hated him and would always hate him, he saw. At least he would repay her for that bitter change of sentiment by destroying her beloved. After that, it only remained for him to do for Chuck Parker, regain possession of Captain, and all would be well. He could leave men and the ways of men with a carefree heart, knowing that he had balanced all scores.

As for the girl? Well, for a time no doubt the loss of her would sting his heart, but greater sorrows than that had been forgotten — and he was adept at putting the woes of the past behind him, out of sight and out of mind.

He spent the rest of the evening and the early night roaming on from group to group along the line, amusing himself with listening to the comments of one section after another on the events of the day, or stopping near the center of the line where the new arrivals reported as they rode up. Though some men had left the watchers when they heard of the agreement to wait for two days, most of the others remained, believing that The Shadow would not remain in concealment so long, but that he would make a break before, driven to it by the pangs of hunger.

It was well past midnight, and a full half of the watchers were sleeping, when The Shadow came again to the east end of the woods. He found two lanterns burning on the raft, on which were half a dozen men, and on each shore there were many others, some of whom lay resting on the ground; but always a certain number industriously watched every sign of movement on the water.

In the meantime, the east wind was steadily increasing in force, until now it blew a fair-sized gale. On that wind he was depending as upon an ally. He drew from his pocket a block of matches, seemed to be busy separating one from the rest in order to light a cigarette which was in his lips, and in the effort the whole block caught fire by the friction.

With an exclamation of dismay, he stepped back and flung the block from him. The wind sent it sailing, a streak of light. Had he thrown it far enough? It landed on the ground. All was black. Was it even in the tall grass?

"That was a fool thing to do," a tall man near him said severely. "You might of started a — By the Lord!"

The last exclamation was called forth by a crackle and then a spurt of flame. The long grass was on fire. A shout of alarm started a score of men toward it, but the fire was running almost as fast as a man. In another moment it struck the pines in a wave, and with a great crackling, the fire fed on the pitch and leaped high in the air in masses of flames.

Chapter Forty-Three

Incredulous Rescuers

Meantime, in the house of Jefferson Lander all was confusion. The good rancher had arrived at his house not knowing whether his fellow traveler was a madman or a dying man or both combined. When he appeared at the front door of his respectable house and kicked that door open and strode inside, carrying a limp form slung over his shoulder and that form covered with crimson stains, his wife instantly fainted.

An elder son showed greater nerve and presence of mind, however, and between him and his father they soon had the victim of The Shadow lying on a bed. There they washed and bandaged, to their clumsy best ability, the ghastly wound in his head while he lay in his faint.

They had hardly ended their ministrations before he was raving again.

"The Shadow!" he would cry, rolling back and forth on the bed. "The Shadow ain't The Shadow!"

"That's the kind of nonsense he's been talking all the time," said the rancher, shaking his head. "He's sure gone nutty — poor feller!"

"The shadow ain't the shadow?" said the son.

346

"I guess he's just delirious. Look at his eyes!"

At that moment the wounded man opened his eyes and looked wildly about him. It was not delirium, however, that set his eyes rolling now. As he came out of his swoon there was newly awakened in him his fierce determination to tell the world, before harm had been done, that the posse was chasing the wrong man. No matter how blind the world might be, they would have to respect information gained at the expense of bloodshed.

Therefore, when he saw the two faces above him, he cried instantly: "Is he dead? Is he dead?"

For it seemed to him, wakened from the trance, that he had been arguing and pleading with these men for a long time to induce them to save the fugitive.

"Is who dead?" asked the father.

"Is The Shadow dead?"

"He's talking about the outlaw all this time," said the son. "They's some sense in him, anyways. No, The Shadow ain't dead, but he will be soon, thank Heaven. Here's the doctor come to fix up that busted arm of yours, partner!"

As he spoke, the door opened, and there entered the neighboring veterinary, who had many a time before done duty as a physician. Indeed, he had all the credit and honor among his fellows that generally goes with the title of physician.

"Curse the doctor!" cried Harry Lang. "I'll have no doctor till I've made sure that they know the truth — that The Shadow ain't The Shadow and —"

347

The veterinary exchanged wise glances with the other two and pointed significantly to his head.

"Curse your eyes!" shouted Harry Lang. "I ain't crazy. I'm sane and talking sense —"

"Certainly. Certainly." The doctor nodded and approached to take charge of the patient. He added softly to the rancher: "A common hallucination! But watch yourselves. The poor fellow has to be treated as though he were insane and —"

"It ain't the fever, I tell you," pleaded Harry Lang. "It ain't the fever that's making me talk, though it will be the fever pretty soon! Just now I've got it pushed out of my head in some way, and I'm as clear-minded as any of you. I've got about one minute to tell you what I know. Will you listen?"

"Wait until I've set this bone," said the doctor calmly. "As soon as that's done, you can talk to your heart's content. Steady, now!"

"I tell you," cried Harry Lang, "that I've got to tell you!"

He thrust the doctor away with his good hand.

"The Shadow," he began, "is —"

"Hold him," said the doctor. "Hold him firmly. The delirium is going to be a violent one. I'm glad that I have this chloroform to —"

But, at the sight of the handkerchief which the doctor was spreading out on the palm of his hand, and the small phial which he now produced from his case with a professional air, Harry Lang uttered what, in a woman, would have been a shriek, but which, from his deep throat and capacious lungs, was simply a high-pitched roar. It made the poor rancher's wife clap her hands over her ears and turn her eyes up to the ceiling.

As Lang shouted in rage and despair, he made a terrific effort to start up from the bed, only to be caught in a trice and held moveless by the powerful hands of the host and his son. In their brawny grips, he would have had much ado to stir, even had his full strength been with him; but in his weakened condition he was as helpless as a child.

The struggle, also, had sent the pulses pounding in his head again and raised his fever to a high point instantly. He was in danger of falling once more under the dark blanket of the delirium, even if the doctor's chloroform should not blot out his consciousness.

"Doctor," he said, "for Heaven's sake give me half a minute for talking. After that you can do what you want, and I won't raise a hand. But —"

"Certainly," said the doctor, pushing up his spectacles a little and looking benignly down upon his patient. "Hold hard now, if you please!"

His plan was apparent. He would soothe the patient with promises of any nature while he went on to finish his operation in the swiftest manner possible.

There remained for the unlucky Harry Lang only a few breathing spaces in which to tell his story — though on the telling of that story, it seemed, depended the life of Tom Converse.

In the other room he could hear the woman

saying to her daughter: "They've cornered The Shadow at last. Steve Wycombe stopped in as he was going past, and says that they have him hemmed in against the quicksands down by Curtin. They'll finish him this time, it looks like!"

"No, no, no!" shouted Harry Lang. "They have the wrong man, and the real Shadow is in the posse helping them corner and kill a gent that never was The Shadow —"

Here he saw the doctor wink broadly at the others, and this drove poor Harry Lang nearly frantic.

"Jim Cochrane is The Shadow!" he yelled at them. "He told me before he shot me. Jim Cochrane is The Shadow. And, if the other gent dies, you'd ought to be hanged for it. If —"

He got no further. With a determined frown the doctor stooped over him. The grips of Lander and his son increased to a paralyzing force, and the handkerchief was dropped over the mouth and the nose of Harry Lang. His next breath dragged deep into his lungs the stupefying fumes of the chloroform. He still struggled to speak, to yell — then his senses swam.

It seemed only an instant later when he wakened, still with words of protest on his lips. But he found that the room was black, and that he was alone. His right arm was secured in a heavy splint, and a bandage was turned neatly and firmly around his forehead, while another bandage passed around the top of his head and was secured beneath his chin.

He made out these things by degrees, for his head was still reeling with the fumes of the chloroform. He propped himself a little in the bed. Around the door he could see a yellow line of light. It was not so very late, then. Others in the house were awake.

He shouted for them.

The door instantly opened, and a blinding shaft of yellow light struck his face. Lander and the doctor came beside him.

"Now will you listen?" cried Harry Lang. "Will you let me talk now?"

"He seems to be still in it," said the doctor. "Strange how the illusion hangs on with him!"

"But I ain't in it!" groaned Harry. "I tell you I'm as clear-headed as any of you, except for that chloroform. I can tell you everything that's happened since you found me on the road, except for the times when I fainted. Doctor — Lander — for Heaven's sake listen to me, or there'll be the death of an innocent man on your heads!"

The solemnity of that appeal shook even the doctor, but he instantly recovered from the shock.

"I've known them to talk even more reasonably than this," he remarked. "The best thing for me to do will be to give him something to put him to sleep, and then —"

"Wait a minute," growled the rancher. "Maybe you know a whole pile about sicknesses, doc, but I figure that I know enough myself to tell when a gent is talking out of a clear head! And this man seems to talk sense to me. Go on, son. You

351

keep right on talking so long as you figure that it does you any good!"

"Lord bless you!" gasped Harry Lang. He reached out and caught the hand of the rancher in a feverish grip. "Hold tight and listen, before I drop out ag'in!"

And then, as rapidly as he could, and as clearly, though waves of weakness and darkness assailed his mind and stopped him from time to time, he told the story of how Jim Cochrane had lured him out of the camp, and of how the attack on the men at the camp fire had been made, leading up to the story of the encounter with Cochrane, the savage burst of words in which the latter had delivered the truth about himself, and the explosion of the rifle which had wiped out the consciousness of Harry Lang.

Before he was half finished with his narrative, there were gasps of excitement from the others. At the end both the doctor and Lander were growling with rage. They believed him, for there was no possibility of disbelieving what he said as he lay there gasping out his words, white faced, but with his eyes on fire with eagerness.

At the conclusion Lander expressed the determination common to both of them.

"We'll get there as fast a hoss can take us! It ain't more'n five miles over the hills to Curtin marsh. We'll be there in half an hour!"

"Let me go with you!" pleaded Harry Lang. "You can lay me in the back of the rig. If you two gents go, maybe the crowd won't believe you. They'll think that you're simply friends of The Shadow. He has got friends around here and there. But if I go, he'll be more'n human if he don't weaken when he sees me. And, besides, I'll be there to tell the crowd how I got these wounds. Will you take me?"

"Can it be done, doc?" asked Lander.

"It ought not to be."

"But I tell you he's right. Them folks over the hills think that they've got on the trail of the real Shadow and cornered him. It'll take a whole lot to make them know that they've been wrong."

Here an excited exclamation from one of the women in the next room startled them.

"Look out the window. Look over the hills!"

They ran to the window and looked out. There was a reddish glow on the northern clouds where they swept low over Curtin quicksands.

"They've set the trees on fire. They're burning him out. Lander, we're too late!" groaned the doctor. "Oh, what a fool I was not to let that boy talk out before!"

"Maybe we're too late," said the farmer firmly, "but we'll keep right on trying to get there — and we'll take him with us!"

Chapter Forty-Four

Forced Out

When Tom Converse, in the edge of the woods near the river, saw the girl reach the top of the hill and wave back to him from the midst of the crowd, he himself turned back and went deeper among the shadows of the trees, vastly relieved. He felt that the end of his great trial had come. If they had agreed to give her the necessary two days he was saved, for she could return well within that time with a thousand proofs of his identity.

Besides, since the strange and joyous five minutes which their interview had comprised, it seemed to Tom Converse that he could not possibly die now. Life promised too happy a future to him with Sylvia Rann. How simple, how direct, how straightforward she had been! In that crisis there had been no time for fencing. She loved him, and he loved her; and that ended one great question. There remained only the problem of saving his life — and that seemed a simple, silly thing in comparison.

He went far back in the woods in recognition of that truce when it was no longer necessary for him to keep so strict a watch on his enemies, and there, as the darkness came on, he drew his belt very tight so that he could forget his hunger, curled up on a bed of pine needles, and went to sleep!

Strange as that might seem, stranger things have been done by strong men in times of peril. Not only did Tom Converse sleep, but he slept with dreams through which pretty Sylvia Rann walked and danced and laughed beside him.

He wakened with a confusion of distant voices in his ears, very like the roaring of the wind, and then he smelled a sweet scent of wood smoke — the purest of all fragrances when there is only a trace of resinous smoke in the atmosphere. But, as his senses cleared, he made out that the voices were loud in great excitement, and next he saw that everything around him was brightly illumined.

Speedily he rose from the ground, amazed and shaking his head. Had the sun risen as early as this? Had his sleep been so short?

In the midst of his wonder he saw a mist rolling toward him through the trees, blown by the east wind. It came toward him white and dense; it curled around the near-by trees, shutting them almost out of sight; and then it reached him.

Instantly he was coughing, choking, gasping. It was not a fog but a cloud of rolling smoke, and the light which played around him and through the mass of the smoke was the light of a fire. The trees of the swamp were burning!

He realized this as he darted to one side out

of the path of that prone, crawling pillar of smoke. Then he rested with one hand against a tree and tried to make head and tail of the mystery.

The swamp was burning, but who could have fired it? To be sure, such things had been done before when men hunted criminals of the most terrible kind. But had he not just concluded an agreement, through the agency of the girl, with those men on the top of the hill? They were to delay two days. That certainly had been the meaning of the triumphant gesture with which she had turned toward him. That, also, had been the meaning of the shout of the men when she had thrown out her arms toward them.

But now the woods burned, and the rolling of the white cloud of smoke toward him could mean only one thing — death! When he issued from the trees, he could not expect them to let him come safely among them. No, their agreement had simply been to forbear from attack for two days. If, in the meantime, he showed himself, there were among them too many injured men who had lost relatives and friends through the butchery of The Shadow, and one or more of these would be sure to shoot him to death on sight.

Accident, perhaps, had started that fatal fire. But now he had only a scant half hour, perhaps, in which to review his past sins and make ready for death. Still there was no element of resignation in the mind of Tom Converse. He felt behind this the same hand of fate which had taken hold of him when he first came into the town of Silver Tip. What would it do with him now, or attempt to do? He felt, beforehand, that he would be thrown on the mercy of those men who waited for him along the hill. But before that came, he would use the last scruple of his strength and his brain power to avoid the inevitable.

First of all, he must go as far from the fire as possible. So he retreated to the very end of the little forest, where it narrowed to a sharp point beside the banks of the stream. There, he saw, the main body of the great posse had gathered. They knew that he could not possibly make headway through those flames. The best he could do would be to get as far from their path as circumstances permitted and then make a final desperate rush.

But when he rushed, he would have to wade through rank after rank of those determined fighters. He saw before him a good five score of cowpunchers and ranchers and townsmen, all more or less expert wielders of weapons, and all keen from one motive or another to be the death of the outlaw.

The fire behind leaped wildly up into the air and illumined the grim faces, and Tom, in an ecstasy of rage, shook his big fist at them. What right had they to back him against the wall and strike him down like a beast?

In the meantime, the heat was growing with every moment. He took the sole remaining chance

— how small it was! — and cut a long branch of willow, as small and as straight as he could find. He rolled this until he could draw out the pith. There remained a long tube of bark. Next he stripped off his outer clothes, took up the tube, and stepped to the edge of the water. Before him slid the dark waters of the stream, filled with black bits of wood which had fallen from the burning trees farther along. A screen of shrubbery sheltered him from the spying eyes which crowded the shores of the stream below and jammed the rude craft which had been anchored there, like the raft above the forest.

Through the shrubs he slipped down into the water. Behind him on the bank lay the rifle and the revolver, his last guarantees. He was discarding them for a single final weapon — chance! Then the cold water rippled up about him, and he headed down the current.

In his mouth he carried the end of the tube, and he swam slowly, rather to keep himself a certain distance under the water than for the sake of speed. The drift of the current must be fast enough for him.

His position was far better than he had imagined. He could expel the air through his nostrils and draw it in comfortably through his mouth. It was strange to be immersed in that chilly silence while above and beyond him roared the fire and the clamor of the crowd.

A long minute, perhaps, had passed, when the tube was driven hard into his mouth and almost torn away, and when he attempted to draw in another breath, no air came. Some passing branch had broken the tube!

There was nothing for it, then, but to roll over and swim like mad as far as he could, and only pray that, when he came up for air, he would come up beyond the raft.

Then began the agony of that swim under water while his lungs, only partially filled with air, began to swell and ache for lack of oxygen.

But when at length he was forced to come up to the surface, he was past the raft! He could look up among a score of heads, all turned toward the fire upstream. He could see on either shore the moving crowds. If only he could expel his breath without noise!

But no, the held breath burst out noisily, and he drew in a second lungful with a gasp that brought half a dozen quick heads around.

"The Shadow!" they shouted.

While he saw half a dozen guns drawn, he turned and dived down with an effort that threw his legs high out of the water even as the guns exploded. No bullet struck him, but around one of those legs there was suddenly whipped a tight grip from which he could not pull himself free, and presently he was jerked swiftly to the shore.

He had been snared, by luck, with the cast of a lariat!

In an instant they were around him. A score of hands gripped and held him. A score of angry, surprised faces crowded above and about him.

"Tie him fast, the snake!" advised a commanding voice. "He's slippery. And if he gets to talking, don't listen to him!"

Tom Converse looked up. He distinguished the face of Joe Shriner among the others. Truly there would be neither mercy nor delay in his death if that man had the control of it!

The news, in the meantime, was spread in all directions, and with a thunder of shouting, the rest of the posse began to focus on the place of the capture. Scores of excited men flocked toward him, while his immediate captors swathed him in ropes, binding his arms in wrappings that extended from his wrists to his elbows, and tying his legs with rope that would have held an elephant. Then they raised him, threw him like a sack across a saddle, and carried him to the top of the hill.

There, awaiting them, was Sheriff Algie Thomas, and the sight of his withered old face was a welcome one to Tom Converse. But the first words of the man of the law were not so encouraging.

"Tom," he said, "if that's your right name, I'm sure sorry to see you all tangled up in ropes that way. But I can't help remarking, son, that I'm sure glad that my last trail has wound up plumb successful!"

As he spoke, the men around him burst into an impromptu cheer for Algie Thomas. They took off their hats and swung them with a will. They had reason, for not a man there but felt that the question of supremacy had been settled. Algie Thomas had proved himself a greater man than The Shadow; the power of the law had triumphed!

Chapter Forty-Five

The Shadow's Legacy

For a man's last glimpse of earth before dying, there was never a gloomier scene than that which the eyes of Tom Converse looked upon. The east wind had at length blown long, stringing clouds across the sky, and, in addition, continuous billows of smoke rolled up from the burning swamp and swept away, adding to the gloom. Around the prisoner, the lanterns were gathering, hurrying along the slopes and coming to a bright focus around him — scores of lanterns held up at arm's length and shining on the baffled, desperate face of Tom.

The chill of horror which he had felt when he saw the jail in Carlton returned to him now. It was not the thought of death which paralyzed him. It was the certainty that he would die without a chance to struggle for his life. What were they doing now? Why was the whole crowd drifting down the hill, shutting out the sight of the fire?

The murmur around him was saying: "Get him under the highest branch. We want him to hang up where folks can see what we been doing. We want the youngsters in these parts to know what happens to gents like The Shadow in the end!"

The drift of the mob did not cease until they were under a tall tree. It seemed to go up to the middle of the cloudy sky as Tom lifted his eyes, and he saw above him a great, far-reaching bough. No doubt he would be swung from that bough. Already a dozen lariats were being flung across it. A hundred pairs of hands would reach for the rope which would jerk The Shadow out of life.

Looking around him in despair upon those iron-hard faces, he saw the true Shadow standing rubbing his chin — and smiling! Tom Converse dropped his head. Truly the man was the devil. He had won, after all. And now he stood with his hand on the shoulder of Chuck Parker. He had made friends with Chuck Parker, of all the crowd. That friendliness was a sure sign that Chuck would soon be lured to his death, and the toll of the three would be complete!

The old sheriff was speaking. "Boys, if you admit that I've run this here chase pretty well, I'm going to ask you to all get behind me and help me to do the thing I want to do now. I want to keep this boy here safe until them two days that we promised to the girl are ended!"

A growl of dissent answered him.

"Ain't we made a promise to a lady?" asked the sheriff sharply. "And ain't other folks in other parts of the country going to shake their heads when they hear how the men of Silver Tip and Carlton and Curtin couldn't keep the word that they'd given to a girl! I ask you that!"

It was a facer for even the most ardent advocate of killing in a hurry. Even Deputy Sheriff Joe Shriner had no desire to be remembered as advocating lack of faith to a pledge given to a woman.

There was only one man there unscrupulous enough to whet the edge of the crowd's appetite for mischief and revenge. That man now stepped into the inner circle, and all eyes fell upon the sallow face of Jim Cochrane. He had lost the girl he loved in this contest with Tom Converse. He had lost the guns with which he had learned to fight; he had lost his peerless stallion, half his strength, in that same battle. There remained to him, as the price of these sacrifices, only the chance of destroying the man who had cost him so dear, and The Shadow was determined that that head should fall.

"Gents," he said, "I sure don't like to talk up loud at a time like this. All I got to say is: Where are we going to keep this gent for two days more?"

"Give him to me!" pleaded Joe Shriner. "I've got the jail that'll hold him!"

"Have you? How long did you hold him before? Didn't he walk into your jail and out again?"

Joe Shriner could not answer. And now a dozen of the older men pressed forward.

"Algie," they said to old Thomas, "we got a world of respect for you and what you want to do. You're most generally right. But we put it up to you: Wouldn't it be plumb foolish to give

364

this slippery snake a chance to get away again? Wouldn't every one of us rather lose an arm than lose the chance of hanging The Shadow now that we've waited for him and fought for him? Sure, I know it's pretty to keep our word to a girl — but we couldn't figure that the wood would burn and throw him plumb into our arms, could we?"

The sheriff was shaken; so were the others in the crowd. The Shadow stepped in with the deciding weight.

"Billy Tompkins would've been glad if The Shadow had given him two days. Carl Mack would've been glad to've got even a couple of hours before the hound cut his throat. And what about your cousin, Steve Macintosh? Did he get two days? And you, Chalmers? D'you remember the time The Shadow went through you and got only five dollars, and then sent a slug through each of your legs because you didn't have more? Ain't you walked with a limp ever since?"

These pointed recollections of his own deeds brought a shout of rage from the entire crowd, and, as they surged in, the old sheriff, Algie Thomas, wisely gave way. After all, he had done his part for the poor girl. Better, indeed, that the horrible work should be finished while she was away.

Thomas retired, turned his back, and calmly rolled a cigarette. He looked up to the windows of the house in whose back yard the tree stood. One of the upper windows was blotched with three white faces. Women were there to watch the end of The Shadow, after all!

What nerve the man had! Behind him he heard the voice of Tom Converse crying: "If you swing me, you'll have the real Shadow on your hands again inside of a week, and Chuck Parker will be the first one to die by his hands. Mind you that. Where's Parker?"

He was pointed out, the real Shadow leaning on his shoulder.

"That gent beside you, Parker, will cut your throat!" cried Tom Converse. "When you feel the knife-edge, remember me! Gents, is there one of you that'll carry my word to Sylvia Rann when she comes back and finds me dead?"

"Ay, lad. Talk out but talk short."

"Tell her I know she's the gamest in the world. Tell her I know that she ain't going to forget me in a day or a week. But tell her that, because she's got so much courage, I know she'll keep right on with her head up high. Tell her I met her twice, seen her face once, and will keep on seeing her forever. Amen. Gents, let 'er go!"

The cords that bound him had been removed, and he waved a brief signal to them with his right hand, while with his left he adjusted the noose around his own neck and set his teeth prepared for the shock when they jerked from beneath him the soap box onto which he had been forced to climb.

"Wait!" called half a dozen voices on the outskirts of the circle. "Here comes a wagonload of gents to see the party. Maybe they been driving all night long to get in at the finish, and it'd be plumb wicked to keep 'em from a sight. Maybe they got gents there that have had doings with The Shadow. They got a right to have a look before the finish!"

This was so manifestly fair that the crowd even gave back a little, and there was a raising of lanterns which exposed to view a buggy drawn by two galloping cow-ponies who were guided by one man while another mercilessly laid on the lash. Between them, wedged into the wide seat, they supported a third man, whose head was wrapped in white bandages.

They brought their horses to a halt. They flung down from the seat and half carried the man who had sat between them, toward the main group around the hanging-tree.

It was the doctor who shouted with stentorian lungs: "Sheriff Thomas! Algie Thomas! For Heaven's sake stop the boys and take the rope off of that man's neck!"

"Doc," said the sheriff, who apparently recognized the newcomers, "they'll bear witness that I done my best to save the prisoner, but they took him from me by force of numbers and wouldn't let the law run its course."

"Where's Jim Cochrane?" cried the doctor now. "Where's the man called Jim Cochrane?"

The Shadow had slipped back in the crowd. But he suddenly found the men in front of him stepping aside, and he was exposed to a revolver held in the nervous hand of Sheriff Algie Thomas.

"There he is," said the sheriff. "I sure been watching that gent for a long time. If you want him, speak up and say why!"

"I want him," said the doctor, "because he's the real Shadow, and not the gent you got there!"

Cochrane stepped forward jauntily enough.

"We've heard a lot of that talk before," he said. "I guess the girl stopped off and had a talk with the doc, sheriff."

"No," said the doctor. "We got our information from another source — a better source — a man who learned to know you at the point of a gun! Look here!"

And, having covered Harry Lang before from sight, he now stepped aside and presented that haggard face, to the eye of Jim Cochrane. The latter fell back with a cry which was well-nigh a scream of terror.

"A ghost!" he cried. "A ghost!"

"Grab him!" cried the doctor. "Don't you see what he's doing?"

"Grab me?" cried The Shadow, drawing himself up to his full height. "There ain't enough of you."

So saying, he flung himself sidewise toward the ground, and in the split part of a second he would have been among the crowd. What would have happened then — perhaps an escape in the confusion — no one could have told, but Sheriff Thomas changed his aim with even more speed than The Shadow changed his position in that sidewise dive. His revolver exploded; The Shadow

368

whirled over and over, then lay doubled in a knot with pain.

When they straightened him out and took his weapons from him, it was plain that he was about to die. The bullet had driven straight through his breast. Why he had not died instantly seemed a miracle.

"Quick!" he whispered. "Where's Tom Converse?"

Tom Converse was brought. They gave way instinctively before the coming of a man who had stood so lately at the door of death. Tom kneeled beside the dying outlaw. The latter made a weak gesture, and Tom lowered his head close to the lips of the outlaw.

"Let the woman go," whispered Jim Cochrane. "She passed me up, and she might pass you up in a pinch. But Captain — be good to him! They's nobody in the world but you worthy of him. One thing more — give me your hand. Converse, forgive me if you can. You've beat me fair and square, with me fighting crooked. You're a man!"

He pushed Tom away with a feeble gesture, then raised himself a little on his elbow.

"Gents," he said, in a voice made audible only through a great effort, "here's my last will and testament. Captain goes to Tom Converse; and the gent that keeps the hoss from him, I'll come back and haunt with fire. Be damned to you all! Tom, good-by!"

There was one convulsive quiver of his body, and he was dead.

Under that tree on the second day, standing close to the new-made grave, Tom Converse looked down the valley road and saw a girl riding rapidly toward him on a shining dappled chestnut. He looked away from her and up through the interlacing branches above him and beyond to the quiet blue of the sky.

Max Brand ™ is the best-known pen name of Frederick Faust, creator of Dr. Kildare™, Destry, and many other fictional characters popular with readers and viewers worldwide. Faust wrote for a variety of audiences in many genres. His enormous output, totaling approximately thirty million words or the equivalent of 530 ordinary books, covered nearly every field: crime, fantasy, historical romance, espionage, Westerns, science fiction, adventure, animal stories, love, war, and fashionable society, big business and big medicine. Eighty motion pictures have been based on his work along with many radio and television programs. For good measure he also published four volumes of poetry. Perhaps no other author has reached more people in more different ways.

Born in Seattle in 1892, orphaned early, Faust grew up in the rural San Joaquin Valley of California. At Berkeley he became a student rebel and one-man literary movement, contributing prodigiously to all campus publications. Denied a degree because of unconventional conduct, he embarked on a series of adventures culminating in New York City where, after a period of near starvation, he received simultaneous recognition as a serious poet and successful popular-prose writer. Later, he traveled widely, making his home in New York, then in Florence, and finally in Los Angeles.

Once the United States entered the Second World War, Faust abandoned his lucrative writing career and his work as a screenwriter to serve as a war correspondent with the infantry in Italy, despite his fifty-one years and a bad heart. He was killed during a night attack on a hilltop village held by the German army. New books based on magazine serials or unpublished manuscripts continue to appear. Alive and dead he has averaged a new one every four months for seventy-five years. In the U.S. alone nine publishers issue his work, plus many more in foreign countries. Yet, only recently have the full dimensions of this extraordinarily versatile and prolific writer come to be recognized and his stature as a protean literary figure in the 20th Century acknowledged. His popularity continues to grow throughout the world.

The employees of G.K. HALL hope you have enjoyed this Large Print book. All our Large Print titles are designed for easy reading, and all our books are made to last. Other G.K. Hall Large Print books are available at your library, through selected bookstores, or directly from us. For more information about current and upcoming titles, please call or mail your name and address to:

G.K. HALL
PO Box 159
Thorndike, Maine 04986
800/223-6121
207/948-2962